She watched him for a moment, her eyes on his strong, sensitive hands. He molded the metal with a deft and delicate touch, using the flame of a gas lamp to soften each sheet and his fingers more than tools to shape it.

He was in shirtsleeves again today, his coat discarded over a nearby chair, and in the bright light of day the white linen emphasized the breadth and power of his shoulders.

The painting and photograph she remembered so well had caught that power in him, that innate strength and vitality even while he was still. Accustomed to powerful beings, Felicity was wholly fascinated by John Sinclair, because the strength and intensity in him were of mind and muscle and sheer force of will; he owed nothing of what he was to anything that was not utterly, completely human.

And very, very male.

She had never expected to meet him in the flesh, never prepared herself for the shock to her senses that was his voice. And she had certainly never allowed herself to even imagine his touch.

But he was alive. *Alive*. And here, with her. A hundred years no longer stood between them. Age and the dusty finality of death no longer stood between them.

And the word *impossible* no longer seemed so undeniable.

Bantam Books by Kay Hooper

Haunting Rachel

Finding Laura

After Caroline

Amanda

On Wings of Magic

The Wizard of Seattle

My Guardian Angel

Bantam Books by Marilyn Pappano

Some Enchanted Season

Father to Be

Bantam Books by Michelle Martin

The Long Shot

Stolen Moments

Stolen Hearts

And coming in February 2000:

You Were Meant For Me

Bantam Books by Donna Kauffman

The Legend Mackinnon

And coming in March 2000:

The Legend of the Sorcerer

Yours 2 Keep

Kay Hooper

Marilyn Pappano

Michelle Martin

Donna Kauffman

Jill Shalvis

Bantam Books

New York London Toronto Sydney Auckland

YOURS 2 KEEP

A Bantam Book / October 1999

ISBN 0-553-58167-8

Published simultaneously in the United States and Canada

Bantam Books are published by Bantam Books, a division of Random House, Inc. Its trademark, consisting of the words "Bantam Books" and the portrayal of a rooster, is Registered in U.S. Patent and Trademark Office and in other countries. Marca Registrada. Bantam Books, 1540 Broadway, New York, New York 10036.

PRINTED IN THE UNITED STATES OF AMERICA

OPM 10 9 8 7 6 5 4 3 2 1

Contents

Arts Magica

Kay Hooper

For all the readers
who asked for another Wizard story

1

Seattle
December 31, 1999

Felicity Grant circled the artifact slowly, studying it from every angle. It resembled nothing so much as a doorway, minus surrounding walls and a door itself. Just a thin frame of some kind of metal, fastened to an oval base that seemed to be made of smooth, polished stone. The metal had a greenish patina.

"It's obviously a gate," she announced with the confidence of the young and untried.

Richard Merlin, who was sitting on the edge of his desk looking through a very old and heavy book, lifted his gaze to his Apprentice. "Thank you," he said dryly.

Felicity had the grace to blush, but kept her chin high. "Well, isn't it?"

His black, curiously brilliant eyes held a slight amusement. "Touch it," he instructed.

She obeyed, and almost immediately jerked her hand away. After a moment, she touched it again, her fingertips resting gently against the metal. "Power," she whispered. "It feels . . . There's almost a heartbeat."

"Yes. After at least a hundred years."

Felicity turned quickly to stare at him. "You said it was

uncovered just a few months ago, but couldn't someone else have found it—used it—in the last century?"

"I think not," Richard replied. "It was discovered in a sealed room within Sinclair's house in London. Until the present owner began to remodel and knocked down a wall, this artifact had been entombed since the turn of the century."

"And they notified you?"

He smiled. "The present owner is on the Council of Elders, and knew very well my interest in Sinclair. He thought I'd be the best person to investigate."

"Did the Elder touch this? Did he feel the power?"

"Of course. His opinion is that this artifact is partially wizard-made."

"But you believe Sinclair built it."

"Yes."

Felicity cast herself into a chair near the artifact and frowned at it. "Well, that doesn't make any sense. John Sinclair was an inventor, yes, even a visionary and an undoubtedly brilliant man ahead of his time, but he wasn't a wizard. Was he?"

"No."

"You're sure?"

"Quite sure."

"And a hundred years ago," Felicity mused, "it was more or less the way it is now, with people of power hiding their abilities from powerless people. So it isn't likely he knew a wizard—or was aware that he knew one."

"According to our records," Merlin said, "Sinclair was never approached by a man or woman of power. He was known to the Council during his time because of his fine intellect and remarkably forward-thinking views, but his power was totally of the mind and quite human. Interesting to us, but hardly something we would have interfered with in any way."

"Then how was this artifact influenced by someone with a wizard's power?"

"That is the puzzle, isn't it?"

Felicity steepled her fingers together and stared at the artifact over them. "Hmmm."

Merlin studied her as she studied the artifact. A young woman with an unusual beauty, she had long hair so fair it was nearly silver, catlike green eyes so vivid they were almost iridescent, and an expression of such life and vitality that even strangers couldn't help but smile at her.

For the past five years, since her eighteenth birthday, she had lived in this house as the Apprentice of Merlin and his wife Serena, both Master Wizards. She'd been a late bloomer as a wizard, coming into her full powers in her late teens rather than years earlier as was the norm, and because of that and her few years training, she was still lacking in control. She was as apt to destroy with her powers as to create, and had to be monitored carefully, especially since those newly unleashed powers were rather remarkable.

If she didn't learn complete control soon, it was possible her own raw ability could destroy her. But both Merlin and Serena believed in her, and they were committed to teaching her.

As he watched, Felicity pulled herself from the chair and went over to a small wooden crate near the artifact. "All this stuff, these books and papers, belonged to Sinclair?"

"They were found with the artifact."

"Then they might tell us if it is a gate, and what he used it for—or intended to use it for?"

Merlin nodded. "Possibly, although we won't know until everything is studied. I thought you might wish to be the first to go through the box."

"Yes. Yes, I would." Felicity felt heat rise in her face. She was more than a little disconcerted to realize that her Master was aware of what she had believed was her secret obsession. She'd thought herself able to hide her own feelings from even a Master Wizard. She had been wrong, obviously.

If her blush betrayed her further, Merlin gave no sign of seeing it. His voice was calm with self-possession, which came from an absolute mastery of his incredible powers. "I know you weren't looking forward to the party tonight, so if you'd rather, you may remain here and go through the box."

"Serena won't be upset with me?"

"No, of course not." He closed the book and set it aside on

his desk as he got to his feet. "But keep everything here in the study, understand?"

Felicity did understand. This room was insulated, protected by Merlin's own power; like the workroom upstairs, it would contain any uncontrolled surges of energy. "You mean you think something in this box may hold power just as the artifact does?"

"I think it's best to be safe," he said, moving toward the door with easy grace, the deceptively lazy movements almost concealing the astonishing strength that helped make him the most powerful wizard to walk the face of modern-day Earth. "Treat anything you don't understand with respect, Felicity."

Alone in the quiet room, Felicity stood for a moment just gazing toward the wooden crate. Then she drew a breath and went to a particular section of the bookshelves. Most of the shelves were filled with books and scrolls that were literally ancient and virtually pulsed with power, containing as they did the history and wisdom of an ancient and powerful people. But this particular section held more recent books, on subjects other than wizards and wizardry.

The book Felicity chose was clearly well read, a biography of a remarkable man named John Sinclair. Born in London in 1865 to wealthy, unusually learned parents, he had demonstrated his own precociousness by mastering several languages, higher mathematics, and at least three sciences before he reached his teens. By his mid-twenties, he had invented half a dozen gadgets that had made factory production more efficient, had written and published five books—three of them novels with astoundingly accurate predictions of what the world would be like in the coming century—and was well known as a passionate and outspoken advocate for reforms designed to improve the lot of the common man.

And woman. A man definitely ahead of his time, he had also championed women's rights, and worked to change both laws and attitudes to give women more rights and freedoms.

Despite that—or perhaps because of it—he had never married. His biographer had found evidence of many friendships with women, and a few more intimate relationships, but either John Sinclair had never met the right woman, or his energy and attention had been taken up with his scientific, creative, and political pursuits.

The book Felicity was holding opened naturally to a page that had often held her attention. Her fascination, if she were honest about the matter.

On the left-hand page was a painting of Sinclair at twenty-one; on the right-hand page, a photograph taken of him before his thirty-fifth birthday in 1900. Not long before he vanished without a trace.

The younger Sinclair was smiling, his eyes bright and direct with confidence, almost arrogance. He was dark; his hair was black and his skin unusually swarthy for an Englishman of the last century. Broad shoulders spoke of physical power just beginning, and his relaxed, easy stance indicated an uncommon grace. His hands were beautiful, strong and long-fingered, while his face . . .

Felicity loved his face. It was not conventionally handsome; there was too much strength of character in it for that. His black brows slanted upward toward his temples, flying above eyes a clear, pale gray. His nose was strong and clearly defined, his mouth just hinting at sensitivity in the curve of the fuller lower lip, and his jaw was determined.

It was a face of a brilliant, complex man.

But it was the photograph that had haunted her dreams since she'd first seen it months ago. Taken more than a dozen years after the painting was done, this picture was of a mature man, broad shoulders heavy with physical power realized, still graceful in stance, still confident in attitude.

But there was something different about him. Whereas the painting showed a confident young idealist, this picture was more ambiguous. The confidence was there, yes, but the idealism seemed worn, partially eroded by the years and the inevitable failed attempts to change the things that were wrong in his life and his world.

Still, though his optimism might have taken a bruising, his brilliance was, if anything, stronger and more acute. It burned in his eyes, an intellect so dynamic it had a life all its own. His face was harder, the planes of it smooth, the angles sharp, and that sensitive mouth was held more rigid in a control earned over years.

And the expression on that face . . . It always caught at Felicity's heart and stopped her breath. She had never been able to define it, but it was so subtle and wrenching it drew her back again and again to stare and wonder.

She touched the picture gently, then placed the book back on the shelf. Why did this long-dead man from another time obsess her so? She didn't know.

"Felicity?"

She turned quickly to see Serena come into the study. Merlin's wife was dressed for an evening party in a beautiful red dress that flattered rather than clashed with her vivid coloring, and only the merest curve to her belly gave evidence of her pregnancy.

"I hear you aren't going to the party," she said with a smile. Her face was so serene it was clear her parents had named her well. Although according to her, it had taken her many years, and a tumultuous relationship with Richard Merlin before they were married, to earn that priceless contentment.

"Richard said I could stay here and go through all this stuff from Sinclair's secret room."

"Seems a quiet way to ring in the new year—and the new millennium," Serena said gently. "But very like you. Are you sure? Your friends will be there."

"I know. I just . . . I don't feel much like a party."

Perceptively, Serena said, "Richard told you about the Council's warning."

Felicity returned to the chair near the artifact, and grimaced. "Yeah. It's their judgment that I've had enough time and training to know how to control my powers, and the fact that I haven't yet been able to do so consistently indicates that it may be an ability I'll never have." She recited the damning words with a coolness she hardly felt. "They've given me six months more. After that . . ." She shrugged. "After that, they step in."

"The most they would do is reduce the level of your powers to bring them within your control. Richard did tell you that?"

"He told me. But, Serena, I don't want to lose any of it. My powers are *mine*. They make me who I am. If I give up any part of them, then I'm diminished. I'm less than what I was meant to be. How is that fair?"

"It isn't, of course. But the Council has to consider the rights and needs of all wizards, not just one. And if your powers escape your control at a time when neither Richard nor I am there to dampen the results, it could have an effect on all of us, Felicity. You know that."

She knew. But it didn't make the judgment of the Council easier to bear. "Dammit, why can't I find the switch? I imagine Richard always had a finger on his, but you said you didn't find yours until you were older than I am now."

Serena hesitated, then said slowly, "Yes, at a moment of great personal pain and turmoil."

Felicity scowled. "Well, if I don't find mine in the next six months, my moment of great personal pain and turmoil will come when the Council calls me before them to take away part of my powers."

"We'll find a way, Felicity."

"I know you'll try. So will I." She managed a faint smile. "Anyway, that explains why I'm not in the mood for a party, even to ring in the new millennium. I'll make myself a pot of tea and spend the evening trying to figure out if John Sinclair built this and what he intended to use it for. It should occupy my mind."

"He usually does, doesn't he?"

The question had been quite mild, but Felicity felt herself blushing again. Dammit, did everybody know?

With dignity, she said, "He was a fascinating man."

Serena nodded gravely. "Yes. He was."

Felicity tried to think of something else to say, but she was rescued when Merlin stepped into the study, dressed for the evening all in black and looking as handsome as usual.

"Ready to go, love?" His voice was different when he spoke to his wife, lower and softer, and his face and eyes reflected a depth of emotion that even the least observant could define easily. He adored his wife, and he was not in the least self-conscious about it.

Serena turned toward him, her smile changing, her eyes glowing with a matching love, and Felicity felt a stab of pure envy.

"I'm ready, darling." She went to join him.

Felicity sighed. "Have fun, you two."

"Keep this door closed," Merlin reminded automatically.

"Yes, Master." It was only a little bit sarcastic.

Merlin sent her a look, brows slightly raised, but didn't comment. He shut the study door behind him and Serena, and a few moments later the front door quietly closed.

Alone in the silent study, Felicity carefully built a fire in the fireplace and was more relieved than she wanted to admit when she conjured a normal blaze rather than the inferno she had created the last time she'd tried. She fixed herself a pot of tea the old-fashioned way, and then settled down in her chair with the small crate of John Sinclair's papers and books within easy reach.

It was a rainy, fairly miserable night, but as time passed Felicity was less and less aware of the outside world. She sorted the contents of the crate first, stacking books and gathering papers together in a pile. There were several journals, which she reluctantly put aside for later, one surprising and fanciful book on magic, one on electricity, and a final volume that seemed to be a workbook filled with diagrams and notes in John Sinclair's clear and beautiful handwriting.

Most of the sketches and diagrams were beyond her understanding, though she did recognize what looked like an embryonic radio and television, something that might have been a radar, and a primitive computer. The notes made little sense, as they went far beyond her own scientific knowledge, until she found on one page what she slowly realized was the theory of relativity. The date on the page was 1898.

"Wow, John. I think you had the jump on Einstein." She felt an odd little thrill of pride. The famous scientist hadn't advanced his theory until after the turn of the century.

On the following page, scrawled as though it had been a

fleeting thought, was the equation $E=mc^2$, a foundation stone in the development of atomic energy, and also credited to Einstein.

She wondered what would have happened if this workbook had been discovered just after Sinclair's disappearance, how history might have been changed. It was a sobering thought.

Felicity was about to put the workbook aside when a slip of paper fell out, and she saw with another jolt a diagram of the artifact just a few feet away from her.

His notes identified it as a portal, and she gathered that his intent was to build a teleportation device—a way of moving instantaneously from one place to another. He had chosen to fashion the frame from beaten copper, thin plates of which were molded around a delicate wooden skeleton, and the stone base was taken from the ruins of Stonehenge.

Felicity blinked. Stonehenge? The base stone must be a fragment that had broken away from one of those huge stones.

Sinclair didn't explain his reasons for choosing such a stone, though Felicity couldn't help wondering if he had believed there was an unusual energy in that ancient place. He wouldn't have been the first, though certainly the first she knew of to try to harness some of that energy.

According to his notes, Sinclair planned to connect his invention to a source of electricity, thus providing it with the power necessary to teleport a person to another place. As far as Felicity could tell, his plans had not advanced to the point of providing some means of determining just where the portal would deliver that person. Was that another reason for the base stone? Had Sinclair believed a traveler would end up at Stonehenge? Perhaps. It made a kind of sense.

Felicity hesitated. It would be, she knew, totally irresponsible of her to experiment with the portal while she was alone. Totally. Merlin would not be happy with her, especially if something went wrong.

But what could go wrong? She was in Merlin's study, safe and protected from even her own wayward powers. And she really wanted to be able to tell her Master Wizard the precise capabilities of the portal when he came home. And nothing was going to go wrong, anyway.

Besides, she really wanted to know if Sinclair's most ambitious invention actually worked.

A small voice in her head reminded her that he had disappeared without a trace, possibly as a result of stepping through a faulty portal, but Felicity didn't let that stop her. She was a wizard, after all. Besides, she had no intention of stepping through the device herself.

Not until she knew if it would work.

She left the study to get what she needed, noting in passing that the grandfather clock in the foyer showed just past eleven-thirty. It would be at least a couple of hours before Merlin and Serena got home. Good. That should be enough time.

She found the set of modified jumper cables right where she'd left them months before, when she'd been conducting a few experiments to better understand the nature of electricity. A wizard could not control what she did not understand, so study was necessary, and electricity was something about which she was still uncertain.

She took the cables to the study and shut the door. It took her a good ten minutes to maneuver the heavy portal close enough to the nearest electrical outlet. Then she carefully fastened the positive and negative clamps into place on the copper part of the portal, following the general ideas in Sinclair's diagram.

"If I blow up the house," she muttered, "Richard will kill me. Worse, the Council will take away a large portion of my powers."

That possibility made her hesitate, but only for a few moments. Curiosity drove her. Keeping her distance from the portal, she cautiously plugged the other end of the cables into the outlet.

There was a sort of swooshing sound, a shower of sparks fell from the copper frame onto the base stone, and a low, vibrant hum filled the room. As she watched, the greenish copper began to glow, not hotly but with a weird radiance.

"Wow." Felicity circled the portal slowly. She thought she could discern a very faint, shimmer in the center of the portal. Excited, she looked around until she found something she could use to perform a little test, and settled on a paperback book she had brought into the room earlier. Standing well back, she tossed it into the center of the portal.

It disintegrated with an angry hiss.

"Yikes. That isn't good." She frowned. "But John would have tested it, too. Surely he would have. Maybe there's too much power. . . ."

The words had barely escaped her lips when she heard the grandfather clock in the foyer chime the hour of midnight. Promptly, all the lights in the study flickered, dimming and then going much too bright.

"Oh, jeez—the Y2K bug strikes." The portal was glowing brighter and brighter. The only thought in her head was that she had to unplug the portal quickly, before the power surges destroyed it. Being a wizard, she instinctively reached her hand out and sent her powers to grab the cables.

As her energy stream flowed through the device, she saw the glowing doorway change, saw the color suddenly turn from green to bright red. The shimmer in the center became a mass of swirling colors, and tendrils of those colors shot out both sides, as if reaching for something.

A tendril touched Felicity's outstretched hand.

The tendril of energy captured her, and within the space of a heartbeat pulled her into the portal.

It was like falling into a black well.

2

The trip might have lasted seconds—or months. Felicity saw colors she'd never seen before, heard sounds she couldn't define, and knew she was totally at the mercy of a force she had unthinkingly set in motion.

Then, abruptly, it was over. She felt her weight as if she'd just stepped down from something high, felt dizzy and disoriented and a little sick. The silence was absolute.

She realized she had her eyes closed, and opened them very cautiously.

For just an instant, she thought she was still in Merlin's study. There were books on shelves, a big desk cluttered with papers and more books, a fire burning in the fireplace. But that's where the resemblance ended. The light in the room came from old-fashioned sconces on the walls and an oil or kerosene desk lamp. The rug on the floor was different, and the two tall windows looked out on darkness, with hints of a skyline she dared not recognize.

"Dear God."

The voice, though it was strained with shock, affected her oddly, seeming to brush along her nerve endings in a caress that was more than pleasant. She wanted to enjoy it, to take that voice and wrap it around her, but she had a strong hunch she had more imperative things to attend to.

She realized her hands were gripping the frame of the portal, that she was standing squarely in the center of the stone base. Unnerved, she released the portal and stepped quickly out of it, then turned to see who had spoken.

He stood a few feet to one side, holding in one hand a fair duplicate of the cables she had used. He was in shirtsleeves, and something about their style struck Felicity as a bit off. It wasn't wrong exactly, just different. But she wasn't all that interested in his clothes; she was more caught by his face, which she knew almost as well as she knew her own.

John Sinclair.

The powerful emotions created in her by his picture in a book were nothing compared to her reaction to the living man standing before her. For a moment, she couldn't breathe. The feelings were a strange and restless tangle inside her, so strong they were almost painful, and the only thing she recognized clearly was an attraction so instant that she actually took a step toward him before she could stop herself.

It was like the instinctive pull toward the warmth of candlelight shining in total darkness.

"Who are you?" he asked slowly, that beautiful voice still strained. "Where did you come from?" His pale eyes flicked to the portal and then back to her, and in them was both the excitement of an inventor whose creation has performed beyond his wildest expectations—and the utter disbelief of a man of reason in the fantastic.

Felicity drew a breath and tried to keep her own confusion and panic under control. What had she done? What on earth had she *done*?

"My name is Felicity Grant. And I came—through the portal."

"How is that possible?"

She crossed her arms beneath her breasts, thinking absently that the way she was dressed—in jeans and a sweater—was probably a shock to him. "Well, you tell me. You designed and built the damned thing."

He seemed to realize he was still holding the cables, and cast them aside as he took a couple of steps toward her. "You know who I am?"

"You're John Sinclair." She concentrated on keeping her voice calm and level, deciding for the sake of her sanity to take this one step at a time. "Listen, before we get into anything else, I have to know something. Where am I?"

He blinked. "My home in Grosvenor Square. London."

She swallowed. "And the date?"

"The date? The twenty-eighth of December, 1899."

A hundred years. No—more than a hundred years.

She frowned at him, trying to make sense of what she didn't understand. "That isn't right. It's three days until New Year's Eve. How could I . . ." Her gaze strayed to the portal and the discarded cables, and she had a thought. "Is this the first time you've connected that thing to electricity?"

"Yes."

"Then that must be it." She looked at him and drew another deep breath. "Surprise. Your portal works. Only it doesn't just move people from place to place. It also moves them through time."

"That isn't possible," he said, taking another step toward her.

"Time is relative, remember? I believe that's a pet theory of yours." There was a wing-back chair nearby, and Felicity went to sit in it, feeling more than a little shaky.

He frowned. "How do you know that?"

"I know it because I looked through your workbook and saw it written there. And I know you, because I read about you in a book. A history book. A hundred years from now."

Sinclair didn't move a muscle for a long while, but then he came forward far enough to be able to study her carefully, which he did. The shock was lessening, but he was still obviously far from convinced. "I must admit, your manner of dress is unfamiliar to me. And your voice, your way of speaking—"

"I'm from America."

"I've never met an American before."

Felicity suddenly felt like a zoo exhibit, and had to smile. "I've never met a Brit, if it comes to that. But here we are.

The things is, I'm supposed to be thousands of miles and a hundred years away from here."

"I'm finding it very difficult to believe that you came from the future."

"You saw me come through the portal?"

"I—saw you appear, yes."

"Where did I come from?"

He hesitated, then said, "From another place, obviously. But another time? The portal was not designed for such travel, even had I believed it possible."

Felicity considered the matter, calling on all the discipline of an Apprentice Wizard to concentrate when too many emotions and sensations pulled her in other directions. "I think there was a glitch—a problem you couldn't have anticipated. I'd connected the portal to an electrical source a hundred years from now, and there was a power surge."

"You connected the portal?"

She didn't blame him for being confused. "A few months ago—in my time—your portal was discovered in a sealed room in your home. This house, I gather. It was sent to—to a man who was interested in your work. I was the one who went through a crate of your books and papers, and found a diagram of the portal. Just as an experiment, I . . . hooked it up to an electrical source."

Long accustomed to hiding from powerless beings the fact that she was a wizard, Felicity was uncertain now if she should tell this man. If the gate worked purely on electricity . . . But she had a hollow feeling that it was her own energy directed through the portal that had thrown her back in time. And if that were so, then she would need the same energy to get home.

Assuming she could get home.

She drew a breath to quash the surge of panic. "And the next thing I knew, I was here."

"A hundred years in your past."

"Yes."

Sinclair shook his head.

Felicity leaned back in the chair and stared at him. Quietly, she said, "A lot of your . . . dreams have become reality. We can sit hundreds or thousands of miles away from where a . . . play is taking place and watch it on a little box in our homes. It's called television. We fly in jet-powered airplanes, crossing the oceans of the world in just hours, and communicate with one another almost instantaneously. We sit at our desks and use machines to collect and sort information and to send electronic messages to one another, and that's just a tiny part of what computers do."

She paused, then added, "And many of the social reforms you've fought for have come about. We still have poor and disadvantaged people, but at least in your country and mine we also have social programs to help them, and laws to protect them and their rights. No more workhouses. Fewer class distinctions as you know them. As for women, we have the right to vote and own property in all the free countries of the world, and we can be educated and work at any profession we wish. As a matter of fact, your own country had a woman serving as prime minister until a few years ago."

That last seemed to satisfy rather than astound him, and his mouth curved in a slight smile. "It sounds like Utopia."

Felicity gave a half laugh, half sigh. "No. No, the world I live in is far from perfect. We have plenty of problems, both old and new. But I have to believe the world is improving, even if only in fits and starts."

He fell silent once more, then said, "I cannot believe this."

Felicity made up her mind. "It gets better," she told him, not without sympathy. "Or worse, depending on your point of view. I'm not exactly an . . . ordinary woman."

"I can well believe that."

She felt heat rise in her face at something in his voice, but kept her own matter-of-fact. "I don't think you'll believe this. I'm a wizard."

Sinclair put a hand out to find a chair and sat down carefully. "I see."

"Told you you wouldn't believe it." She sighed. "But that I

can prove. If, that is, I can control—Never mind." Remembering the book on magic she'd found among his belongings, she said, "Do you know anything about magic?"

"I know it is sleight of hand." The faint note in his voice told Felicity he'd been disillusioned, and it made her hopeful.

She stood up, pleased to find her legs no longer so shaky. "Okay. Is this sleight of hand?" With a slight, graceful gesture, she conjured her long black Apprentice's robe and donned it.

Sinclair blinked.

"I see you aren't convinced. Let's see . . ." She didn't tell him she had to choose carefully. Some basic spells demanded little energy, and she was confident of her ability to control it. Other spells were more demanding, and she dared not risk attempting them.

Felicity spent the next ten minutes convincing John Sinclair that magic was indeed real. She moved books off his shelves, levitated objects—including the chair, with him in it—made the fire in the fireplace blaze high and then die down to embers and blaze high again, formed a ball of energy between her hands and made it arc and swirl, and turned his favorite footstool into a pile of ash.

"Damn! I'm sorry."

"Think nothing of it." Astonishingly, he smiled. His eyes were very bright. "So. A wizard."

Felicity got rid of her black robe with a slight gesture and sat down again. "A wizard. And I think your portal sent me back here because I accidentally used some of my own energy at the exact moment there was a power surge. Now, I don't know much about the space-time continuum, but I'm guessing that because this was the first time you connected the portal to electricity, you opened a doorway into this time. And because I was . . . experimenting with the very same portal a hundred years from now, I inadvertently opened the other doorway—and got pulled into it."

Sinclair leaned forward, elbows on his knees, and stared at her, vivid interest in his eyes. "So in order to become a vehicle for time travel, there must be two doorways—the same portal in two different time periods—both activated with electricity simultaneously."

Felicity chewed on her lower lip. "I think so. Damn, I hope the Y2K bug didn't crash the power at home. If it—"

"Y2K bug? What on earth is that?"

She shook her head. "It's much too long a story to go into. Let's just say that with advancing technology come some very . . . interesting problems. The point is, if the portal in my time remains activated, I should be able to get back home. I think." She turned her brooding gaze to the portal, looking at it clearly for the first time since her arrival. And went cold.

"Wait a minute." She got to her feet and went to the portal, moving slowly. "This isn't right. It isn't finished." The wooden frame was covered with copper sheathing in only two spots—where Sinclair had attached the power cables, most likely.

He joined her, a little puzzled. "It isn't?"

Felicity tried her best to remember his diagram. "You planned to encase the entire frame in copper."

Sinclair went to his desk, then returned to her with a piece of paper. On it was the diagram Felicity had seen—but without the penciled note stating the entire frame would be sheathed in copper. "I had no such plan. The copper plates on either side of the frame were intended only to create an electrical field, not to enclose the entire structure."

Felicity looked up at him, far more aware of his nearness and its effect on her than she wanted to admit to herself. "But the portal we found was completely encased in copper. When I attached the cables, it glowed, and there was a shimmer in the center, a distortion of—of space and time, I guess."

He nodded slowly. "It makes sense that more power and a larger electrical field would be required to transport a traveler through time rather than simply over distance."

"Do you have enough copper to finish the job?"

"No, but I can have it delivered tomorrow."

They looked at each other for a moment in silence. Felicity fought a sudden and almost overpowering urge to slip her arms around his waist and lean against his powerful body. She wanted to touch him, and badly.

She took a step back, removing herself from temptation and trying very hard to think logically. "What bothers me is the fact that I don't have enough power to duplicate an electrical surge." *Not power I can control, anyway.* "If we can't match the conditions exactly, I don't think it'll work. Either I'll end up somewhere else, maybe in another time or place, or . . ." She remembered the book she'd thrown into the portal and watched disintegrate, and swallowed hard.

He lifted a hand, hesitated long enough to make them both conscious of it, then placed it on her shoulder and squeezed gently. "Then we shall find a way to duplicate the conditions," he said. "Don't be frightened, please. Somehow, I will see that you get home, Miss Grant."

"Felicity." She managed a smile. "My name's Felicity."

Grave, he said, "Felicity. Thank you."

This time, her smile was easier. "Manners are much less formal in my time. You'll have to forgive me if I appear to break all the rules of etiquette. Do you mind if I call you John?" She didn't add that she'd been calling him by that name in her mind for months before her trip here.

"Of course not. Please do." His hand squeezed again, then released her, but he didn't move away. His gaze held concern. "As much as I would enjoy talking to you for the remainder of the night, Felicity, you must be exhausted. We cannot do anything further with the portal until tomorrow. I think we both need to sleep."

"And find, with any luck, that all this was just a dream?"

"Somehow, I doubt that will prove to be the case."

She half nodded. "Yeah, I don't believe it, either. This is as real as it gets." She moved away from him, trying to seem casual. "What time is it, anyway?"

Sinclair returned to his desk briefly, leaving the diagram there and picking up a pocket watch. "Just after two. The servants will be up in another two hours.

"Oh, damn, I forgot about them. John, they can't see me. Can't know anything about me, not even that I'm here."

He shook his head. "My servants are discreet—"

"They may well be, but think about it. A young woman appearing without warning or explanation in your house in the middle of the night, and dressed like this . . . I'm obviously not English, and even if I was crazy enough to pretend otherwise, I'd be bound to make mistakes in my speech and manner they'd spot right away. Now, I don't know about you, but I'm reasonably sure even the most discreet servant would want to talk about a stranger like me. They can't know about me. If word gets out, it could—could change history, somehow."

"Felicity, they live in this house. What would you have me do?"

"Well . . . can you give them a few days off? Or maybe send them to your country house? You have one, don't you?"

"Yes, but it is more than adequately staffed."

"Never mind that. Would they go? For a few days, maybe a week?"

"Of course, if I required it of them. But—"

"It's important, John." She looked at him with pleading eyes. "I've already made a mess of things by being here. If something I do changes the future, I'll never forgive myself. Please? I just don't want to take any chances."

"Very well. But it is an unusual action to take, and it will be noted even outside this house."

"Better a small mystery than a big one."

He smiled. "I suppose." Picking up the lamp on his desk, he returned to her side. "Come, and I'll show you to a guest room."

She went with him silently, noting as they passed through the foyer and went up the curved staircase to the second floor that there were electrical light fixtures here and there on the walls, but all of them were off. It wasn't until he opened a bedroom door and turned on the switch to light that room that it occurred to her he had probably turned off all unnecessary lights before connecting the portal to electricity.

"I believe you'll be comfortable here," he told her, his voice low. "There is a connecting bathroom rather than a dressing room, and should provide you with anything you need." Then his gaze turned doubtful. "That is . . ."

"Don't worry," Felicity reassured him. "I can create anything I need, remember?"

He nodded. "Good. Lock the door. The maids will be up and about early, and it will take some time even after I talk to my butler to have them all out of the house." He paused, then added with a flicker of a smile, "I do hope your ability to create extends to meals, or we shall be reduced to eating raw whatever we find in the larder."

"I think I can keep us from starving." She found it difficult to create food from nothing, but was confident of her power to conjure meals from raw edibles.

"Good night, Felicity."

"Good night, John." She closed the door and locked it, then leaned back against it and surveyed the bedroom with a feeling of decided unreality. Was she here? Really here, in 1899? She wouldn't have believed it possible, and yet she knew without a doubt that this was no dream. As she'd said to Sinclair, this was as real as real got.

Tired beyond belief, she took only a few moments to look inside the bathroom, which was fitted out in Victorian style with actual furnishings and was much larger than the average bathroom a century later. She was amused by the water closet with its wooden box designed to hide its parts, and impressed by the size of the enameled, cast-iron tub complete with shower.

Good as a shower might feel, she had a hunch that plumbing in this time worked neither as efficiently nor as quietly as what she was used to, and she had no desire to rouse the household by making too much noise. So she merely used her powers to get cleaned up and change into a nightgown, created a brisk fire in the fireplace to take the chill off the room, and climbed into the big bed.

It was comfortable enough, but even so, for a long time Felicity found it impossible to fall asleep. Worries and questions swirled in her mind, and fear made her feel cold and very alone. What if she did something to change history? Worse, what if she was stuck here?

She reminded herself that if the situation became desperate, she could—very, very cautiously—seek out the wizards living in this time and place. A being of power could recognize another, so it would only be a matter of time before she was able to locate at least one other wizard. And that wizard would most likely do his or her best to help her. Time travel was uncommon among wizards, and frowned upon due to the dangers inherent in the practice, but it was knowledge taught to every wizard by his or her Master.

Felicity hadn't quite reached those chapters in her own study, so all she knew of the matter was that it was dangerous, that changing history could have terrible consequences—and that Merlin was going to kill her when she got home.

For the first time, she wondered if Merlin and Serena would realize what had happened. If so, the minds of two extraordinary Master Wizards would be considering the problem and how to solve it from their end.

She hoped.

Partially reassured by that, she felt herself drifting off to sleep. She was almost there when she had a last clear thought, and it followed her into dream.

According to the historical record, something she had totally forgotten, John Sinclair had, without explanation, sent his servants away for a week in the final days of 1899. And when they returned, it was to find him vanished without a trace.

History, it appeared, was so far on track.

Sinclair returned to his study, moving slowly. It was late, and it had been a long day, but he had never in his life felt less need of sleep. Or want of it.

He was half convinced that if he closed his eyes for only a moment, he would open them to find it had all been a dream. All of it. That she had been a dream.

He stood staring at the invention that had been conceived in a moment of frustration with London traffic, and shook his head in wonder. Never in his wildest dreams had he expected a visitor from the future to step through the portal, to look at him with vivid green eyes alive in a face so lovely he knew it would haunt him always.

And not only a beautiful woman from the future, but a wizard, a woman of power. A woman who had donned a long black robe with a sweep of her hand, and with the same graceful ease had lifted him and the chair in which he sat so that they drifted in the air with the lightness of a feather.

He told himself that a man of science should not believe in such strange and unearthly powers—but he was not a man to doubt the evidence of his own eyes. Her powers existed, every bit as real as she was herself.

Sinclair went to his desk and sat down, but kept his gaze fixed on the portal on the other side of the room. Just a bit of wood and copper affixed to a plain, ancient stone, such a simple and innocent doorway to have allowed wonder and magic to pass into his life.

And it would also allow that magic and wonder to pass out of his life all too soon.

He looked down at the hands that had built the portal, watched them close slowly into fists. A man's hands might open a doorway into time, but they could never master time. The hours would pass, inexorably, and the future would reclaim the haunting visitor it had so briefly sent him.

And leave him alone once again.

After a moment, Sinclair forced his hands to relax and reached for his workbook. He turned to a blank page near the back, and began sketching. Under his skilled fingers, Felicity's lovely face took shape, filled with all the life he could create with spare lines and shading and longing.

She woke to dim sounds she didn't recognize, and for a few minutes lay with her eyes closed trying to identify them. Then, as she remembered the previous night, her eyes flew open, and Felicity sat up hastily in bed. The room was quiet, the house beyond her locked door quiet, but the windows . . .

She got out of bed and crossed the room, and for a moment stood staring at the scene out in the street. Carriages and horses and people bustled along, noisy and brisk. It was obviously a chilly day, judging by the way the people were bundled up.

She shook her head and turned away from the window to quickly get dressed, creating for today a long tunic sweater in a flattering shade of gold, and dark brown slacks. She even put her hair up in a style that looked casual but elegant.

"Idiot," she muttered to herself, hardly unaware of what she was doing. "Just because he disappears in a few days doesn't mean he comes back to the future with you. That's an absurd thought. And dangerous. He probably just decides on a trip after you're gone."

She pushed speculation out of her mind, knowing it was unspeakably dangerous; she could not betray her knowledge of his future to Sinclair, because doing so risked changing what had to be. Whatever the cause or reason for his disappearance, she could not influence either him or events to make it happen—or not happen.

She left the bedroom cautiously, listening but hearing no sounds to indicate the presence of servants. A grandfather clock in the upper hall told her it was nearly ten o'clock, and she relaxed somewhat as she realized there had been time for the servants to pack up and leave.

It was easy enough to find her way downstairs; once in the foyer, she remembered the way to Sinclair's study. In fact, she found the doors open, and Sinclair already at work carefully bending thin sheets of copper around the frame of his portal.

She watched him for a moment, her eyes on his strong, sensitive hands. He molded the metal with a deft and delicate touch, using the flame of a gas lamp to soften each sheet and his fingers more than tools to shape it.

He was in shirtsleeves again today, his coat discarded over a nearby chair, and in the bright light of day the white linen emphasized the breadth and power of his shoulders.

The painting and photograph she remembered so well had caught that power in him, that innate strength and vitality even while he was utterly still. Accustomed to powerful beings, Felicity was wholly fascinated by John Sinclair, because the strength and intensity in him were of mind and muscle and sheer force of will; he owed nothing of what he was to anything that was not utterly, completely human.

And very, very male.

She had never expected to meet him in the flesh, never prepared herself for the shock to her senses that was his voice. And she had certainly never allowed herself to even imagine his touch.

But he was alive. *Alive.* And here, with her. A hundred years no longer stood between them. Age and the dusty finality of death no longer stood between them.

And the word impossible no longer seemed so undeniable.

He looked around suddenly, as if feeling her gaze or her intensity, and that hard, strong face lightened a bit. His mouth curved in a smile that was a bit wry, and his brilliant eyes reflected both satisfaction and something else she couldn't quite define.

It made her heart skip a beat.

"So you are real. I was half afraid I'd dreamt you."

"I'm real enough." She tried to keep her voice casual. "Good morning. I gather the servants are gone?"

"Yes, they left more than an hour ago." He nodded to a silver tray on a nearby table. "There's coffee, although it's cold by now."

Felicity knew he watched her as she went to the tray. She didn't make a big production of it, just put her hands on the silver pot briefly and then poured steaming coffee into the cup beside it. Then she turned to face him, sipping the coffee.

He let out a breath as though he'd been holding it. "I told myself it was incredible enough you had come from the future, that I must surely have dreamt the rest."

"Afraid not. I am a wizard." Absently, she conjured the only meal she was good at creating from nothing, a sausage biscuit, and took a healthy bite.

Sinclair looked as if he wanted to say something, but instead went back to his work. It was several minutes later when he finally asked, "Are wizards common in your time?"

"No more so than in yours." He sent her a quick, startled glance. "Oh, yes. Wizards have always walked the earth. We've just learned to hide our powers."

"Remarkable," he murmured.

Felicity set her coffee cup aside. "John, something occurred to me last night. The circuits in this house are probably overloaded quite easily, aren't they?"

He looked at her in comprehension. "You don't believe there will be power enough to activate the portal?"

She chewed on a thumbnail, then made herself stop. "I have no way of measuring, but I'm afraid there might not be."

"You said your own energy was added as well."

"Yes." She didn't even want to think about that, because she was desperately afraid she would not be able to control what she had unthinkingly created before. "But that was after the power surge. There *has* to be enough sheer electrical power." Even as the words left her lips, a memory surfaced, and she felt her heartbeat increase.

"I can tap into the main line," Sinclair said slowly. "But even that is unlikely to increase electricity to a high enough level."

Felicity drew a breath. "There's something I just remembered. I've been researching electricity lately—or was, in my own time—and I remember reading that here in London something unusual happened just at the turn of the century. On New Year's Eve, 1899, just at the stroke of midnight, three separate power stations here in London experienced an unexplained power surge."

"Just as power surged in your time."

"Yes. With one difference, I think."

Sinclair waited, brows lifting.

"In my time, it's purely a matter of technology getting in its own way. I think the power surge here in London is caused by me. I think the only way we're going to get enough power to this portal is if I draw it here myself."

3

His hands fell away from the portal, and he gazed at her with eyes like tarnished silver. Very quietly, his face utterly still, Sinclair said, "You would be killed."

"Not necessarily. Wizards enhance and use the electrical energy of our own bodies. It's quite possible for us to channel pure electricity safely. If we're careful." She knew her own fear was obvious, and cursed herself silently. If she had learned to control her powers as she should have, learned to find the "switch" somewhere inside herself, there would be nothing to be afraid of. As it was, she knew only too well that with the slightest loss of control, of concentration, the electricity would indeed kill her.

"There must be another way," Sinclair said.

"I can't think of one." She moved closer to him and the portal, and sat on the arm of a chair. His coat lay over the back, and she resisted the urge to stroke the material just to feel it beneath her fingertips. "Today is December twenty-ninth, right?"

"Yes."

She collected her thoughts and continued slowly. "The doorway on my side is tied to a very specific date, a moment in time when a massive power surge combined with my own powers to activate it."

He frowned slightly, his brilliant mind almost visibly at work behind the intensity of his eyes. "So we must attempt to return you to your time only moments after you left—while the power connected to that portal is still surging. While that side of the doorway remains open."

She drew a breath. "I have to aim for a very small window of opportunity. And I can't alter history to do it, or the entire future could be at risk. So, if I'm right about the power surges at the London power plants on New Year's Eve, we have until midnight on December thirty-first to get this portal ready."

Sinclair glanced at the portal and assessed his work so far. "The remainder of the copper should arrive by afternoon, and it should not require many hours to mold it into place. Tapping into the main power lines will be more difficult and time-consuming—if I'm to do it without attracting notice."

It wasn't a question, but Felicity nodded. "Definitely without attracting notice. And it would be far better to make sure we leave no evidence of what we're doing, to be found and puzzled over by someone else at a later date. Just . . . in case something goes wrong, I mean."

They were both aware that where there was electricity, there could be fires and explosions deadly enough to destroy everything in the vicinity.

"In that case, it may require the better part of a day." He looked at her. "Still, I believe we can be ready to make the attempt by midnight of December thirty-first."

She almost winced. "Attempt. The problem is, I think . . . I'll only have one chance at it."

"Why?"

She hadn't wanted to tell him, but he needed to have all the information. "When I first connected the portal in my time to electricity, I threw a book into the doorway to see what would happen. It was destroyed. Instantly."

His face tightened. "I see. Then we must be very sure before you step through the portal."

"How can we be sure of anything? I have no idea why it

destroyed the book and then later just—just!—sent me back in time."

Sinclair smiled slightly. "It is my invention, Felicity. It may have performed far beyond my expectations, but I designed it, and I will calculate every variable necessary to assure your safety."

For the first time since her unexpected journey had landed her here, Felicity felt a real sense of confidence, and if it was fleeting, at least it gave her some comfort. "In that case, why don't you get to work on those calculations. I don't understand enough about electricity, to say nothing of math or physics, to be able to help you with the brain work, but I think I can handle the copper plates."

Sinclair was agreeable, and after showing Felicity exactly how to mold the copper around the portal's frame, he went to his desk and got to work. The room was not silent; he asked her a number of very specific questions as to the appearance of the portal just before she had come through it, as well as several about electricity in her time. She could answer some of the questions, but had to guess at others.

"Will it matter?" she asked him.

He frowned down at papers on which his calculations were beginning to take shape. "I believe I can compensate for the—gaps in my knowledge."

Felicity turned her attention to her own work. Rather than use the oil lamp flame to soften the plates, she was letting some of her own power flow as gently as she could manage from her fingertips, and the results were quite good. It was some minutes before she remembered her conversation with Merlin, and his statement that the Elder who had discovered the portal believed it was partially wizard-made.

Looking at her fingers molding the copper gently, feeling the pulse of her power, she murmured, "Mine. It was partially my own power I felt when I touched it."

After a century.

"Felicity?"

She looked across the room at him, and smiled. "Another wizard was certain this portal was partially wizard-made. It looks like he was right after all."

"So power lingers in wizard-made objects?"

"Always. Only wizards can sense it, and even we can't always distinguish between something a wizard made and something with innate power of its own." Her fingers smoothed the copper gently. "A hundred years from now, this portal retains so much power it feels as if it has a heartbeat."

"Then your power must be considerable."

"When combined with electricity, at least." She sent him a quick smile. "I doubt it was all mine."

He bent his head to his work for some time, then looked up with another question. "You said wizards create and use the electrical energy of their own bodies. Is the power positive or negative?"

"For me, negative. For all female wizards, as a matter of fact. Males have positive energies."

"Always?"

"Always."

"Then a male and female can combine their power? Be stronger together than separately?"

"If they trust each other enough, yes. It's a tricky thing, trust between wizards. And especially between the sexes. Males and females can combine their power, but they can also use it against each other. It has been known to cause . . . problems in the past."

"Do wizards ever . . . marry?"

Felicity kept her gaze firmly on the portal. "Sure. Most marry powerless mates, perhaps because of the question of trust. But there are mated pairs of wizards. As a matter of fact, I study with one pair."

"And you?"

She glanced over her shoulder to find his eyes on her. "What about me?"

"You aren't married?"

"No." She drew a breath. "I've been studying hard the last five years, and there hasn't really been time . . . Even if I had the inclination, I've hardly had a chance to meet anyone."

"I see."

Felicity forced herself to look away from him and appear

to be paying attention only to her work. "And it's a bit problematical, anyway. Just confessing to a powerless man that I'm a wizard will be difficult enough. And for him, hitching his fate to a being of power isn't the easiest thing in the world to do. Our art demands so much of our time and attention, for one thing. For another, we have to live in a world that denies our existence and disbelieves in our abilities."

"A secret life," Sinclair said.

"A life with secrets, at any rate." She watched her fingers gently smooth the gleaming copper. "We have to obey the laws of man—and the laws of wizards. And sometimes the two don't mix very well."

"For instance?"

"Oh . . . it's difficult to explain. As wizards, we're expected to practice, to perfect our abilities, and yet we're always forbidden to expose ourselves to the powerless. So we take planes when teleportation would be so much faster and easier. We buy clothing instead of creating it. We hold down normal jobs and at least appear to live normal human lives. At the same time, the Council of Elders enforces laws that have bound wizards for millennia."

"Laws that ban your interference in the lives of the . . . powerless?"

"That's a large part of it. Laws designed to hide or disguise what we are. To protect both our society and that of the powerless from the . . . unbridled ambition of any wizard."

"So there are wizards who would use their abilities to control others?"

"Wizards can be very human in that respect. Once one gains superior abilities, it's not a very big step to imagine oneself as having superior wisdom. The Council makes very sure that none of us exerts undue influence over the powerless or each other. All of us are under observation, and they take away powers if they have to. Both the control and the punishments of the Council can be . . . severe." She paused, frowning, then went on in a lighter tone, "We haven't had any serious problems among wizards for generations, literally centuries."

Sinclair watched her intently, absorbing the fleeting

expressions that crossed her face as she talked, the rise and fall of her musical voice. "You know the punishment of the Council firsthand, do you not?"

Felicity half turned to look at him in surprise. A little laugh, not entirely humorous, escaped her. "Am I that transparent?"

"What did they do to you?" he asked without answering her question.

She hesitated for a moment, absently rubbing the fingertips of one hand with the fingers of the other. "Nothing. Not yet, anyway. Let's just say they have the authority and the power to impose penalties for . . . shortcomings. They expect a great deal of us. Sometimes those expectations aren't easy to live up to."

Slowly, Sinclair said, "You walk a difficult path."

She smiled suddenly, vividly, and it caught at his breath. "Maybe. But I'm a wizard. Believe me, the joys and benefits far outweigh the pains and disadvantages."

"Do they?"

"Oh, yes." She turned back to her work, and this time her smile was both content and faraway.

He watched her still, seeing the lovely shell of a mystery that would, he knew, prove endlessly fascinating. Her kind had walked with his all through history, and yet he knew nothing of her life, of the obviously complex and ancient society of wizards. And what must it be like for her, a woman of power in a world where, undoubtedly, there were still arbitrary limitations placed upon women?

Sinclair doubted very much that a hundred years had changed men convinced by the history of thousands of years of their own superiority. Yet here was Felicity, gifted with extraordinary abilities and what was obviously a curious and highly intelligent mind; how did she reconcile her undoubted superiority over most men with their conspicuous belief in her place as inferior to them?

He wanted the answer to that question. To all his questions about Felicity, about who and what she was. He wanted to understand what made her smile so vividly one moment and so wistfully the next. He wanted to understand why she feared the Council of Elders, why her voice contained both respect and anxiety when she mentioned them. He wanted to learn more about the laws governing wizards. He wanted to ask question after question, just to hear her voice.

Most of all, he just wanted to listen to her voice.

The clock on the mantel told him that time was passing, the minutes and hours ticking away. In the back of his mind, he was automatically calculating all the variables to make certain Felicity could step safely through the portal. On the desk before him, mathematical formulas raced across page after page, and still his gaze lifted again and again to watch her.

How could he have so little time with her?

Abruptly, trying to distract himself from an increasingly painful awareness, he said, "I gather horses no longer provide most transportation in your time? I mean for powerless people?"

"They're mostly used for sport. People ride for exercise, or to show off their ability to ride. And racehorses still run. But automobiles took over the world."

"I see. And this . . . television you mentioned? Transmitting images from one place to another? Is this a large part of everyday life?"

"Is it ever. So are computers."

"Computers?"

At first, Felicity hesitated to say too much because she thought it might distract him from the work he was doing, but it became obvious he was perfectly capable of thinking of at least three things at once—and calculating in longhand at the same time.

He really was a remarkable man.

So Felicity answered his questions, grateful to be able to fill the silence between them with unimportant chatter.

He was endlessly curious, and she amused him several times with her colorful explanations. She amused him even more when she conjured a small feast for their lunch, using no more than some raw vegetables and smoked beef from the kitchen.

"This is not my strong suit," she warned.

"It tastes fine. But what are these?"

"We call them French fries. A delicacy from my time."

"Why are you laughing?"

"Private joke. Eat your lunch."

By late afternoon, the remaining copper plates had been delivered, and Felicity had over half the frame covered. Sinclair had continued to work at his desk, and though he had sworn beneath his breath several times and torn up a number of sheets of paper in apparent frustration, it seemed he was making progress—even while continuing to ask her occasional questions about the future.

As the weak winter sunlight faded into twilight, he got up from the desk to turn on the lights in the room, pausing near the fireplace to eye the brisk fire there thoughtfully. "This fire has burned precisely this way since last night, without any tending or additional fuel."

Felicity stepped back away from the portal and rubbed her hands together absently, only dimly aware of the ache. "It'll continue to do so until I tell it otherwise. A characteristic of a wizard-influenced fire. Remember last night, when I was demonstrating my powers?"

"I remember." He looked at her for a moment, then crossed the room and took her hands in his.

Before she could react except with an indrawn breath, she realized he was examining her fingertips intently.

"That copper has sharp edges," he murmured. "Your fingers must be sore by now."

"A little," she admitted huskily, gazing at his bent head. There were a few threads of silver among the black, and they unaccountably sent a pang through her.

He looked up and met her gaze, and for several heartbeats they were both very still. Then his fingers tightened on hers, and Sinclair's eyes dropped to her mouth. He seemed to lean toward her, and there was something in his face that made Felicity catch her breath again.

Whether it was that faint sound that broke the spell, or some thought of his own, Sinclair slowly straightened and released her hands. His face was still once more, unreadable. "We should stop work for the day," he said formally. "I should be able to complete my calculations tomorrow, and it's clear you will have the portal finished."

She moved away from him toward the fireplace, and stood gazing down at the flames. "That gives you all day on the thirty-first to tap into the major power lines." Her voice was remarkably steady, she thought.

"Yes. Enough time, I should think."

Time. We have all the time in the world. And none at all.

"Good. That's good," she said.

He was silent for a few minutes, as though he, too, didn't know what to say. But then he joined her at the fireplace, standing on the other side, and spoke lightly.

"You've told me a great deal about the future. But you've said nothing about my future."

Felicity kept her eyes on the fire. "If I told you anything about your future, that could change it. I can't say or do anything to change history."

"Won't your mere presence here, the interaction with me, change history?"

"I hope not. I shouldn't even have told you anything at all of the future, but—" She swallowed.

"But?"

"Nothing." She could feel his gaze, the probing scrutiny of that brilliant, questioning mind, and was afraid he would eventually figure out why she felt somewhat safe in giving him a glimpse into the future.

Because he would not be here to change the past.

She hurried on. "Besides, what choice do I have? All I can do is try to stay hidden and leave here as soon as possible. The longer I stay here, the more likely it is that someone else will see me, or that I'll somehow change what has to be."

Sinclair said, "Perhaps your presence here is meant to be a part of history. That is possible, isn't it?"

"Possible—but I can't know for sure." She looked at him finally. "So many things will happen in the coming hundred years. Important things, advances in science and technology.

Discoveries. Wars. And so many of those things happen because of a delicate balance of people and actions. Time is . . . such a fragile thing."

And we have so little of it. He tried not to allow the growing pain of that realization to show on his face. Tried not to reach out and touch her once again, even though he wanted to with a need stronger than anything he had ever felt before. A need he had to fight, to master.

He had no right to even try to hold her here.

He looked at her steadily, concentrated on keeping the conversation going with at least the appearance of ease. "I get the feeling you are counting this experience as a lesson well learned."

"Well, let's just say I won't be experimenting with any more artifacts without adult supervision." She saw his puzzlement, and added somewhat reluctantly, "I'm still in training, still an Apprentice wizard. I had no business connecting the portal to electricity, not without Merlin being there."

Sinclair's brows rose. "Merlin?"

"Richard Patrick Merlin. My Master wizard."

"Not the original Merlin, I gather."

Felicity had to smile. "I don't think so. But he can be fairly enigmatic, so I've never been absolutely sure."

"He is one of two with whom you study?"

"Yes, his wife Serena is also my Master. But Merlin is a tenth-degree Master, superior to both of us combined, in terms of raw power. He doesn't command Serena because they're mates and deeply in love, but he does command me. By my choice and by tradition, I must obey him."

"You fear him?"

"I'm not afraid he'll hurt me, if that's what you mean. He's a great wizard—and a very good man. Far kinder to me than I sometimes deserve. But power and knowledge must be used wisely, and Apprentice wizards should be supervised whenever they contemplate doing something foolish."

"Such as electrifying a portal?"

"Exactly."

He drew a breath. "I'm sorry you feel it was a mistake."

Felicity made herself look away from him. "How could it be anything else? Not only have I broken a rather important law of wizards by traveling through time without permission or even supervision, I risk changing history and—and I've disrupted your life."

He took a step toward her. "You have not *disrupted* my life, Felicity. Brought magic and wonder into it, yes. Taught me there are fascinating mysteries yet to be explored, yes. Renewed my faith in the future of mankind . . . yes."

"I did all that?" She managed a smile, but still didn't look at his face. She could see his hand gripping the mantel, powerful and beautiful and tense, feel him close to her.

"And more." He paused, then went on steadily, "Yesterday I was finding life decidedly . . . uninteresting. There had been too many failures recently, too many disappointments. I found myself wondering if I—if any man, any person—could make a true difference."

"You can. You did."

"Did I?"

The wry note in his voice made her smile again. "You have to remember, I read about you in a history book."

"And from your point of view, in your time, I'm long dead."

Felicity shied away from thinking about that. He was so alive, so vital and intense beside her, she simply could no longer think of him as a man existing only in the pages of history. If she ever had.

Without responding to what he'd said, she changed the subject abruptly. "I think I'll go down to the kitchen and see what I can find for our dinner."

"Yes. Of course."

Still without meeting his gaze, she turned away and headed for the kitchen. Giving herself something to do helped focus her thoughts, but her emotions were so turbulent that her wayward energies destroyed two lights in the kitchen and totally wrecked her first attempt to conjure dinner.

She sat down and put her head in her hands, trying

desperately to get control of herself. The smell of food burnt to a crisp was acrid in the room, and her stomach churned, her head throbbed.

"Control," she whispered. "I have to control this . . ."

Without control of her powers, there was no way she could return safely to her own time. And as tempting as it was to remain here with him, in this time—and, God, how tempting it was!—that was totally impossible. Living in this time, she would without doubt change the future, and Felicity wasn't willing to damage the future and the people she knew for her own selfish reasons, even if she knew she could be happy in this time.

Even if Sinclair could learn to feel for her even a fraction of what she felt for him.

So she did her best to push aside useless longings, and fought to control her powers. As hard as she tried, the inner switch still eluded her; all she could do was gather her energies painstakingly, dampen and redirect them with utter concentration. It took a great deal out of her, and when at last it was done, she sat there feeling shaky and frightened.

She didn't need a mathematician to tell her that even with Sinclair's brilliant mind calculating all the variables, the odds against a successful return to her own time were incredibly high. Because of her. Because she could not adequately control her own powers. And she had an instinctive certainty that failure would not mean being transported to a different time or another place. It would mean her death.

Felicity drew a deep breath and climbed to her feet. She couldn't let herself think about that. There was no choice except to move forward and do what she had to do.

Her second attempt to conjure dinner was more successful, and they ate the meal as they had before, informally and with little conversation. Felicity was too conscious of him and her feelings for him to be able to relax.

When had fascination turned into something else? When he had stood before her in the flesh? When she had heard his voice? When she had looked into his eyes and realized how badly she wanted him to kiss her?

"You are very quiet," he said.

They had returned to his study, and she realized she was staring broodingly at the portal without seeing it. She turned away from it to find him watching her intently.

"Am I? Sorry. Maybe we could play chess or something. It's too early to go to bed." She felt heat rising in her face, and silently cursed the betrayal.

Sinclair remained near the fireplace and kept his full attention on her. "Felicity, I don't mind silence. But you are clearly . . . uncomfortable with me. Was it something I said?"

"No, of course not."

"Then what is it?"

"Nothing. I'm just a little worried, that's all. I'm a hundred years and a few thousand miles from home, and I'm not sure I'll be able to get back." Her voice was brittle and she knew it. "I would say that's enough to make anybody disinclined to talk very much."

"I'm sorry. That was thoughtless of me. Of course you are concerned." He took a step toward her. "I want to reassure you, but—"

"But all those calculations today showed you what I knew already. The odds are against me. It's all right. I do know that. But I don't have a choice, do I?"

Her courage and the wistfulness of her smile nearly broke his heart. He wanted to put his arms around her, to hold her so close not even time would be able to take her away from him. He told himself once again he had no right, but even as he faced that painful reminder, he heard himself speak steadily.

"You could stay."

Felicity chose to read nothing personal in the statement, and answered calmly. "No, I couldn't. Living here, I would most certainly change the future. Besides, I don't belong here. I never could."

"Felicity—"

She abruptly gestured toward the portal. "I've been curious about something. Why did you construct the base using a stone from Stonehenge?"

At first it seemed Sinclair wasn't going to answer, but finally he drew a breath and said, "I visited there as a child, and fancied I could feel a—a throbbing in the stones. I convinced myself that there was an unknown power source waiting to be tapped."

"Maybe you were right. Copper and electricity alone couldn't have done it."

"And perhaps it was simply the power of a wizard."

She shook her head. "No, from the moment I connected it to electricity, there was something . . . something otherworldly about it. My power might have been the catalyst, but your invention would have been remarkable without it."

"As a destructive force? You said it obliterated a book."

"You weren't there to calculate all the variables." She returned her gaze to Sinclair, making herself smile calmly. "But you're here, so we don't have to worry about that."

"Do we not?" His voice was strained. "Then just what is it you are worried about?"

Felicity shrugged jerkily, and sat in a chair. "My part. Even if I remember exactly how much energy I used when I reached through the gate, duplicating it will be difficult. And there are no mathematical calculations to help me do that." She drew a breath. "So . . . the odds are even longer than you know."

Sinclair came to sit on the other chair, leaning forward with his elbows on his knees as he stared at her. His expression was still grim, his voice a bit rough when he said, "You said there were other wizards in this time. Could we find one to help you?"

"No."

"But—"

"John, wizards are very good at keeping their own historical records. They don't leave things out. And there is no mention in the history of wizards of any wizard from this time helping one from the future. It didn't happen. So it can't happen."

"Forgive me," he said, "but I am more concerned with your safety than with the future."

"You wouldn't be if it were your time at risk." She kept her voice steady with an effort.

"You are wrong about that." There was something she'd

never seen before in the depths of his eyes, and his mouth curved suddenly in a smile that was a bit reckless. "Quite wrong."

Felicity felt herself respond, felt her heart leap and pulse quicken, but then she reminded herself sharply that it was absurd to believe he could feel so much for her after so short a time. He simply didn't understand the stakes involved in changing the future, that was all.

She ignored the other little voice in her head that reminded her John Sinclair was not at all deficient in understanding.

With an effort that hurt, she looked away from his clear eyes and got to her feet. "I think . . . I'm really tired. We need to get an early start tomorrow, anyway. Good night, John."

She was at the door before he said, "Good night, Felicity."

4

The following day, December thirtieth, was spent much as the previous day had been. Sinclair worked at his desk, while she worked to finish molding the copper plates to the portal. Conversation was casual, and confined for the most part to Sinclair's occasional questions about either the portal or the future, and her brief replies. Felicity was determinedly calm, even cheerful, and kept such a rigid hold on her emotions that even conjuring the meals they required proved trouble-free.

And when the silences grew longer, as night closed around them and the faint sounds from the streets outside died away, she began talking about whatever entered her head, subjects ranging from some of the more esoteric of a wizard's powers to the very latest thing in twentieth-century marvels.

"Of course, it's difficult to explain the Internet even if you understand how it works, and between you and me I don't believe many people do understand it. But it's an amazing thing, a storehouse of the most incredible information on every conceivable subject."

"Indeed."

She was acutely aware that he had stopped working and turned sideways at the desk to watch her. She could feel his gaze, his absorption in her, and that fixed scrutiny shook her control until she actually felt it begin to desert her. Her fingers trembled as she smoothed and molded the last of the copper plates to the portal, and she felt heat spreading outward through her body. She couldn't seem to breathe properly, and she heard the tremor in her voice when she made herself keep talking.

"Yes, it's fascinating. Of course, there are drawbacks, because anyone can contribute to the information, and you can't always be sure what you're reading is accurate or truthful, but it's still an amazing thing."

"It certainly sounds that way."

She realized he was coming toward her, crossing the room with a deliberate tread.

Quickly, she said, "But technology's gotten so advanced that it does tend to get in its own way. That Y2K bug I mentioned earlier, for instance—"

Sinclair turned her to face him, his hands on her shoulders. Softly, he said, "Stop it, Felicity. Stop it now."

She fixed her gaze on his loosened tie, the unfastened top button of his shirt. "I don't know what you mean."

His hands tightened on her shoulders. "Yes, you do. You believe if you fill the silence and the space between us with meaningless words, you won't have to face what is really there."

"Nothing is there."

"No?" He surrounded her face with his hands and forced her gently to meet his gaze. "Are you sure?"

Felicity wanted to say yes. She knew it was what she should say. In hardly more than twenty-four hours, she would have to turn her back on this man and step through a doorway that would either take her somewhere and sometime else, or kill her. No matter which it was, she would never see John Sinclair again, and it was the height of insanity to even consider a deeper involvement with him in the hours they had left.

"Are you sure, Felicity?"

"Yes," she whispered, achingly conscious of his thumbs brushing gently back and forth across her cheekbones. She wanted to close her eyes and lean into his touch, luxuriate in it, in him.

He bent his head and kissed her, his lips warm and hard and very sure of her response.

Felicity thought her knees probably buckled, because that was the only excuse she could offer herself when her arms slid up around his neck. She just needed the support, that was all. Otherwise, she would have fallen.

But she *was* falling.

She felt his hands sliding down her back to her hips, drawing her even closer, and her mouth opened helplessly beneath the hungry pressure of his. Need burned through her veins like wildfire, and she had the certain realization that some things were worth it, however high the price climbed.

He raised his head slowly and stared down at her, those brilliant eyes darkened and hot. "Tell me that was nothing," he said huskily.

She just stopped herself from making a sound of sheer frustration, and had to concentrate hard in order to speak words that made sense. "You aren't being fair."

His mouth brushed hers again, then retreated. "I have no time to be fair, Felicity. You've come through my life like a whirlwind, and tomorrow you'll be gone. I have no right, no right at all, but I cannot let you go without . . ."

"Without tasting the future?" she whispered.

His entire face softened in a look Felicity knew she would never forget as long as she lived. "No. You. At least . . . a taste. A touch. I've always thought I would recognize the right woman when I met her. I was right." His mouth twisted a little. "And damn fate for taking her away from me so quickly."

"Not—not until tomorrow."

"No. Not until tomorrow. So we have . . . some time left." He drew a breath, and she felt him tensing to pull back away from her. "I had no right, but I won't apologize."

Felicity knew he was about to end what had barely begun, that he was enough in control of desire to be the gentleman he had undoubtedly been raised to be. It was a fundamentally decent and honorable gesture from a bygone age, and for an instant she was almost tempted to let him go. Almost.

"I don't want you to apologize." She let her fingers slide up into his silky hair, and felt a little shiver deep inside her at the sensuous touch of it.

"Felicity—"

"You made me admit it," she reminded him. "And you're right. I was talking to avoid facing how I feel. Even . . . to avoid facing you. But I have to face it now." She moved slightly against him, a seductive action that was wholly deliberate.

Sinclair's eyes half closed and a muscle tightened in his jaw. "How . . . do you feel?"

"It happened just as suddenly to me, but I've had months to get used to it." She raised herself on tiptoe so she could feather her lips teasingly near his. "Ever since I saw a picture of you in a book. I knew then. It was like recognizing the other half of my soul."

One of his hands slid up her back to the nape of her neck, probing beneath her long hair, and his eyes burned down at her. He kissed her, the gentleness rapidly becoming urgent with hunger.

Even so, Felicity could feel him once more attempting to regain control, and knew what was in his mind as surely as if it were her own. Against his lips, she whispered, "It's all right. Please. I want this. I want you."

"Felicity . . ."

"This is not a mistake. It could never be a mistake, John." She pressed herself even closer, allowing her building desire to fuel his.

Sinclair was a strong man, but even he couldn't fight the need in both of them. With a smothered sound, he lifted her into his arms and held her cradled securely as he carried her from the study and up the stairs to his bedroom. A lamp on the nightstand was the only light in the room.

Without thinking about it or even glancing in that direction, Felicity conjured a brisk fire on the grate, even though she wasn't cold. There was heat enough inside her, and that fever was rising.

She wanted him so wildly she knew she was shaking with it, her fingers trembling as she helped him cope with buttons and unfamiliar fastenings. And the hunger in him was just as intense. His kisses held the keen knowledge of how little time they had, his caresses exploring her body as if he meant to imprint what she was on his mind, to see him through a bleak and empty future.

On some level, Felicity was astonished at how strongly she felt his emotions, but on another, deeper level, she understood that her love for him had opened a new door for her, both as a woman and as a wizard. A bond was being forged between them, a connection that would endure as long as they lived.

Passion was the fire of that forge, the affinity of their minds and spirits the iron and carbon, and their aching knowledge of the loss soon to come was the crucible.

Felicity was hardly aware of being lifted until she felt the bed beneath her. She was blind and deaf to everything but him, his face, his touch, the hard strength of his body, and the rough velvet of his voice. And all she could feel was the desperate, spiraling force of her own need.

It surged inside her like a living thing, fed by his touch, by the slow, potent joining of their bodies. Instinct drove her toward some unknown pinnacle of sensation, and when she finally reached it she could only cling to him in wonder.

For a long time, the only sound that disturbed the peaceful silence of the dimly lit bedroom was the crackle of the fire. Felicity lay close to his side, boneless in a physical contentment but wide awake, watching her fingers trace invisible patterns among the silky dark hair on his chest.

His arms around her tightened suddenly, and his low voice broke the silence between them. "How can I let you go now?"

She rubbed her cheek against his shoulder, closing her

eyes against the sharp pain. "There's no choice. You know that."

"I can come with you."

For just an instant, Felicity let herself hope, but then fear for him jolted through her even sharper and stronger than any pain she'd known before. *I can't control my powers. God knows where and when I'll end up, if I even survive. I can't risk his life. If he died because of me . . .* In her mind was the certain knowledge that he would vanish from this place soon, and it terrified her to think he could die because of her.

Had it been her selfishness that had deprived the world of this brilliant man? Had she taken the chance and allowed him to step with her through the portal that destroyed them both? And would she change the future if she chose now, this time, to take that step alone?

How many times had she, would she, make this journey and face these agonizing questions?

Was the journey successful? Had John Sinclair vanished from this time because he had gone to the future with her? Had she died in the attempt, and had he been killed as well, either at the same time or later?

She didn't know the right answer. All she could do was follow her instincts and say what she thought had to be said.

"Felicity, I can come with you. There is nothing here to hold me, nothing I care about."

She turned her head to press her lips gently to his shoulder, then pushed herself up on an elbow and looked down at him. "Your life is here."

"There is nothing here I care about," he repeated.

Felicity drew a steadying breath. "You don't understand. Your *life* is here. You're alive and well here. How do you think I'd feel if I let you come with me—and got you killed?"

He shook his head, vivid eyes fixed on her face with such longing she could hardly bear it. "Without you, what kind of life will it be? I don't ever want to be without this feeling, Felicity. I don't ever want to be without you."

"Do you think I want to be without you? But we don't

have a choice, John. I have to go back, and I won't risk your life when I can't be sure of controlling my own powers."

"Is it not my risk to take?"

"No."

"I built the portal, Felicity."

"Yes. But it was my power that sent me back in time. You know that now, don't you?"

Reluctantly, he nodded. "I completed the calculations. If we draw enough electrical power, we can activate the portal. But that should only send a traveler to another place. Probably to Stonehenge, where the stones would resonate and provide a destination point. To send a traveler through time requires a kind of energy I have no way of creating. Without your power, it is merely a device to transport over distance. Not time."

It was something Felicity had known but hadn't wanted to think about. She nodded. "There it is, then. I might—*might*—be able to duplicate the precise amount of power I used to bring me here. But I can't control my powers with enough certainty to add another person into the equation."

Sinclair opened his mouth to protest, but Felicity added a soft declaration that stopped him.

"It could kill us both."

He would eagerly have risked his own life to be with her, but not if that action put her life in greater danger.

Felicity saw that certainty settle heavily over him, felt his pain and loss, and her own anguish tore at her. She leaned down, pressing herself against him, and kissed him with all the longing inside her.

"Make love to me," she whispered. "It's all we have."

Neither of them slept very much during the remainder of the night. They dozed briefly, only long enough to replenish their strength so they could make love again and again. They said little with words, but their emotions were so powerful and raw they were a language all their own.

Because she was so emotionally distraught, Felicity's

energies surged unpredictably, causing the fire in the fireplace to blaze high one minute and die to embers the next, and bursting the bulb in the bedside lamp as well as those in two sconces near the doorway.

Sinclair was more fascinated than disturbed, but because Felicity was so upset by this continuing demonstration of her lack of control, he soothed rather than questioned.

They left their bed reluctantly not long after dawn. Sinclair was fairly sure it would take him most of the day to unobtrusively tap into three main power lines near his house, and both of them wanted to get that done so they could spend the evening together.

There was little Felicity could do to fill the hours while he was gone. Little except think and question her own decisions and motives. The portal was finished, all the copper plates molded in place, so she had not even that to occupy her thoughts or her fingers. She wandered around his house, not really looking at anything so much as absorbing the most intimate part of his world and his life.

It was early afternoon when she thought of the sealed room in which the portal had been found, and looking for that occupied her attention for a while. Because it was so well hidden, she had to use her wizard's abilities to locate it, discovering the door cannily hidden behind a bookcase in the study.

The small and windowless room housed the remnants of earlier experiments. She couldn't identify most of the gadgets and bits of wire and metal she found in several boxes, but on the worktable near the center of the room, she did recognize the small notebook in which he had kept some of his drawings, notes, and theories.

Felicity looked through that for a few minutes, then left the room as she'd found it and closed it up once again. After that, there was nothing for her to do but wait.

Sinclair returned just before four o'clock, and she met him in the foyer, her heart leaping at the eagerness in his eyes and the strength of his arms as they closed around her.

"God, I missed you," he murmured, nuzzling his face against her neck. "This has been the longest day of my life."

"For me, too."

He drew back just far enough to gaze down at her. "I have to spend a few more minutes outside running the power line into the house and to the study, then I'll be finished."

"We should probably move the portal out of your study to someplace where power surges would do less damage. Why not your secret room?"

He didn't seem surprised that she had found it. Somewhat rueful, he said, "With the other failed experiments?"

"I don't know about your other experiments, but some of your theories will revolutionize the way we look at the world."

That startled him. "Indeed?"

Felicity regretted the words the instant they left her mouth. His theories were no less valid because someone else would get the credit for them, but she was suddenly, painfully conscious of that fact.

Quickly, she said, "Why don't you go ahead and run the power line into that room while I see what I can find in the kitchen. You must be starving by now."

Before she could move completely away from him, he caught her hand. "Felicity? What is it you haven't told me?"

He was too perceptive. "Nothing." She couldn't tell him he would vanish from his own time, and soon. Whatever happened had to happen as it was meant to.

Sinclair let her go, but his expression was thoughtful as he went to finish his work.

By the time he was done, Felicity had a meal ready for them, not confessing that her first attempt had resulted in an inedible mess. Her energies were surging, and she knew it would only get worse as the hour for her departure drew closer and her pain increased.

Dammit, why can't I find the switch?

That question haunted her even as she tried to build enough memories of Sinclair to last her the rest of her life. Assuming she had a life beyond today. She watched him move, listened to him talk, reveled in the touch of his hands. She tried her best to make every moment they had left count.

After they'd eaten, they moved the portal into the secret room.

"You should have put this on wheels," she noted.

"That would make things easier." Sinclair opened the bookcase doorway and went into the room to turn on the lamp on his worktable. When he came back out, he looked at her intently. There was no more warning than that, no preface to his abrupt, calm question. "I have no future in this time, have I, my love?"

She froze. "I—I don't know what you mean."

He came to her slowly, halting an arm's length away. His expression was grave. "Almost from the moment you arrived, what concerned you most was not changing the future. You were determined to do nothing that would alter what had to be. Yet when I asked you questions about the future, you never hesitated to answer them. You told me a great deal, gave me knowledge that could enable me to . . . anticipate the future. If I had one, of course."

Felicity swallowed hard. "I knew you weren't unscrupulous. Knew you wouldn't—"

He was shaking his head. "Simply having the knowledge could have an effect, we both know that. My decisions, my choices, actions—all could be colored by that knowledge whether I wished it or not."

She was silent.

"You know how I die, don't you, Felicity?"

"No," she answered immediately. "I don't know. I don't know that." At once, she realized the answer told him more than she had intended.

Sinclair's eyes narrowed. "Then history doesn't record my death, but my . . . disappearance?"

"I—I don't—"

"When? When do I disappear?"

"John—"

"Is it tonight? Could it be?"

"I can't tell you that! Don't you see? Whatever decisions you make have to be your own, not influenced by me or anything I tell you about what happened."

"Felicity, has it occurred to you that all of this—our being together, the things you've told me, even the questions you answer now—are part of what happened? That you could change the future you know by *not* telling me?"

She uttered a little sound that was almost a laugh. "Has it occurred to me? I've been questioning and second-guessing myself since the moment I got here. I don't know, John. I don't know what to do, other than what I think is right from moment to moment."

He pulled her into his arms and held her tightly. "I'm sorry. I didn't mean to upset you."

She burrowed even closer, holding on to as much of him as she could, then drew back and looked up at him with forced calm. "The only thing I know for sure is that I can't control my powers. And because I can't control them, taking anyone else with me through the portal is a guaranteed death sentence. I won't risk your life, John. Please . . . please don't ask me to do that."

He touched her face, his fingers gentle, then bent his head and kissed her. "All right. I won't ask you anything else." His expression was still, his control obvious. "Why don't we get everything ready for . . . for tonight."

Felicity nodded. She helped him with the portal, warily using just a bit of her power, conscious of how fragile her control was. That task was barely accomplished when they both heard the distant sound of the door knocker.

For a moment, Sinclair looked surprised, but then he remembered. "One of the scientific journals wanted a photograph, and I agreed. That will be the photographer. I can send him away—"

"No, go ahead." Felicity thought she could use a few minutes by herself anyway.

"The study was suggested—"

"That's fine. I'll stay in here. Push the door to and he'll never know I'm here."

Sinclair hesitated, but finally nodded and left the secret room.

The lamp provided all the light Felicity needed, but the

utter silence of the room began wearing on her nerves after several minutes. She went to the door and listened, then eased it open just a few inches.

Luckily, the photographer standing just a few feet away had his back to her, his camera set up to photograph Sinclair standing at the fireplace on the other side of the room.

Felicity started to close the bookshelf door again, but at that moment Sinclair looked past the photographer and saw her. She had no idea what the photographer was saying, and she didn't think Sinclair heard the man, either.

Several moments before the flash of the camera confirmed it, she found herself gazing at the picture that had obsessed her from the first moment she had seen it in a book. Sinclair, handsome and strong, his expression controlled, his head a little turned, his eyes fixed on . . . her. And the look in his eyes that had haunted her, and wrenched at her heart, was love and loss and loneliness.

She made herself ease the door shut and, tears blinding her, felt her way to the chair at his worktable. The sobs that tore at her throat were so painful only the knowledge of a stranger in the next room kept her from wailing out loud. She buried her face in her hands, wondering dimly if a wizard's heart was different, because human hearts couldn't break and she could feel hers tearing itself apart.

The violence of her emotions fed her wayward energies, and they easily escaped her uncertain control. But this time, instead of merely shattering the bulb in the nearby lamp, the unruly stream of power was drawn instantly toward the portal. A shower of sparks fell to the base, and the copper began to emit a faint, eerie glow.

Felicity saw what was happening, and it was just one more reminder that she was caught up in something that, for all her powers, all her wizard's abilities, she could hardly fathom, much less bend and shape to her own will.

No control. I can't stop this, can't change it . . .

Both the past and the future tugged at her. Her life was in the future, her heart here in the past. The only man she had ever loved or could ever love was about to be lost to her forever, and the loss and loneliness she had seen in his eyes was a knife in her soul.

Control. I have to—

Suddenly, as if she had always known it was there and within reach, she found the switch within herself, and gently took control. The only outward sign of what she had done was that the portal stopped glowing and showering sparks. Inwardly, she felt a peculiar peace.

Control.

"Felicity? My love . . ."

She blinked back the last of the tears and focused on Sinclair as he knelt before her. The pain in his face made her reach out to touch him.

"I'm . . . fine," she said.

He rubbed at the wetness on her face. "Are you?"

Felicity drew a breath. "I am now." She held her free hand out to one side and instantly, easily, created a ball of brilliant energy. With precise control, she made it grow and shrink and intensify, then tossed it up into the air and made it vanish.

Sinclair was sitting back on his heels, watching with dawning understanding. "Does this mean what I think it means?"

In wonder, she said, "I found the switch. I know how to control my powers."

He took both her hands in his and repeated steadily, "Does that mean what I think it means?"

Her hesitation lasted only a moment. Selfish or not, her common sense told her that Sinclair alive and well in the future was the best possible reason for his disappearance from this time. And all her instincts told her that he would step into the future with a confidence and fascination few other men could have matched.

Still, she had to ask.

"John, are you sure? Absolutely sure you want to come with me? It's a different world."

"I have never been more sure of anything in my life." His eyes held that certainty.

"In that case . . ." She smiled at him. "According to the history books, when your servants return from the country next week, they will find you have vanished without a trace. It's one of the great mysteries of the past hundred years."

Sinclair got to his feet and pulled her up. He was smiling as well, his face alight. "Well, we mustn't change history."

"Oh, I agree." Her arms went around his waist, and she tipped her head back to add seriously, "I can't be absolutely sure the attempt will be successful, John. I can control my powers, but duplicating by intent something I've only done by accident is chancy."

"Nothing in life is certain." He kissed her. "But I can bear whatever comes, as long as we're together."

"So can I." She felt a rush of sheer joy and almost laughed aloud. "Now, why don't we get the portal all ready, and then find something we can do to while away the next few hours."

"My thoughts exactly," Sinclair said.

In the final seconds of 1899, the portal glowed with power as the connections Sinclair had designed and calculated so carefully did their job.

Felicity had sealed the bookcase doorway behind them so that only by knocking down a wall would the room be discovered, and they had rigged both the table lamp and the power connections to the portal to go dead no later than five minutes after midnight.

She had been amused and satisfied when Sinclair had gathered together some of his books and papers to leave in the room so he'd be sure of having them in the future. She herself had briefly considered leaving her future self a note so as to avoid the agonizing of the past few days, but in the end decided against it.

After all, she had found no note to herself.

Now, as they stood just a step away from the portal, watching the copper begin to glow, listening to the intensifying hum of power, she took Sinclair's hand and said, "Just a few more seconds . . ."

"Felicity? Whatever happens, I love you."

She met his gaze. "I love you."

He kissed her hand, and Felicity stretched out her other one to direct a perfectly controlled stream of energy through the center of the portal.

Epilogue

January 1, 2000

"There have been better parties," Serena was agreeing as she and Merlin came into the house. "But the power surges added a bit of excitement, I think."

Merlin laughed. "I can't help thinking of all those people who were sitting by with candles and flashlights, all ready for the end of the world as we know it."

Serena opened her mouth, but whatever she intended to say was lost as Felicity rushed out of Merlin's study. Their Apprentice's entire face was glowing, green eyes brilliant with happiness, and it didn't require Merlin's wizardry to point out what was obvious.

"You've found the switch. Learned to contain and control your powers."

Serena, more perceptive when it came to some things, said, "More than that. Felicity—"

Felicity grinned at them. "Do I have a story for you. But, first, there's someone I want you both to meet."

About the Author

Kay Hooper, who has more than four million copies of her books in print worldwide, has won numerous awards and high praise for her novels. Kay lives in North Carolina, where she is currently working on her next novel.

Gabriel's Angel

Marilyn Pappano

1

Gabe Rawlins loosened his grip on the steering wheel, then glanced at his watch. Eleven forty-four on New Year's Eve. All the world was celebrating the coming millennium with somebody somewhere—and where was he? Somewhere in northern New York, tired beyond belief, still an hour from Howland and the motel where he planned to spend the night, alone. Happy New Year. Yeah, right.

He switched on the radio but couldn't find anything he wanted to listen to. Shutting it off again, he raised one hand to massage the stiffness that had settled in his neck. He should have stopped in the last town and checked into its lone motel. He could have been asleep by now. But no, he'd wanted to cover as much distance that day as he could, and so he had pushed on. Now he felt as if he'd pushed too hard.

Up ahead, a faint glow tinged the night-black sky. He hoped it came from a restaurant, but he would settle for a gas station or even a soda machine, as long as it came with caffeine. He could use a little artificial stimulation.

As he rounded the curve, he slowed, then pulled into the gravel lot on the left. The neon sign near the highway read simply BAR. The squat, concrete-block building sitting a hundred yards back didn't call for anything fancier.

He drove past car after car, finally parking on the snow-packed grass at the end of a row. After he got out, he stretched his arms high over his head, his joints creaking. The long hours behind the wheel had him feeling his age and then some.

The mountain air was frigid, so he didn't linger. He shoved his hands into his pockets and headed for the bar. As he drew closer, he heard loud music and, nearby, louder voices. Two men were arguing, and it looked as if he was going to walk right into it. But rather than backtrack, he simply hunched deeper in his jacket and kept walking.

When he cleared one row of cars, he saw the men—one to his left, one straight ahead. He didn't make eye contact, tried not to notice details, but the gun one man held was a pretty damn big detail to overlook.

The shot sounded like a cannon, sending shock waves through the air, through him. For an instant he stood motionless, unable to grasp what had happened. He saw the men's mouths move but heard no sound, not even the men's footsteps as they raced away.

Numbly Gabe looked down, past his unzipped jacket, at the stain seeping through his shirt. He touched it gingerly and his fingers came away wet and red. Blood. Jeez, it was blood—*his* blood. Pulling up his shirt in slow motion, he stared in horror at the gaping hole in his stomach.

He'd better sit down—no, better call for help. But when he tried to yell, the only sound that came out was strangled, choked. He tried to sit down but discovered that he was already on the ground, the front bumper of a muddy truck against his back. He couldn't move, couldn't speak, couldn't feel. He couldn't—couldn't—

Oh, God, he was dying.

The square was the most magical place in all of Bethlehem, and there was no time more magical than the middle of the night with snow on the ground. Noelle loved it best then.

She came often just to sit and enjoy the peace. No one ever disturbed her on those nighttime visits. Heavens, no one even saw her unless she wanted them to.

A few minutes ago, the church bells had tolled the midnight hour, and all over town, cheers and songs had filled the air. A new year held such promise. It was a fresh start, another chance to live life right. She loved fresh starts and one-more-chances. She especially loved setting things right.

Oblivious to the cold, she followed the path to the bandstand in the middle of the square. In summer, it was home to concerts on warm evenings. On Christmas Eve, it was the center of activity for Bethlehem's midnight service. Children played there. Lovers kissed there. But tonight it was all hers. She climbed the steps almost to the top, swept her full skirt around her, and sat down. The wood was cold and damp, and the temperature was chilly enough to put fingers and toes at risk. She knew those things, but didn't feel them. Like being noticed, she felt physical discomfort only when she chose to. Tonight she chose only to enjoy the evening.

From the direction of the hospital came the wail of a siren. Noelle listened as it increased in volume, then grew more distant. Some poor unfortunate soul was in trouble this beautiful night, but it wasn't her concern. Still, raising her gaze to the heavens, she whispered a silent entreaty on his or her behalf.

"Mind if I join you?"

When she lowered her gaze, she saw a man standing at the bottom of the steps. Surely he wasn't speaking to her—he couldn't be—but when she looked over one shoulder, then the other, she saw no one else. They were alone in the square. "Are you talking to me?"

His grin was quick to come, then leave. "I don't see anyone else. Do you?"

For good measure, she looked again. "No. No, I don't."

"So . . . can I sit down?"

She gestured to the broad steps, surprised to see that her hand was less than steady, and he chose to sit one step below her, easing down before extending his hand. "I'm Gabe Rawlins."

On impulse, she slipped off her mitten before placing her hand in his. His was big, his fingers long and slender, and the instant they closed around hers, she felt an incredible sense of . . . She wasn't sure what. There was something so familiar about him, something she seemed to recognize deep inside. But how could that be? She knew everyone in Bethlehem—everyone in the county—and Gabe Rawlins was definitely a stranger.

Though he felt like someone she knew. Like someone very important to her.

"I—" She cleared her throat. "I'm Noelle."

"Hi," he murmured.

"Hi."

Moment after moment, they stared at each other. He was handsome, with brown hair carelessly combed, eyes so blue they took her by surprise, and a determined set to his square jaw. His clothes weren't adequate for the cold—jeans, a leather jacket, scuffed boots, no gloves. They were the sort of clothes a man might wear if he didn't expect to be outside long, but he didn't appear uncomfortable. Like her, he didn't appear to notice the cold at all.

But he wasn't like her. And yet he saw her. Spoke to her. Heard her. He touched her, in a way that had nothing to do with his hand clasping hers.

A slight tug drew her attention to their hands. He was subtly trying to pull away. With an embarrassed smile, she let go, then slipped on her mitten again. Her fingers tingled inside the soft fabric.

"Nice town," he remarked. "Do you live here?"

She nodded.

"Do you usually sit alone in a park after midnight?"

"As a matter of fact, I do. It's perfectly safe." And, tonight, perfectly confusing. Her reaction to him was a mix of things she'd never felt before—familiarity, a sense of homecoming, embarrassment. The sort of things a woman might experience upon meeting a particular man. But she was immune to such emotions—or, at least, she was supposed to be.

Adding to her confusion, she shouldn't even be meeting

this particular man. In all of time, she'd never been approached by a human unless she'd planned it, and she certainly hadn't planned this. Which meant that, somewhere, something had gone terribly wrong.

He glanced at her, away, then back again. His jaw might have a determined set but he looked far from determined. There was bewilderment in his eyes. "Can I ask you a question? Is there . . . do you see something . . . odd about me?"

The simple fact that he was there asking proved that there was nothing at all ordinary about him. "Odd in what way?" she answered cautiously.

"I saw some people on the sidewalk over there"—he gestured toward Main Street—"and I spoke to them, but it was as if they didn't see me. And I don't know how I got here. The last thing I remember was stopping at a bar out along the highway, and the next thing I knew, I was walking down the street. And I'm not cold. Are you cold?"

She shook her head.

"But there's snow on the ground. It must be five degrees. When I got out of my car at the bar, I was freezing, but I'm not cold now. How can that be? Where is my car? And how did I get here?"

Noelle thought of the ambulance she'd heard earlier, of that poor unfortunate soul in trouble. Gabe Rawlins looked neither poor nor unfortunate, which was only fair, because he was no longer in trouble, either.

He was in limbo.

Dealing with souls in transition wasn't her job. She'd never even met anyone in transition before. There were others who handled passings, and one of them should have been waiting for Gabe Rawlins. The fact that he'd found her instead meant . . . Well, she wasn't sure exactly what it meant. But she would find out soon enough. Someone was sure to come looking for him.

His dry, mocking chuckle broke the silence between them. "You think I'm crazy, don't you? Or drunk or high. But I haven't had a drink in longer than I can remember, and I never take anything stronger than aspirin." His voice lowered and turned grim. "I *must* be crazy."

She laid a hand on his arm—solid, real, and oh, so pleasing to touch. Ignoring the tingle spreading up from her fingers, she forced herself to sound calm and reassuring. "No, Gabe, you're not crazy. Though, truthfully, when I tell you what you are, you're going to think *I'm* crazy."

He looked at her, his gaze steady, hopeful, and she wondered how best to break the news. But if there was a gentle way, she couldn't think of it, and so she drew a deep breath and blurted it out. "You're not crazy, Gabe. Unless I'm mistaken, you're dead."

He took the news rather well. Of course, it was easy to take news well when you didn't believe it, and Gabe Rawlins didn't believe her. Why should he? He was breathing, talking, thinking—all things he no doubt associated with living. He had no reason to believe that he had died in the last few minutes and didn't know it.

Eyeing her warily, he eased away from her, scooted to the far edge of the step, and asked in a strangled voice, "So . . . you live nearby?"

"Like, in the local mental hospital?" Now she found gentleness and used it. "I'm not unbalanced, Gabe. I understand this comes as a shock to you—"

"Oh, no. I'm not shocked. I had a cousin who swore he'd been abducted by aliens and taken to their mother ship. My secretary's mother is convinced that Elvis pumped gas for her on her last trip out west. Me, dead—that's not such a shock."

"You don't believe me." She wasn't disappointed. She'd had to show proof before, and she would have to again. "Then why didn't those people see you? And why aren't you cold? And how did you get here?"

He shook his head in stubborn denial. "Okay, so maybe I did have a few drinks tonight, maybe more than a few. Maybe I blacked out and I walked into town, and the people were just rude, and—"

Leaning close to him, she sniffed. "You don't smell as if you were anywhere near a bar." In fact, he smelled fresh and clean, with just a hint of spice—a lovely masculine combination. She breathed again, deeper this time.

"I can't be dead. You can't die and not know it."

"Generally not. Frankly, I'm not sure what's happened—a mistake, or perhaps a miscalculation in time or identity. But the mere fact that you can see me is proof that something's gone wrong."

"Why?" His eyes narrowed with suspicion. "What does seeing you have to do with anything?"

Noelle regarded him for a long while. She hated to give him another shock so soon after the first. This one was likely to send him running, when, for his own sake, he needed to stay with her. But there was no getting around it. He would figure it out for himself soon enough.

"Because, Gabe, I'm an angel."

It was too bad, Gabe thought. After a year of not dating, a year of not having anything to do with women beyond facing his ex-wife and her lawyer in court, he finally met a beautiful woman who made his heart beat faster and his blood pump hotter, and she was nuts. A first-class, off-her-rocker, ought-be-locked-up lunatic.

How could he be *dead* when he was sitting there talking to her? When he'd felt the touch of her hand in his? When he could see the silvery wash the night cast over her pale brown hair? When he could smell her fragrance with every breath?

How could he be dead when simply sitting beside her made him feel more alive than he had in months?

So he couldn't remember getting from the bar to the town, and the people he'd said hello to had looked right through him, and he wasn't cold—not his hands, not his feet, not even his nose. He could find a logical explanation if he just gave it a moment's thought.

He *wasn't* dead. And Noelle *wasn't* an angel.

Even if she did look like one. There was an ethereal air about her, as if she were a rare and delicate treasure that should be tucked away and kept safe for eternity. Her hair reached almost to her waist, heavy and straight before curling under at the ends, and made his fingers ache to touch it. Her eyes were brown, and her smile . . . People would pay a fortune for a smile so perfect and white, so warm and sincere and comforting.

What a shame she was nuts.

Easing farther away from her, he looked around. There was no traffic on the streets, no signs of life—er, activity anywhere. Across the street on three sides of the square were businesses, all closed for the night. Behind them was the courthouse and, according to the sign outside, both the sheriff's and police departments.

He stood up and felt none of the stiffness he'd expected. The muscles in his neck had relaxed, and the ache that had settled into his lower back after four hundred miles was gone. He felt as if he could easily drive another four hundred, if only he had a car to drive. Maybe at the sheriff's department he could find some deputy heading out to patrol and get a lift to the bar.

"Well . . ." He looked at Noelle again, felt the pull again deep inside. "I'd like to say it's been nice, but—"

"You can't leave, Gabe."

"Oh, yes, I can."

She shook her head as she got to her feet. Her heavy crimson skirt fell past the tops of her boots, the black coat to midcalf, and the fringe on her scarf swayed. "They'll come looking for you. Until then, it's best that you stay with me."

"They who? Your angel friends? The Angel of Death? Look, Ms.—"

"Not Ms. Just Noelle."

"Look, Noelle, I'm heading over to the sheriff's department to see if I can catch a ride to my car. You should probably go back to wherever you came from. Someone's probably looking for you." Like orderlies with a straitjacket.

He descended the steps to the sidewalk. He was almost at the outer edge of the square when Noelle appeared on the bench just inside the gate. She was sitting on the curved iron arm, her feet on the snow-covered seat, her hands clasped between her knees.

He stared at her, then looked back to see that the bandstand was empty. It was Noelle, all right, and she had just appeared out of thin air.

Games, he thought dizzily. He'd had too much to drink, and his mind was playing games with him. There was no Noelle, no square, no town. In another hour or two, he would awaken—alone, intoxicated, and freezing to death—in his car, parked outside the bar, and he would wonder about the weird dream he'd had.

"If I'm not an angel, Gabe, how did I do that?"

He shook his head. "You don't exist. You're just a figment of my imagination. I'm tired. I need some sleep. When I wake up, you'll be gone."

"How did *you* do *that?*" With one delicate hand, she gestured behind him. He saw nothing out of the ordinary until she pointed it out. "Footprints, Gabe. You just walked across a hundred feet of snow without leaving footprints. How?"

She was right. The snow covering the sidewalk was pristine. Looking down, he lifted one foot and saw that the same was true there. He stomped his foot down hard, then lifted it and looked. He hadn't disturbed so much as a single flake.

Raising his gaze to her again, he opened his mouth but could think of nothing to say. The denials screaming inside him couldn't work past the fear frozen solid in his throat. He couldn't be dead. *He couldn't!* But suddenly, he wasn't so sure.

He was still staring at her, speechless, when a sound drew his attention to the street. An ambulance drove by slowly on Main Street, its red and blue lights flashing distorted shadows on the snow, its siren eerily silent. Either the patient they were transporting wasn't in critical condition, or he was—

A chill swept through him with painful intensity, and in that instant he knew. Noelle wasn't crazy. *He* wasn't crazy. He was dead.

Dead.

The ambulance drove out of sight, and he shifted his

gaze back to Noelle. "What happened?" He tried to put strength into his voice, but instead the words came out hoarse. Frightened.

"I don't know. I've never dealt with the dead before. I suspect there was some mistake."

"I'm dead, and you think it was some *mistake?*"

"I don't know. We'll find out soon enough."

"I want to know *now*!" he shouted, making her flinch. "This isn't some minor little detail that can be taken care of in a day or two! I'm dead, and I damn well want to know why!"

She touched him again, her fingers curving around his forearm. With that simple touch, his fear drained away. He felt . . . stunned. Bewildered. Sorrowful. All his plans for a new start in a new place were gone. Any chance of fixing things with his daughter Jen was shot, too.

"As soon as the problem is figured out, they'll let us know," Noelle said. "In the meantime, why don't we go someplace warm to talk?"

"I'm not cold," he said absently. How could he be?

"I know. But until you become accustomed to—to not being, familiarity can be comforting. There's a diner on Main Street. Come on."

He half expected her to transport them using whatever method she'd used to move herself from the bandstand to the bench. Instead, she jumped down from the bench and started walking.

Harry's Diner was open every day, breakfast through dinner, according to the sign on the door. Its eight P.M. close had come hours ago, and now the place was empty, with only a few dim lights burning over the counter. Gabe looked down Main Street in the direction he'd come, then turned back in time to see Noelle, on the other side of the glass door, pull it open. "How did you—"

She smiled that brilliant smile. "I'm an angel, remember?"

Giving her no response, he stepped inside, then looked around while she locked the door again. There was nothing fancy about the diner, though he'd bet the food was good. An hour ago, he'd been hungry for even a fast-food hamburger. Now, he supposed, he would never be hungry again.

Noelle passed him, then slid into the round booth in the far corner. When he sat opposite her, he rested his hands on the table. It was real. The vinyl bench beneath him was real, too—padded, comfortable. Hell, everything in the place was real. Except him. And her.

He watched as she pulled off her mittens, then unwound the scarf. The black coat came off next, revealing the fitted top half of her crimson dress. "I always imagined angels in flowing white gowns. What kind of angel wears a crimson dress, mittens, and a striped scarf?"

"A stylish one." She smiled charmingly. "I have my share of flowing white gowns."

"What kind of angel are you?"

"A guardian angel."

"Then why didn't you guard me from whatever killed me?"

"Because I'm not *your* guardian angel. And even if I were, if it was your time to die, you would die."

"And was it my time?"

Her expression turned thoughtful, with her mouth flattening into a thin line, her brows drawing closer. "I'm not sure. I suspect not. I think that's why you're here—because no one was expecting you."

With a low chuckle, he shook his head. "This is crazy. I can't believe I'm sitting here in a body that's supposed to be dead chatting with a woman who claims to be an angel."

"You can believe what you want, Gabe, but it doesn't change the facts." Quickly enough to catch him off guard, she changed the subject. "Where are you from?"

"The realm of the living, originally. Also known as Boston."

"Where were you going?"

"Cleveland. I start a new—I was supposed to start a new job on Monday."

"Why were you leaving Boston?"

He delayed answering by looking toward the counter. He wished he had a cup of strong black coffee. It would occupy his hands, steel his nerves, and give him a ready excuse to put off talking. But there was no coffee, and he doubted it was possible to put off an angel. After all, patience was a virtue, and he was fairly certain angels were nothing if not virtuous.

With a shrug he faced her. Now that he was dead, he could answer any questions she asked. He had no reason to worry about opening old wounds, stirring old sorrows. He could talk about his failed marriage without reliving the heartache and disappointment. He might even be able to talk about his daughter.

And even after that silent pep talk, when he opened his mouth, it was the standard evasive answer that came out. "We moved to Boston after college because that was where my wife Cassie wanted to live. I was never that crazy about the city, so, now that we're divorced, I decided to settle someplace else."

"Were you crazy about Cassie?"

"Yeah," he admitted. Even when he'd begun to suspect that she was falling out of love with him, even when he'd heard it from her own mouth, he'd still loved her. Loved her, wanted her, resented her, hated her. He'd spent the year since the divorce putting his life back together, wondering if he would ever look twice at another woman, doubting that he could ever fall in love with anyone else.

Now he didn't have to worry about it. It was just as well, because the first woman he'd looked twice at was off limits. *Way* off limits.

"Was she crazy about you?"

"In the beginning. The last few years she'd found other things—other people—to care about." The words surprised him. He'd never admitted her affairs to anyone else. Even his lawyer had gotten only vague answers to questions about the cause of the breakup. Not that Cassie had minded admitting to the affairs. She hadn't been nearly as ashamed of them as he was. Of course, she hadn't been the one betrayed, the one made a fool of by the one person she'd trusted most.

"Any children?"

"One. Jen is fourteen and lives with Cassie and her new husband, who wants to adopt her." The man was old enough to be Cassie's father, rich enough to own half of Boston, and had no kids of his own to leave his fortune to. He wanted Jen to be the daughter he'd never had, and his terms included bearing his name, growing up in his mold, and breaking off all ties with her *real* father.

Gabe had no problem with Cassie and Jen living like royalty. God knows, he'd never been able to give them a fraction of what they had now. But Jen was *his* daughter, born with *his* name, and he'd be damned if he . . .

Could do anything about it now. With him gone, there was no one to stand in their way. Cassie and her rich-old-goat husband would be in court next week to complete the stealing of his daughter from him, and he couldn't stop them.

As an ache settled in his chest, he wondered why being dead could cure him of physical discomforts like hunger, fatigue, and being cold, but left the emotional discomforts intact. Given a choice, he'd rather be cold than feel this overwhelming despair over all he'd lost.

He forced his attention from himself to the woman/angel/being across from him. "What does a guardian angel do?"

She knew he was deliberately changing the subject—he could read the sympathy on her face—but she let him. "She, or he, looks after those whose care has been entrusted to her or him."

"So why aren't you looking after them now? Why are you hanging out downtown alone?"

"It's not a twenty-four-hour-a-day job. When they need me, I'm there. The rest of the time, I wait and watch."

"So you hang around until they need you, then you perform your magic and fix their problems, and then—"

"Not magic, Gabe. Miracles. And they're not *my* miracles. They're God's. Surely you believe in miracles."

Oh, yeah, he believed. The night Cassie had agreed to marry him, the first time he'd held Jen in his arms, a tiny, wrinkled creature with amazing eyes . . . Those had been miracles. When he'd seen Noelle in the square, sitting there with her gaze lifted heavenward, his immediate thought had been that she couldn't possibly be anything less than a miracle. In that instant, he'd wanted to simply stand there and stare, to sit beside her, to touch her, draw her close, hold her safe. He'd wanted things he couldn't express, in ways he couldn't imagine.

And it was a good thing he couldn't express them, because he didn't think such all-encompassing desire was the appropriate response when meeting an angel for the first time.

"What kind of miracles do you grant?"

"Small ones. Grand ones. They're one and the same. I help people fall in love, resolve their differences, regain their faith. I help create families and heal wounded hearts."

"You help," he repeated.

"Well, I can't do it for them. What good would it be if I said, 'Here's a miracle. All your troubles are solved'? They have to want it, to work at it. People always value what they work for over what they're given."

"So you're the Cupid of the angel realm."

"Not exactly. Cupid is a mythological figure."

"Some people say angels are, too."

"Some people are wrong." She smiled serenely, and took on that breathtaking beauty that could bring a man to his knees. His fingers ached to touch her face, her lips, any part of her. He wanted to capture that smile, that warmth, that incredible feeling, to keep with him throughout eternity. He was reaching out to do just that when a rumble from the back of the diner startled him, made him jerk away.

It was just the furnace coming on. Gabe felt the air from the register above ripple across his skin, felt the warmth in it, but he was already plenty warm from looking at Noelle. The change in room temperature had no effect on him. He didn't grow warmer, didn't think about taking off his leather jacket. His comfort level remained unchanged, which made his *dis*comfort level rise a notch or two.

It was unsettling, this business of not being. Although he'd been in limbo for more than a year. It had started with the shock of finding out about Cassie's affairs, had persisted through the separation, the divorce, the battles over Jen. He'd gotten through *that* limbo one day at a time. He'd promised himself that things would get better tomorrow, and when tomorrow had come with the same hurt, he'd made promises for the next one, and the next.

Now there would be no more tomorrows. He'd traded one limbo for another, and this new one might never end.

2

Noelle gazed out the window at her town—peaceful, still, secure. Her charges were all sleeping soundly, except for the few stirring in preparation for the new day. Everything was calm and quiet, as it should be. Even Gabe Rawlins.

Then she amended that thought. He was quiet, but she wasn't sure about the calm part.

For the last few hours, he'd remained slumped on the bench across from her, his head tilted back, his eyes closed. He looked as if he were sleeping, but he had no need for rest now. More likely he was trying to understand the tremendous change he'd undergone. Though he was no longer denying his death, she suspected that he was currently engaged in regretting his life. It would have been easier for him if everything had gone smoothly, if he'd been met by those whose responsibilities included the transition from life to death. Instead, he'd been left with no one but her to ease the way.

A noise from the back startled him and made him straighten on the bench. "What . . . ?"

"That'll be Harry coming in to get ready for the day. This

is his diner." She gestured toward the sidewalk, where an older woman was briskly approaching the door. "And there's Maeve. If Harry's the heart of this place, then Maeve is the soul."

"Shouldn't we leave?"

"Why? They won't notice us."

The bell dinged over the door as the waitress let herself in. At the same time, Harry came through the swinging door from the kitchen. "Mornin', Maeve," he greeted her as he tied apron strings around his middle.

"Mornin', Harry." Maeve slipped off her coat, straightened her uniform, then checked her hair in the mirror behind the cash register.

"Harry's wife is gone, and his children have moved away," Noelle said as the two went about their business. "The diner is his life now—that, and his friends. Maeve's husband is dead, too, and she's got a daughter and one granddaughter. She's loved Harry for ages, but he sees her only as a good friend and an outstanding waitress."

"So why don't you help her get his attention?"

"You don't have to whisper, Gabe. If they can't hear me, they certainly can't hear you. When the time is right, I'll give them a hand. When it comes to love, timing is everything, you know."

"No kidding," he replied dryly, his mouth turning up in the faintest of smiles.

Wanting to see a full-fledged smile, she offered a suggestion. "Hey, you want to watch the sun rise? It's one of the most beautiful sights most people never see."

"Sure. Why not." He started to slide out from the booth, but before he'd moved more than an inch, they were already in her favorite place for watching the sun clear the mountains to the east. Wearing a startled, wide-eyed look, he nearly stumbled. Though she knew he could catch himself, and couldn't do himself any harm even if he didn't, she grabbed his arm to steady him. She'd advised familiarity, and physical contact was familiar to most humans. It brought them comfort, reassurance. And it made her very pores flutter.

"What-where are we?"

"This is the roof of the First Church, so named because when Ezekiel Winchester built it over two hundred years ago, it was Bethlehem's first church. I helped persuade him to build it."

He jerked back from his perusal of the town to stare at her. "You're over two hundred years old?"

His surprise made her laugh and sent pleasure through her. "I'm an angel, Gabe. I'm ageless."

Looking for something solid to lean against, he found it in the cupola that housed the bell. "Were you ever alive?"

"No. I've always been an angel. Since the beginning of—well, the beginning."

"If you've never been alive, then you've never fallen in love, healed your broken heart, or regained your lost faith. How can you help someone do those things when you've never experienced them yourself?"

She boosted herself onto the low wall that provided support to the posts and roof of the cupola. It gave her a good view of the coming sunrise. It also placed her close to him. "I feel emotions, Gabe—at least, some. I've never known hatred or anger or jealousy. But I do know love. I worry about the souls in my care. I can be happy for them, and sad and impatient and disappointed. I feel a lot of things." And was experiencing new sensations every day. "Look, here it comes."

She gestured to the east and he obediently looked that way. The sky lightened and brightened and turned every soft, rosy shade known to God. First, one brilliant golden ray appeared, then more, until the sky was lit with molten gold. When the sun finally cleared the horizon, forcing the night to recede, she gave a delighted clap of her hands. "That was a miracle, Gabe. Could you feel it?"

She stole a glance at him. He wasn't smiling, but he looked . . . relaxed. As if he'd glimpsed peace for the first time in too long. When he became aware of her attention, he gave her a sidelong look and pretended cynicism. "The sun rises every morning. It sets every evening."

"Yes. Think of it: two guaranteed miracles every single

day. Isn't that grand?" Sliding to her feet, she changed the subject. "Would you like a tour of Bethlehem?"

"That depends on how you give it. Popping onto rooftops makes me a little queasy."

"We can walk, if you'd like." She transported them both to the sidewalk in front of the church, linked her arm through his—for familiarity, of course, not flutters—then started toward Hawthorne Street.

"You said last night that the mere fact I could see you was proof that something had gone wrong with my death. Does no one ever see you?"

"Only when I want them to. I can appear as human as you—well, as you before last night. I can take on substance and give voice to my voice. I can walk, talk, eat, drink, everything."

"Do you ever want to stay that way?"

She gave him a curious look before turning her attention to the question. She'd never thought about being human, a fact that struck her at that moment as rather amazing. Humans' lives were so different from hers. They held such potential for joy. Few of them fulfilled it, granted, but the possibility was always there. They felt everything, and felt it intensely. They were blessed with so many miracles—holding a new baby in their arms, getting a sloppy kiss from a toddler or an embrace from the one they loved best. They had sunrises and sunsets, newly bloomed flowers, warm sunshine, and cool rain.

Oh, yes, they held such potential, and her job was to help them fulfill it, not covet such opportunities for herself. But now that he'd asked, she couldn't help but wonder. What would it be like to be a woman in love with this man? Sharing his heart and his life, bearing his name and his children, working together to build hopes and dreams? What would it be like to hold his hand, to talk late into the night, to be kissed, held, desired, needed?

She wasn't sure that she'd ever blushed before, but now she felt the heat in her cheeks. Angels didn't have physical needs. They didn't have that kind of emotional needs, either.

And there, she thought, was where humans were luckier.

"No," she replied at last. "I've never wanted to stay that way." But the next time she took on human form, she would consider it again. She would wonder if she was missing out on something incredibly special.

Stopping at the intersection of Fourth and Hawthorne, she gestured to the house across the street. "That's where the Winchester sisters live. Miss Agatha and Miss Corinna are Ezekiel's great-great-however-many-greats-granddaughters, and they're the closest thing you'll ever find to angels on earth. In the blue house over there live Nathan and Emilie Bishop and their four children. I helped them become a family two years ago." There was pride in her voice, but not enough to be considered excessive. "Actually, three of the kids belong to Emilie's sister. Poor Berry has a problem with alcohol and drugs. You can bet her guardian's got his hands full looking out for her."

"How many angels are there?"

"As many as are needed."

"And everyone gets one. Even alcoholic drug addicts."

She gave him an earnest look. "The weak and the troubled need assistance the most, don't they?"

As they crossed Fourth, he shoved his hands in his pockets and gave a shake of his head. "I'm not sure I approve of a system that gives as much to the sinners as the saints."

"I find that most people have varying degrees of both in them. Even the worst criminal generally has a soft spot in his heart for someone, and even the most righteous person has usually committed some wrong." She stopped in front of a solid brick house with Christmas lights glowing. "This is the McKinney house. Maggie and Ross were *this* close"—she held her fingers up a breath's distance apart—"to ending their marriage and losing each other for forever. Now they've rediscovered their love and renewed their commitment, and they couldn't be happier, although, of course, they will be, when their little girl is born later this year."

Gabe's expression turned distant—because, she suspected, his thoughts had traveled all the way to Boston. Wondering why Maggie and Ross had gotten to save their marriage, while his had been lost?

"Some marriages are fated to last," she murmured. "Others are fated to end."

"And some things are fated to never be at all." He was studying her intently when he spoke, the way a man might study a woman who meant something to him. It sent a shiver skittering down her spine. "If you weren't an angel . . ."

When he didn't go on, she wanted to prompt him, to grab his shoulders and shake the words out of him. What would he do if she weren't an angel, if he weren't dead? What would he want?

But he started walking again. She had no choice but to let the questions go unanswered and catch up.

They walked block after block, with Noelle pointing out businesses and homes and filling him in on all the details of the lives of those under her care. Their meandering journey took them from one end of town to the other and back again—not that distance mattered. They could walk ten thousand miles and finish no more short of breath than when they'd started.

At City Park, she left the sidewalk and crossed the snow to the swing set. Bending, she blew lightly and every flake of snow disappeared from the seat. Beside her, Gabe brushed the snow away from a second seat and left it undisturbed. He tried again, then gave her a challenging look. "How did you do that?"

"I'm an—"

"Angel," he finished for her. Ignoring the snow, he sat down, straddling the seat so he faced her.

Before he could speak, she did. "What did you do in Boston?"

"I was an engineer."

"Did you enjoy it?"

"Not particularly." Anticipating the question she was about to ask—*Then why did you do it?*—he went on. "I'd had the job a long time. The income was good, the benefits were good, and it was all I was trained to do. Of course, if I'd known I was going to die at thirty-six, I would have looked at something else, something I'd enjoy."

"Life is short? Live each day as if it's your last?" She gave a chastening shake of her head. "You humans . . . Every day is precious whether it's your last or there are ten thousand more to follow. Dying at thirty-six with a career you didn't like is wasteful. Dying at ninety-six after putting forty or more years into a career you didn't like is that much more wasteful."

"Guess I don't have to worry about it either way, do I?" His smile was regretful. "I would have done a lot of things differently if I'd known, but, hey, who thinks about dying?"

"Actually, in most cases, it's more, Who thinks about living?" Bracing her feet, she turned the swing to face him. "If you could change one thing, what would it be?"

The expression that fell across his face was as sweet as it was sad. "I'd try harder to fix things with Jen. I didn't want to die knowing that my little girl doesn't . . . love me anymore."

Noelle wished she could reassure him that of course his daughter loved him, but unfortunately, there was no *of course* to it. Some kids had a tremendous capacity for love and forgiveness, like Emilie Bishop's nieces and nephew. Others didn't, and though it pained her to think it, Jen Rawlins could be one who didn't.

"My turn to ask a question," he said. "If you could experience one human thing, what would it be?"

She didn't have to think about her answer. Of all the wonders that filled humans' lives, there was one that had been on her mind since she'd laid eyes on Gabe, one so sweet and full of both promise and heartache, one that she would like very much to experience. "Love."

"I thought—" He cleared his throat to chase the huskiness from his voice. It didn't work. "I thought angels knew love."

"We do, of the universal angelic sort. I'm talking about the romantic sort." Her face grew warm again. "The hearts-and-flowers, grand gestures, commitments, ups-and-downs, happily-ever-after sort." The love of a woman for a man, the being-loved feeling she got from him in turn. The love that made life worth living.

"My turn again," she rushed on, and though he looked as if he might protest, he didn't. Barely able to think, she blurted out the first question that popped into her mind. "What did you do in Boston when you weren't working?"

It took him a moment to shift gears from her answer to her new question. "I like—I mean, *liked* to sail and to read. I used to have a workshop in the garage, where I built things—bookcases, tables, deck chairs. I liked history."

"There's a lot of that in Boston."

"And you probably saw some of it as it happened."

She shrugged modestly. "Want to hear the *real* story behind Paul Revere's midnight ride?"

After his chuckle faded, his blue eyes softened. "I liked taking Jen to the Red Sox's opening game every spring and tucking her into bed at night and seeing her face when she caught her first fish every summer. Until baseball, getting tucked, fishing, and her old man all lost their appeal for her."

"I like to fish," Noelle said with enough enthusiasm, she hoped, to lighten the moment. Then honesty forced her to clarify. "Well, I like to go to the lake, sit in a boat, and enjoy the beauty while others fish."

"What else do you like?"

"I like the peace in the square after midnight. I like the sound of the stream tumbling over the rocks in the evening near J.D.'s house. He's a psychiatrist here in Bethlehem. He and his wife Kelsey live outside town with four children whom they're adopting and J.D.'s son from his first marriage and his father, and they're expecting a baby soon. It'll be a girl, and they'll name her Faith because they have it."

"Let me guess—you helped them find it."

"And each other." She set the swing in motion, gliding gently forward, then back again. "I like being present when the babies are born. Babies are the best miracles of all. And I like watching friends greet friends, seeing families gather, and people helping each other, and the respect and compassion that fill their lives. And I like—"

Gabe waited for another greeting-card-sweet sentimental

favorite, but, while watching him from the corner of her eye, she gave a completely different answer.

"No, I *love* cotton candy."

The unexpectedness of the statement made him laugh aloud. "Cotton candy?"

"Mmm. It's pink and blue and sticky and melt-in-your-mouth sweet. Have you ever had it?"

"Not in a long time." Not since Jen was little enough to enjoy carnivals and Cassie was happy enough to find pleasure in such an outing. "You're easy to please."

"Simple pleasures are the best."

"Sounds like a song," he said dryly, humming a few off-key bars. Truth was, he agreed with her. He'd rather be sitting there in the park talking with her than anything else he could think of—except both of them sitting there alive and well and mortal and talking. He couldn't remember the last time he'd felt so right, the last time disappointment, hurt, and frustration hadn't dogged every minute of his day. It had been before the discovery of Cassie's infidelities, before the disillusionment of Jen's growing up and away. Literally, it had been another life.

But this morning he felt at ease. Darn near peaceful. He still wished he hadn't died, wished he could have accomplished more in his life, wished he could have met Noelle in human form when he could have done something about it. But being dead wasn't *all* bad.

"Are you an only child?"

Back to Twenty Questions, though she probably preferred Twenty Thousand Questions. "Don't you angels have some sort of database that tells you everything you need to know about your people?" he asked mildly as he left the swing to lean against the frame.

"I know everything about my humans," she boasted with a teasing grin. "But you're not—" Her grin faded, and regret slipped into her expression. "You're not mine."

If it was up to him, he would happily volunteer to change that. The fact that nothing was up to him anymore gave him a regret of his own.

"I'm an only child," he said, deliberately distracting

himself. "I grew up in a small town in Rhode Island and had the perfect childhood. I was a Cub Scout, a Boy Scout, captain of the high school football team, and dated the girl next door until she decided to go to college in Virginia. I went to school in Kingston, where I met Cassie, and we moved from there to Boston. Did you have a childhood?"

"You mean, did I start life as a cherub and eventually grow into a full-fledged angel?" She shook her head, making the scarf fringe swing and her hair shimmer. "This is what I am. I've never been younger and I'll never grow older. One of the perks of the angel realm."

"And you'll never die. But you'll never really live, either. Until you've fallen in love, you won't know what living really is."

Again, that faint regret darkened her eyes, and tightened his chest. She brought the swing to a stop by dragging both feet, then gracefully stood up. The way she moved reminded him of a dancer—such confidence and ease with her body. Ironic, since she didn't *have* a body, not really. He could see her, could even touch her—and proved it by brushing a strand of hair from her cheek—but it wasn't real. *They* weren't real.

But she damn well felt it. Her hair was like cold silk, her skin warm satin. He tucked the hair behind her ear, then followed its curve down to her jaw. So delicate, so real, so . . . "Are all angels beautiful?" His voice was unusually hoarse, his hand oddly unsteady.

Her own voice was breathy, underlaid with a hint of confusion. "All of God's creations have beauty," she said in that angelic-pronouncement way of hers, then immediately, in a more womanly way, asked, "Do you think I'm beautiful?"

"Very."

"I think you're beautiful, too."

For a moment they simply stared at each other. His gaze moved from her brown eyes, with such clarity and sincerity in their depths, over high cheekbones and creamy china skin, to her mouth, lips slightly parted, perfectly shaped for breathtaking smiles, for sweet, breath-stealing kisses. All he had to do was move one step closer, bend his head, bring his own mouth—

Abruptly, he jerked back, turned away. His eyes popped open wide, and his heart thudded in his chest. Breath-stealing kisses? She was an *angel*, for Pete's sake! Men didn't go around kissing angels! Surely it was a mortal sin to even think about it.

But dead men weren't supposed to go around doing anything, and yet there he was.

She placed her hand in the center of his back, and he swore he felt the heat—*felt* it. It traveled through his jacket, through his shirt, through every layer of his dead body, and it felt good. Alive.

When she spoke, her voice was subdued. Because she knew what he'd been thinking and disapproved? Or maybe because she *didn't* disapprove? "Why don't we go back downtown? There will be some people out and about."

He turned, and her hand slipped. Before she could pull it back, he caught it and held it tightly between his. "Can you find someone who knows what happened last night? Can you tell me how I died?"

She was silent a moment, no doubt debating the pros and cons. But surely a dead man deserved to know how he got that way. Surely he wouldn't have to spend eternity wondering. "All right," she said. "Probably the best place to start is Harry's. All the local gossip makes it there eventually."

He thought they might walk back, stroll along holding hands like any normal couple. He would have liked that. But they didn't stroll anywhere. One moment they were standing in the park. The next they were in the diner.

There was a fair crowd in for a holiday breakfast. Noelle left him the lone empty stool at the counter while she perched on the glass cabinet that held the cash register.

It was an eerie feeling, sitting in a crowded room utterly unnoticed by anyone. People walked past him, looked through him. When a tall man in uniform came in, Gabe thought for an instant he was going to sit right on him. He scrambled to vacate the stool milliseconds before the man sat down.

"It wouldn't have hurt," Noelle said as he leaned against the counter beside her. "You wouldn't have felt a thing, and neither would he."

"Maybe not." But he'd still rather not have a grown man sitting on his lap.

"That's Sheriff Ingles. He comes in for breakfast most mornings. Let's see what he has to say."

There was an expectant air around the man, but the other diners waited until he'd placed his order and gotten a sip of hot coffee before one finally said, "Heard there was some trouble at the Hillside Lounge last night."

The sheriff took another swallow of coffee before looking up. His expression was grim and weary. "We had a shooting just before midnight."

"Who was it?" another diner asked.

"Don't know who did it. The victim was a stranger—from Boston. Just passing through, I guess."

Gabe looked around the room, searching the faces for some sign of relief that the dead man was no one they knew. He didn't see it, not on one single face.

"A senseless death is always cause for sorrow," Noelle said quietly, "regardless of whether you know the person."

"What happened? Was there a fight?" Harry asked.

The sheriff shook his head. "We have a witness who says the dead man—Gabriel Rawlins was his name—had just pulled into the parking lot. He was on his way inside when there was a gunshot. He was alone on the ground when they found him."

"Poor man," Maeve murmured. "Such a waste."

"Do you remember?"

Gabe looked at Noelle. "Maybe." Though he wasn't sure he really remembered or merely imagined it.

"Would you like to go to the bar?"

Before he could think twice about it, he nodded, and once again he and Noelle disappeared, then reappeared. The process seemed easier this time. He wasn't quite so dazed to find himself standing in a gravel parking lot, with only part of the town visible in the valley below.

He looked at the neon sign, the building, and his car, and, without fanfare, with no blinding flashes, he remembered. He looked down to find that his T-shirt was intact. There was no bullet hole, no bloodstain, no agonizing pain. But there on the ground, sprinkled over slush and gravel, were a half dozen drops of faded red. His blood, marking the spot where he'd died.

He dropped to his knees and touched one trembling finger to the biggest, brightest drop. There wasn't enough to transfer to his skin, unlike last night, when he'd pressed his hand to the wound to stanch the flow and blood had dripped from his fingers to soak into his clothes.

The trembling spread through his body and into his voice. "It hurt so bad. I couldn't talk, couldn't move. I knew I was dying, and I didn't want to. I was too young. I had too many things left to do. I still had to deal with Jen."

For a long time she stood there and said nothing. He didn't *want* her to say anything. He just wanted comfort. Her hand squeezing his. Her arms around him. Gentle murmurs of reassurance. All the things he'd done without for a long time and now would do without for eternity.

But no sooner had the thought of eternal despair entered his mind than she chased it away. She knelt in front of him and wrapped her arms around him, and, in that simple act, offered peace he'd never known. Eyes closed, barely breathing, he savored her touch, her nearness, her heartaching sweetness. He felt safe, protected, as if *this* were the place he'd lived his whole life to get to. He felt an incredible sense of oneness, of rightness, that grew too quickly into an incredible sense of need, heat, hunger—

Abruptly, he pushed her back, jumped to his feet, and stalked to the edge of the parking lot, forcing himself to concentrate on his surroundings and not on the turmoil inside. The bar behind him was an eyesore, but everything around it was breathtaking—snow-covered mountains, evergreens softening the leafless branches of hardwoods, the valley below. The air was cold and fresh, with no pollution, and he felt as if he could see forever. There were worse places to die.

There was a slight disturbance in the air behind him, and he knew she was there—too close, not close enough, and totally out of reach no matter what. "Why do you push me away, Gabe? Back at the park, and again here . . . I want to help you. I want to ease your pain. I want . . ." She moved to face him and nervously moistened her lips with the tip of her tongue. "I want to touch you. Don't you want me to make you feel better?"

He thought of touching her, of losing his pain as well as himself in her, and of how wrong it would be, and groaned. "Aw, hell, Noelle, this isn't fair."

"Life isn't fair, Gabe. Why should death be?" After a time, she reached out and laid her hand on his arm, curving her fingers to fit him. "You feel it, too," she murmured, then wistfully added, "don't you?"

He wanted to sputter a dozen responses, but settled for only one. "Feel what?"

"This—this connection." She shrugged. "In all of time, I've never felt these things I feel with you. I've never thought—never wanted—"

"You're an angel. You're not supposed to want."

"And you're in limbo. You're not supposed to want, either. I know it's unusual—"

In spite of his frustration, his longing, his sense of unfairness, he couldn't help but laugh at her understatement. "You mean dead men don't fall in love with angels every day?"

Her responding smile was womanly. It did incredible things to her face, and even more incredible things to his body. "In love?" she echoed. "You're falling in love with me?"

Once more he touched her, drew his hand across her jaw, and found that his fingers already knew her, as if he'd touched her a million times, and they already craved her, as if he might never touch her again. Slowly he fitted his palm to her cheek and grazed his thumb across her lips. "I don't know about love. I thought what Cassie and I had was love, and look where it got me. But . . . my first thought when I saw you last night was that you were the most beautiful woman I'd ever seen. That there was something incredibly special about you. That there could be something incredibly special between us. Then you told me I was dead, and that changed everything . . . and nothing." He raised his other hand, cradling it against her, holding her face gently between his palms. "You'd think a man would stop wanting once he's dead, but . . ."

His mouth brushed hers, and a jolt swept through him. Surprise that he'd closed the distance between them when he didn't recall moving? Shock because somewhere in the universe, there had to be a law against what he was doing, with dire consequences, maybe even eternal damnation, for breaking it? Or pure satisfaction because she tasted so sweet, because he'd hungered so long for this, because it was so good and right that *incredibly special* didn't even begin to describe it?

She brought her hands to his, but not to push him away. Her fingers curled around his wrists with surprising strength, and her mouth opened to his, and she pressed closer still. Freeing one hand, he slid his arm around her, held her close, and marveled over how slender, delicate, and perfectly angelic she—

Angelic. Good God, he was kissing an angel—needing, wanting, seducing an *angel*!

With more conviction than he knew he possessed, he forced her back. Her lips parted in protest, and her eyes fluttered open, their expression dazed, dreamy, womanly. "Gabe," she whispered, reaching out.

He folded his fingers around hers and was searching for the words—the strength, the resolve—to keep her at a distance when movement behind her distracted him. As quietly and quickly as a breath, a woman had appeared in the parking lot. She looked old enough to be his mother, and was dressed in colors so bright that they made him wince. A wildly patterned turban covered her hair and lent her face a regal look, while her ebony skin accented the brilliance of the smile that split her face. She was a striking woman—an intimidating woman—and she was looking straight at him. "I've been looking for you. Nice of you to come back to where I lost you."

"Norma!" Startled, Noelle tugged her hand from his and whirled around. It took her a moment to regain her composure. "It's—it's good to see you again."

"Likewise. And you, Gabriel Rawlins . . . I turn my attention away for one minute—*one minute*—and you go and get yourself into trouble." She gave an exasperated shake of her head before offering her hand. "I've known you all your life, but I guess now is as good a time as any for formal introductions. Gabriel, I'm Norma. Your guardian angel."

The seconds ticked by as he stared at her. Just when he'd started to recover from the last awful year of his life, he'd died. He'd finally met the woman who embodied his hopes and dreams for the future, and she was no woman at all but a guardian angel. And his own guardian angel was a Cicely Tyson look-alike named Norma who'd managed to "lose" him at the most critical point in his life.

Who said God didn't have a sense of humor?

3

"He looks a bit dazed," Norma pronounced as they watched Gabe pace the parking lot from their seat atop the bar's peaked roof.

And well he should, Noelle thought, if that kiss had affected him half as much as it had her. That was the first time in all of time that she'd ever been kissed, and it had been splendid. Breathtaking and knee-shaking. And, most likely, wrong. Though how anything that felt so good could be wrong was beyond her understanding.

But she wasn't put here to understand. She'd been given a job, and she was supposed to do it. Period.

"Under the circumstances, I'd say he's handling things rather well." She drew a breath that tasted of him, and enough heat rushed through her to melt the snow where they sat. "So . . ." She cleared the huskiness from her throat. "I take it what happened last night—the shooting and his dying—wasn't supposed to happen at all."

"Well, the shooting was, but he wasn't supposed to die. It was that darn computer glitch. You know, that millennium thing they've carried on about the last few years. The local nine-one-one system went down, and it took a lot longer to get the ambulance up here than it was supposed to. I was tied up in Boston, and I didn't get here in time. It was a busy night for us city angels." Norma gave her an exasperated look. "I suppose the only disturbance you had was the sweet ring of church bells at the midnight hour."

"Plus a few rather boisterous renditions of 'Auld Lang Syne.' " And a handsome stranger wandering into her existence. "If he wasn't meant to die, what was the purpose behind his getting shot?"

"Gabriel's a small-town boy at heart. He grew up in a town much like Bethlehem, and he's missed it every day he's been away. He was never happy in Boston, but once he decided to leave, what did he do? He went and got another job he doesn't like, in Cleveland, another city where he's not going to be happy, where he's not going to find the things he's searching for."

Noelle swallowed hard. "So he was meant to stay in Bethlehem." She would have seen him every day, would have watched him fall in love with someone else. She would have watched him get married and have kids, and known that she could never have those things. She could never have *him*.

Of course, if things had gone according to plan, he never would have died. She wouldn't have spent all these hours with him, felt his touch, or known his kiss. She wouldn't have learned that she wanted him, wouldn't have known that she even *could* want him.

Which would be sadder? Seeing him with a woman and knowing that he could never be hers? Or never experiencing these new strange and wonderful feelings?

That was an easy one to answer, she thought with a secret smile as she touched her fingertips to her lips.

"Besides," Norma went on, "the man who shot him—a fellow by the name of Adams—needed a wake-up call to turn him from the path he's been following. Nearly killing Gabriel was it."

"So what happens now?"

"Well, he *is* dead. I suppose they could decide to leave him that way. Or they could undo what went wrong. It's not my decision."

"Undo what went wrong," Noelle suggested quickly. "He has so much left to do, so much to give. He should be allowed to live every second allotted to him. His death was caused by a computer problem. He shouldn't have to suffer because a stupid computer failed."

Norma gave her a long, steady look that made her want to squirm. "He's not suffering, Noelle."

Noelle looked at him, standing motionless now, staring at those half dozen red drops on the ground, and her throat tightened. "Yes, he is. He deserves another chance, Norma. He deserves to be happy."

Norma got to her feet and walked down the steep, snowy slope of the roof. "It's a busy time. There was a lot of chaos last night, which leaves us with a lot of chaos to sort out today. They'll make a decision sooner or later. Since I have to get back to Boston, and you have such"—she looked at Gabe, then Noelle, then carefully chose her words—"concern for him, perhaps you can give a city angel a hand and keep an eye on him until they let us know."

"I'd be happy to." Thrilled, in fact, but she didn't say so. Of course, there were other things she shouldn't say, but she bumbled ahead with one of them. "Norma, have you ever felt . . ."

The other angel paused, one foot extended past the gutter. Her red high heel, with its delicate strap around the ankle, looked outlandish hanging in midair. Slowly it returned to the roof, where it looked just as silly in two inches of snow, and Norma turned to face her. "Have I ever felt what?"

Her face as red as the shoe, Noelle shook her head. "Never mind. I was just wondering . . . It's nothing."

Norma looked from her to Gabe, then back again, her brows drawn together with suspicion and disapproval. "Don't forget yourself," she said very quietly. "Whether they return him to life or send him on over, he's here for only a very short time. You're his friend, his guardian, his guide. Do you understand?"

Hating her answer, Noelle reluctantly forced it out anyway. "Yes, ma'am." She *was* those things—and more. Gabe wanted more. *She* wanted more.

She *wanted.* The admission struck her with wonder. And fear. And sweet, tingly pleasure.

"We'd best get back to our charge," Norma said, emphasizing the last word. Together they paused at the edge of the roof, watching as a car turned off the highway into the parking lot and headed straight for Gabe. He leaped out of the way, bringing a laugh from Norma, who descended to the ground directly in the car's path. It passed through her before coming to a stop near the front door. "You're dead, Gabriel, and while there aren't many advantages to your condition, there *is* one—you can't be killed again. A thousand cars could drive through you, and you wouldn't feel a thing. You stay with Noelle. I'll be back when I find out something."

"What do you mean, find out something?" he demanded, but Norma was gone, so he turned to Noelle. "What did she mean?"

She debated how to answer. On the one hand, she wanted to give him hope, to assure him that the life he'd lost so unexpectedly would once again be his. But what if the decision was to leave him as he was, with his life prematurely ended because technology had failed? It seemed too cruel to give him hope, then take it away. It would be like dying twice, and the first time had been hard enough for him.

Angels couldn't lie, but unless he figured that out and asked point-blank questions, she could skirt around the truth. "It's a busy time," she said with a shrug. "Last night was the biggest celebration the world has ever seen. You humans seemed to think that the millennium was a big deal. They'll get to you as quickly as they can."

His gaze locked with hers for a while, as if he knew she wasn't being entirely honest with him. Then, with a shrug, he agreed to let her keep her secrets. "Unlike you angels, most humans are lucky to see a millennium end. Of course it's a big deal."

"There's some disagreement about whether it really is," she remarked. "The millennium, I mean. Did we reach the end of the twentieth century last night, or did we merely begin the last *year* of the twentieth century—in which case the true millennium isn't for another year?"

"Then they can have another big celebration."

And maybe he would be around to see it, happier than he'd ever been before. Maybe this New Year would be no more than a bad memory tempered by sedatives and pain-killers, and his time with her wouldn't be a memory at all.

Over the years she'd been forgotten by thousands without so much as the slightest regret. That was the way her job worked. But the idea of Gabe forgetting her filled her with a very unangellike sadness.

Shrugging it aside, she forced a smile. "Where would you like to go now?"

"It doesn't matter." Hands in his pockets, he started walking along the shoulder of the road, and she went along. He didn't seem in the mood to talk and neither was she, so silence accompanied them step by step down the mountain and into the valley. She assumed he was lost in thought far away from her, but halfway into town, he took her hand and held it tightly. She liked the possessiveness of it. She liked it much too much.

When they reached the square, they turned as one into the park. They climbed the steps to the bandstand and sat down side by side on the top step, and finally he broke the silence. "What were you and—" He hesitated, as if the name didn't come easily. "Norma talking about?"

"The plight of a city angel versus a small-town angel. Computers. Chaos."

"What did she say about me? What's going to happen?"

"She doesn't know, Gabe. It's not her decision to make."

"What happened? Did somebody screw up? Was it a mistake or a miscalculation in time or identity, like you suggested, or am I supposed to be dead? And if I'm supposed to be dead, why am I here? Why haven't I gone on to wherever dead people go? Why haven't I—"

She laid her hand against his face, and his words dried up. He turned his head slightly, just enough to bring his lips in contact with her palm. His skin was warm, bristly with beard stubble, and his mouth was incredibly soft. The contrast sent tiny waves of pleasure all through her hand, from there to the rest of her body.

"How well does Norma know the angel business?" he asked hoarsely.

"She's been an angel since time began. Why?"

"She said one of the advantages of being dead is that you can't be killed again. Is that true? Because if you don't let go of me, I'm going to kiss you again, which surely must be against every rule in the book." His grin was charmingly rueful and made him more handsome than ever. "If you break the rules enough times, sooner or later you have to face the consequences. I'd hate for God to strike me dead when I've already died once, but I can't think of a better reason to die again. Can you, angel girl?"

Wide-eyed with anticipation, she shook her head. Smoky-eyed with desire, he studied her. Are you falling in love with me? she had asked, and he had replied, I don't know about love. But that wasn't true. *She* knew about love, and she knew that was what she saw in his beautiful blue eyes as he drew her near. It was the same heartfelt wonder she'd seen in the eyes of every couple she'd ever helped find love, the same awed, amazed look reflected in her own eyes. In her own heart.

He brushed his palm over her hair, and sparks shot through her, like fireworks on the Fourth of July. Sliding one hand under her hair, he fitted his fingers to curve around her neck and drew her to him, and from no more than that touch, heat seeped through her. Her lungs tightened, her nerves trembled, her heart pounded.

And then he kissed her—little kisses, little miracles that brought tears to her eyes with their absolute perfection. Yet instinctively she knew there was more—more satisfaction, more intimacy, more temptation, more fascination—and she wanted it.

He coaxed her to open her mouth, and his tongue slipped inside, making her breath catch in her chest. Oh, yes, more intimacy. Definitely. But she still wanted. He could give her more than this, could teach her so much more about love and pleasure, and she wanted to experience it all. She wanted to know what it was like to be human, wanted desperately to be human with *this* human.

Never in his life had Gabe found such satisfaction—and torment—in a kiss. Given half a chance, he would carry her off someplace private, place her on the softest of beds, strip off their clothes, and make love to her more tenderly, more exquisitely, than love had ever been made. He would bury himself inside her, would become so much a part of her that nothing—no person, no time or place—could tear them apart.

But that was wishful thinking, some small voice inside him whispered. They could and, eventually, would be torn apart. Look how easily he'd been snatched from life. He could be sent back just as easily, or sent on. Only one thing was sure—he wouldn't be allowed to remain in limbo.

He wouldn't be allowed to stay with Noelle.

With a soft sound that was equal parts frustration and regret, he ended the kiss, then dragged in a lungful of air mixed with her delicate fragrance.

"Gabe? Did I do something wrong?"

With a weak smile, he opened his eyes and found her watching him, looking well kissed. "Oh, darlin', you did everything just exactly right."

Her lower lip eased out into a pout. "Didn't you like kissing me?"

"More than you can imagine."

"Then why did you stop?"

He lifted her onto his lap and found that, while some physical discomforts—such as being hungry, hot, or cold—hadn't accompanied him into limbo, at least one had. But it was a pain that was pure pleasure, and as long as she sat still . . . "Because if I hadn't stopped now, I wouldn't have stopped at all."

With a sigh, she rested her head on his shoulder. "That would have been all right. I understand why humans like kissing so much. We could do it some more, if you'd like."

Gabe's chuckle was half groan. She'd been around since the beginning of time. She knew things he couldn't begin to imagine, had powers he couldn't understand. But in some ways she was as innocent as a newborn. Multiple millennia old, and never been kissed before that day. Never made love to at all.

The thought created amazing desires inside him.

So did the fear, not for himself but for her, if he acted on those desires.

"Gabe?"

He settled her more comfortably in his lap, then used his free hand to stroke her hair. "You're an angel, Noelle, and while I don't know a lot about your kind, I feel fairly certain that this sort of thing is against the rules."

"It's not rules so much as just believing. No one ever *told* me that I couldn't have feelings for a human, that I couldn't love or want or need. I believed it because angels just don't do those things. I believed we weren't capable of *wanting* to do them. In all of time, I've never known of an angel who did." She laid her hand against his chest, directly over his heart. "Until now."

"Well, I'm pretty sure there's a strongly held opinion somewhere that angels shouldn't make love."

"Oh, no, we make love all the time—at least, some of us. That's our job—" Abruptly, her cheeks turned crimson and she lowered her gaze. "Oh. You mean, *make love*. Um, no, I'm pretty sure that's frowned upon. I mean, no one's ever *said*, but I've never known anyone—never heard whispers about anyone—But, of course, I don't know the fallen."

"The fallen?"

All the remaining pleasure drained away, leaving her still in his arms. "The fallen angels," she whispered. "The ones who have failed at their jobs and—and been banished."

Banished. The word made him swallow hard. Whatever happened to him, please, he silently prayed, *please* don't banish her. None of it was her fault. She wasn't responsible. If anyone had to be blamed for what happened, it was him.

So gradually that it took him a few seconds to realize what was happening, the sky grew darker around them until it was black as midnight. Casting a curious look about, Noelle eased out of his arms, and they got to their feet. The street lamps had come on and the traffic had disappeared. Over at Harry's, all the lights were off except those few over the counter, and the sign on the door was turned to CLOSED. Everything was exactly as it had been last night when he'd first wandered into the square and seen the most beautiful woman in the world sitting alone there.

Except for Norma. She was sitting on the railing, legs crossed, with one purple high heel dangling from her toes. Her long formal dress was iridescent and sprinkled with what looked like confetti, and her glittery silver top hat tilted at a jaunty angle over one arched brow. She was an amazing sight.

One he wished he'd never had to see again.

"What did they decide, Norma?"

Though it was Noelle who asked, Norma directed her answer to him. "It wasn't your time, Gabriel. They're sending you back."

Gabe's chest tightened, but the protest that rose inside him couldn't escape the lump in his throat. He wasn't ready. He needed time, needed to talk to Noelle, to tell her—

"You can't stay in limbo, Gabriel. And you can't stay with Noelle." Norma fixed her gaze on Noelle. "They want to see you, my friend. And Gabriel? You—rather, the physical manifestation that represents you is waiting for us up there on the mountain."

Finally he managed to swallow, to unclench his jaw. "Can I have a minute?" His voice was thick, and it trembled as unsteadily as his hands. When Norma gestured impatiently, he turned his attention to Noelle. She stood on the other side of the bandstand, her hands clasped tightly, her gaze downcast. Her lower lip quavered, and tears sparkled on her lashes. She was exquisitely beautiful. Exquisitely sad.

He reached her in three strides, wrapped his arms around her, held her tightly as if it could stop him from being taken. Her slender body shuddered, then sagged against him, and she hid her face against his chest. He stroked her hair gently and murmured into her ear, "Remember this morning, over by the McKinneys'? You said some marriages are fated to last and some aren't. And I said—"

"That some things are fated to never be at all."

"And then I said if you weren't an angel . . ."

She looked up at him then, her eyes welling with tears. One more drop, and they were going to spill over. "What?"

Her voice was little more than a whisper. "What would you do?"

"We would find out what this is between us, and then we would spend the rest of our lives making the most of it. We'd do the hearts-and-flowers, grand gestures, commitments, ups-and-downs, happily-ever-after routine. We'd have babies and dreams and grow old together, and we'd have at least two guaranteed miracles every day."

His words touched her, and saddened her. "You'll have all that, Gabe, but not with me. With—with someone—" The first tear slipped free, but he stopped its slide down her cheek with a kiss.

"I don't want someone else."

"You won't remember me."

He smiled the best smile he was capable of, one that didn't even hint at the pain he felt inside as he pressed her palm to his heart. "I'll always remember you. Always, Noelle."

Behind them Norma cleared her throat. "Gabriel, we must go. It's time."

He glanced at her, then back at Noelle. Distance was growing between them and he couldn't stop it. He couldn't reach her.

The pain came from nowhere, an incredible jolt of agony that made him stagger back. He tried to see, but his vision was blurred. He tried to cry out, but the only sound he managed was strangled, choked. He couldn't move, couldn't speak, couldn't feel. . . .

Oh, God, he was alive again.

Noelle sank onto the step where Gabe had kissed her only minutes ago and buried her face in her heavy crimson skirt. "I'll miss you, Gabe," she whispered sorrowfully, her voice breaking.

The words echoed around her, gathering strength with every sob. Carried on her tears, they traveled through the night up to the heavens, then drifted back down, frozen into crystals so beautiful they took her breath away, so fragile that the slightest thought might cause them to shatter.

Like her all-too-human heart.

The snow started shortly after midnight on New Year's Day and continued without ceasing, sometimes in single flakes drifting to the ground, at others in fierce swirls that raced across the ground with fury. Or anguish, Gabe thought as he watched from his hospital bed. It made him feel his own sorrow more intensely, so much that he remembered yesterday's surgery only occasionally.

They had changed everything—Norma and whoever. The ambulance had arrived within minutes of the shooting, and he'd been rushed to Bethlehem Memorial where a surgical team had been waiting. How convenient that half the hospital's staff had been celebrating the millennium—or *not*-the-millennium—at a party less than a block away.

He'd spent most of New Year's Day sedated, and the nurse who'd checked on him an hour ago had told him to buzz if he needed another shot. He didn't. What he needed was—

Out of his reach. Existing in some other realm. Noelle.

"You are *not* a good patient, Gabriel Rawlins."

If he pretended to not hear the voice, would she go away? Probably not. Norma didn't seem the type to give up easily. Scowling, he shifted his gaze to her, standing at the foot of the bed with his chart open in her hands.

"Hmm. Says here that the doctor wants J.D. Grayson to stop by and see you in the morning." She looked up and matched his scowl. "He's a psychiatrist. They're concerned about your mental state. You're *alive*, Gabriel. You're going to survive this stronger and healthier than ever. You should be grateful!"

"I'm grateful. I *am*." How could he not be? He had been dead, and now he was alive. He'd been given another chance, a chance to do things right this time. But it took two to do things right, and he was utterly alone and destined to stay that way.

He breathed as deeply as the incision on his stomach—and the pain around his heart—would allow, then quietly asked, "Is she all right?"

Norma crossed to the window on gold rhinestone heels that clashed with the austerity of her white dress and buttoned-up lab coat. "She's about like you," she said grudgingly, shaking her head. "Noelle was always so competent and efficient, so compassionate without the least bit of envy of you humans. Whoever would have guessed that she would fall in love? And with a human who doesn't have the sense to be thankful he's alive."

He didn't argue his gratitude again. He needed to convince himself before he tried convincing others. "What's going to happen to her?"

"She'll be fine. I'll see to her myself." Briskly rubbing her hands together, she turned to face him. "Get some rest, Gabriel. Even with all our miracles, recovery from a near-death shooting takes its toll. I'll be checking on you regularly. Try to be kind to those who helped save you."

She disappeared before he could tell her that he always tried to be kind, before he could ask her to answer one very important question for him. They'd brought him back from death, given him this second chance, saved his life, but for what? Without Noelle, with no hope of seeing her, kissing her, holding her again, what exactly did he have to live for?

The town of Bethlehem was buried under more snow than it normally received all winter, and yet the flakes still fell. The First Church bore a load heavy enough to threaten its two-hundred-year-old roof until Norma waved one hand and sent most of it cascading to the ground in gentle drifts. Humming rather loudly to announce herself, she leaned against the cupola and waited. A minute or two after she fell silent, so did the sniffles coming from inside the bell tower.

"Ah, Noelle, come out and look at what you've done."

For a time, there was no response, then slowly the other angel stood up. She looked a sight as she stood there, a fat tear streaking down her cheek. Norma caught it between her thumb and finger, watched it turn to ice, then gently blew it away. "Angel tears," she murmured. "Since before time, I never knew . . ." Giving herself a mental shake, she put on her all-business voice and expression. "He's doing well. The ambulance arrived right on schedule, and the surgery went off without a hitch. He's going to be fine. So why are you sad?"

"I miss him," Noelle whispered.

"You've dealt with thousands of humans. Why him? What's different about him?"

"I don't know."

"You took some risks."

Finally Noelle looked at her. "I would risk anything for him. I would give up anything."

"Even being an angel?"

For a moment Noelle looked scandalized, as if such a thought had never occurred to her. Then certainty replaced shock. "Yes, if such a thing were possible."

"*Why?*"

Her smile transformed her. It made her look *womanly*. "Because he makes me *feel*."

The answer was as simple and complex as time itself. All angels felt. How could they show compassion without feeling? But Noelle was obviously referring to so much more. Though she feared it was hopeless, Norma continued to argue the point. "But angels are immortal, Noelle. Humans' time is limited. You could have sixty years together, or only six hours."

"Even six minutes would be worth it."

"And you would have no regrets?"

"None."

Norma studied her intently. It was no surprise that Gabriel had fallen in love with her. Even among angels, her beauty was breathtaking. Perhaps it was no surprise, then, that *she* had fallen in love with *him*, because even among angels, her heart was extraordinary.

Norma wagged her finger in warning. "You have to be

very sure, Noelle. Once the decision's made, there's no going back. You can't try it out for a few days or months or years, then decide it doesn't suit you. You make the choice, and you live with it. You understand? You live with it, and forty or fifty or sixty years from now, you die with it."

"What choice, Norma? What are you talking about?"

"You've heard of the fallen."

"The fallen angels." Noelle caught her breath. "The ones who have been banished."

"Not banished. They've merely . . . left us."

"Left? Why? And where have they gone?"

The girl looked totally perplexed. Norma knew the fallen were only whispered about in private, but she hadn't expected a guardian as capable as Noelle to be so completely in the dark regarding them. "Do you think you're the first angel to fall in love?" She gave a rueful sigh. "It happens. Not very often. About once in a millennium. And when it happens, the angel is given a choice: to forget and continue with his or her duties, or to . . . to become mortal."

Noelle's face lit up. Her eyes became brighter, her smile more dazzling, her beauty more breathtaking. "You mean I can be with Gabe."

"It's a big decision, Noelle."

"It's no decision at all. I would give up anything for him."

"Even being an angel." Norma said it with some sadness, because she knew the answer. But if any human could make Noelle's sacrifice worthwhile, it was Gabriel. And if any human deserved his own personal angel in residence, it was him.

For a moment they simply looked at each other, then Norma drew her close for a long, tight hug. When finally she released Noelle, she sniffed. "I guess this means that the guardian angel has a guardian angel of her own now. And don't you worry. I'll take good care of you two."

Before Noelle could blink the moisture from her eyes, the world tilted and she found herself facing a pale green wall. A look around confirmed that she was in a hospital, outside a room in the surgical intensive care unit. The door swung open and a nurse came out. "I just gave Mr. Rawlins a sedative," she said to the woman seated at the desk. "Sleep's the best thing for him now." After making a notation on the chart, she looked up. "Can I help you?"

Noelle glanced around, then realized that the woman was speaking to her. People could see her now—not just her charges to whom she was deliberately appearing, but everyone. She was no longer invisible. She was human—and next to being in love, it was the most wonderful feeling she'd ever experienced. "I-I'd like to see Gabe."

"Are you family?"

She nodded without hesitation, then offered, "I'm Noelle."

The nurses exchanged looks, then one of them shook her head while the other said, "Well, I'll be . . . He was calling for you when they brought him in, when he came out of surgery, when he came out of recovery. No one knew who you were or how to get hold of you. Go on in. He may still be awake enough to understand that you're here."

Noelle's hand trembled when she pushed the door open, her knees went weak when she walked into the room, and her heart swelled when she saw Gabe lying in the bed. Such wonderful feelings, every one of them, and they were hers forever.

Like Gabe.

His eyes were closed, his breathing shallow but steady. He looked weak and handsome and dear. She leaned over the bed to brush his hair from his forehead, and his lashes fluttered. When she bent lower to press a kiss to his cheek, he murmured, "Noelle?"

"Yes, Gabe, it's me."

"I told you I'd never forget. . . ." He felt blindly and she took his hand in hers, holding it tightly. "They let you come back?"

"Yes, I'm here."

With great effort, he forced his eyes open, forced them to focus on her face. "For how long?"

"For the rest of our lives," she whispered tearfully.

"For the rest . . ." His eyes closed again as the medication-induced sleep pulled him deeper. "I love you, angel girl," he whispered, soft as a breath. "For the rest . . ."

Of our lives.

The house was nothing fancy—two stories and an attic, white with black shutters, a wide porch across the front, and some of the oldest trees in Bethlehem in the yard. It had been listed as a fixer-upper, and for once, there'd been truth in advertising. In the two months they'd lived there, Noelle and Gabe had spent much of their time stripping, painting, repairing, and replacing.

It had been the best two months of her life.

It was the middle of March, early on a quiet, unseasonably warm Sunday morning. Noelle had left Gabe sleeping peacefully and come outside in shirtsleeves and bare feet to pick up the morning paper. She was halfway back when an elegant figure seated on the rooftop stopped her in her tracks. "Good morning, Norma," she greeted the angel cheerfully.

"That it is. I would ask how you're doing, but it's amazingly obvious. Come up and talk with me."

"I'd rather talk from down here," Noelle said hastily. "Poor Mrs. Deavers across the street still hasn't quite gotten over the shock from the last time you popped me up there to talk."

"Very well." Effortlessly Norma moved until she was seated just at the edge of the roof, her feet dangling over the edge. "The house is coming along nicely."

"Yes, it is. Jen's coming to visit next week. I told her she could do her room however she wanted." Noelle was both eager and apprehensive about meeting Gabe's daughter. She knew the girl could try the patience of a saint—and Noelle was nowhere near that status these days—but she had high hopes. When Gabe had called Jen from the hospital and told her flat out that she was *his* daughter and he wasn't relinquishing his rights to anyone, she'd retaliated by refusing to come to the wedding. But maybe a little firm fatherly control was exactly what the girl had needed. At least she'd apologized to them both when she'd called to ask if she could visit during spring break.

"Jen's learning that an endless supply of money isn't everything," Norma said. "She could use a little unconditional love."

"I have plenty of that," Noelle said with a laugh. She wiggled her toes on the brick walk. It was a little too chilly to be out without shoes. "Want to come inside?"

"Don't tell me you're cold. Why, it's a beautiful day. I couldn't be more comfortable." Then the angel grew serious, her gaze intense. "I just wanted to ask you—what's it like, Noelle?"

Noelle knew immediately what she meant. She thought of all the endless ways she could try to describe the love she shared with Gabe, but most of them would bear little significance to an angel who'd never experienced such love. She thought of words to express how one man could be more important to her than all eternity, but they were inadequate, too.

Then he appeared in the doorway. He wore jeans and a shirt that was unbuttoned, revealing the long, neat scar from his surgery. His hair was mussed, his eyes were hazy with sleep, and his smile when he saw her . . . Ah, his smile was pure bliss. "Hey, angel girl. Come inside. I've made coffee."

"I'll be right there." She watched him go back in, watched until she could see nothing more, then looked up at the other—no, not the other angel, the *only* angel—and murmured, "Heaven, Norma. It's like heaven."

About the Author

Known for her intensely emotional stories, Marilyn Pappano is the author of nearly forty books with more than four million copies in print. She has made regular appearances on bestseller lists and has received recognition for her work with numerous awards. Though her husband's Navy career took them across the United States, they now live in Oklahoma, high on a hill that overlooks her hometown. They have one son.

Stuck with You

Michelle Martin

1

Rather than lounging on her couch in flannel pajamas and watching *We're No Angels* with Humphrey Bogart and Peter Ustinov on Turner Classic Movies, Lauren Alexander stood, pretty much against her will, in the middle of what was billed as San Francisco's biggest New Year's Eve party. Because the party was actually a costume ball, she wore a white, short-sleeved, full-skirted evening gown just like the one her namesake Lauren Bacall had worn in *The Big Sleep*, and had styled her dark blond hair in a 1940's sweep ending in curls against her shoulders. After all, the movies *were* in her blood.

Lauren sighed as San Francisco's rich, powerful, and famous hobnobbed all around her in the spectacular mirrored ground-floor ballroom of the new Millennium Tower and Hotel, which was celebrating its grand opening tonight. She was here because, as an up-and-coming criminal trial lawyer with a couple of high-profile cases under her belt, she needed to be seen at a major social and civic function, to kiss up to the city's politicos, and to curry the rich potential clients who helped pay for her pro bono cases. She had come to work.

Her friend Charlene Tuttle, who was also the private detective Lauren used on her cases, wore a replica of one of Josephine Baker's more notorious costumes. It barely covered her ample brown flesh which was, of course, the point. Charlene had come for the fun, the food, and the men.

Her elbow jabbed Lauren in the ribs.

"Ow!"

"Try smiling. You might actually find yourself having a good time."

"Charlie, you're the only person I know who could enjoy this kind of party," Lauren retorted, rubbing her ribs.

"What's not to like?" Charlene demanded. "We're in a beautiful setting with beautiful people, the orchestra is hot, the champagne is cold, the food is free, and there's actually a decent collection of single heterosexual men of many delectable hues here tonight. You just don't know a good thing when you're hit over the head with it."

"I came to schmooze, which I hate, not to find a bed partner to ring in the new millennium, or to find a future husband for the aforementioned millennium."

"You have an appalling lack of ambition when it comes to your personal life."

Lauren laughed. "I just don't have your predatory urges."

Charlene draped an arm over her friend's shoulders. "Lauren, honey, I've known you for almost ten years, and from what I can tell, you don't *have* any urges."

Lauren scowled at her. "I'm building a career, Charlie."

"But that's no reason you can't have a little fun now and then. Let me introduce you to Mark Watkins. He's *very* fun."

"No!"

Charlene looked her slender friend up and down. "You're such a timid little thing when you're not working on a case."

"You're confusing timidity with morality. I don't believe in casual relationships. If only I could say the same thing about my mother," Lauren said with a sigh, her blue gaze fixed on a stunning mature blonde, costumed and coiffed convincingly as Jean Harlow. She was hanging on the arm of their host—English developer and hotelier Montgomery

Vance—with a crowd of Caesars, cowboys, Robin Hoods, one hairy-chested Tarzan, and a Superman with skinny legs.

"Piper Blake, as I live and breathe," Charlene said. "What's your mother doing so far from Hollywood? I thought she got nosebleeds if she was more than ten yards away from a movie studio."

Lauren grimaced. "She flew up this morning to spend the dawn of the new millennium with me, she says, and to lend a touch of glamour to this event, she says. But really, she's here because she's dating Monty Vance and she wants to make him and his billions Husband Number Six."

"She could do worse," Charlene said with a shrug.

Lauren grimaced. "Trust me, she has. My mother has the worst taste in husbands this side of Elizabeth Taylor."

As a girl, Lauren had dreamt of finding a man who was strong enough to protect her from her childhood nightmares, a man who was passionate enough to stir her passions, a man who could make her laugh in spite of herself. Ever practical, she'd told herself that such a fantasy man couldn't exist in real life, but she'd kept on dreaming all the same . . . until her mother's marriages began stacking up.

Her father and each of her four stepfathers had looked good on the surface, but underneath they had been either narcissistic (her father), alcoholic (stepfather number one), eager to spend her mother's hard-earned fortune (stepfather number three), or womanizers (stepfathers two and four). By the time Lauren entered college, they had killed her dream of love and happiness.

She had found sanctuary in work. Now her dreams were about justice and her career. But they lacked the power to warm her at night, or to make her feel safe, as her earlier dreams had done.

Piper Blake—the star of twenty-four feature films and two successful television series, including America's currently top-ranked television drama—spied her daughter through the crowd, waved gaily, whispered something in Montgomery Vance's ear, and then began making her way toward the two women, her shimmering silver satin gown outlining every inch of her voluptuous body as half the ballroom watched her progress.

"Lauren, dearest!" Piper cried, air-kissing her daughter on both cheeks. "You look splendid, simply splendid. But my darling daughter, this *is* a costume ball. Couldn't you have found—"

"I'm dressed as Lauren Bacall in *The Big Sleep*, Mother."

"Oh. Oh, of course you are!" Piper said gaily. "And Charlene Tuttle, aren't you scandalous!"

"You've got to properly display your wares if you want to attract any buyers," Charlene said with a grin.

"You always were the most audacious girl," Piper said with a fond smile. "If only a little of that audacity had rubbed off on Lauren. I don't understand it. Her father and I bequeathed her the best genes in Hollywood, I took her with me all over the world, wherever my movies took me, I sent her to the most progressive schools, and look at her! Wasting all of those gifts as a *lawyer*." Piper shuddered slightly.

"As a *good* lawyer," Lauren corrected her.

"Well, of course," Piper said, beaming at her. "You couldn't be anything but brilliant with my dramatic talent in your veins. I just wish you would do something outrageous now and then."

"But, Mother," Lauren said with a wicked smile, "you do outrageous so well. I couldn't possibly compete."

"But, my darling daughter, a little healthy competition, particularly between parent and child, is *good* for you. It spurs you to take chances, to push forward, to *do* something."

"But no one can compete with the great Piper Blake. Your Oscar and two Emmys prove that. And I *am* doing something. I'm helping people and I'm serving society. That satisfies me just as much as all of your glowing reviews satisfy you."

"Oh, stop making sense when you know I'm right," Piper said with a scowl. "You think too much, Lauren. Sometimes you just need to *act*."

"Mother, you're not a psychiatrist. You just play one on TV."

"The tart tongue she gets from me," Piper proudly informed Charlene. "Well, I'd better get back to Monty before he forgets that he's madly in love with me."

"Fat chance," Lauren said fondly.

"You can be such a dear sometimes," Piper said, kissing her cheek. "Get her drunk, won't you?" she said to Charlene, and then she walked—with a sultry gait that had three-quarters of the ballroom staring at her—back to the man she intended to marry.

"Wow," Charlene said as she and Lauren watched Piper's progress through the ballroom.

"She's the most amazing woman I've ever known," Lauren agreed with a smile, "and I grew up in Hollywood."

"Since a lot of what she said made sense," Charlene said, snagging two glasses of champagne from the tray of a passing waiter and handing one glass to Lauren, "drink up."

"Corrupter of the innocent," Lauren said, raising her glass in toast.

"Slave to the Protestant work ethic," Charlene said, clinking her glass against Lauren's. They both laughed and then took a sip of champagne. "Why are you grimacing?" Charlene demanded. "This is good stuff."

"I just saw Griffin Sloan again. Every time I turn around in this throng, there he is," Lauren complained.

"That is not a problem. The guy is very easy on the eyes. Where is he now?"

"Over there," Lauren said, pointing to a clutch of city politicians. Her grimace turned to a ferocious scowl. "How dare he? How *dare* he?"

"What?" Charlene asked in confusion.

"He came dressed as Humphrey Bogart in *Casablanca*!"

And *she* had come as Lauren Bacall. How humiliating.

It didn't matter that, at a little over six feet, he was taller than Bogart. It didn't matter that he had all the beauty Bogart had lacked.

Tonight, Griffin Sloan looked like Humphrey Bogart. He certainly held himself with all of Bogart's assurance. It drove her crazy. Sloan didn't have to say anything. He just *looked* as if he knew more than anyone else. Including how to please a woman in bed. The man was lethal. He could hold a jury, and sometimes even her, spellbound in court. Even now, it was hard to look away from the man, and she hated looking at him!

Like Bogart, Sloan had a long face with a strong nose, a jutting, downright pugnacious chin, and long, thick eyebrows over brooding dark eyes. Like Bogart, he had brushed his black hair back from his high forehead. He wore the white dinner jacket and shirt, black slacks, and bow tie Bogart had worn in *Casablanca*. But unlike Bogart, Griffin's dark brown eyes, fringed by thick black lashes, had only two expressions, at least when directed at her: arctic ice, or a blazing glare that could melt the polar ice caps.

Their first trial with him prosecuting and her defending had set the tone for their relationship this last year. She had passionately believed her client was innocent, he had passionately believed her client was guilty, and the jury had sided with her. She and Griffin had been butting heads ever since.

"*Nice* buns," Charlene said with an appreciative sigh.

"Good looks mean nothing," Lauren informed Charlene. "He's a cold-hearted, self-righteous *bastard*. He sees the world in black and white. He has no understanding, let alone appreciation, for the layers of emotion and history and strength and weakness that make us who we are and determine how we act. Take the Jessica Kirby case. He pushed hard for life without chance of parole, and got it!"

"But Mrs. Kirby was guilty, Lauren. She killed her husband."

"I know that! But she didn't deserve that sentence, not after what her husband had put her through. Assistant District Attorney Sloan, however, can only see the cold, hard letter of the law, not the human beings it touches."

"There is nothing cold about *that* guy. Griffin Sloan is a hunk."

For just a moment, glaring at him across the ballroom, Lauren tried to see Griffin through Charlene's eyes. She saw his long legs and broad shoulders, and the most sensual mouth this side of Frank Langella. Then she heard in her inner ear his deep, powerful voice in the courtroom last week, damning Jessica Kirby to life in prison.

"How can you like someone with a heart of stone?" she demanded.

"Lauren, give the guy a break. He's a good man, and you know it."

"I don't care if he's Gandhi, Superman, and Tom Hanks rolled into one," she retorted. "The only break I'll give Mr. Sloan is something painful . . . with a baseball bat."

Lauren drank the last of her champagne just as Mark Watkins—an ex-Giants third baseman turned city councilman—walked up to them dressed in his old baseball uniform.

"Charlene, you look stunning," he said. "May I have the next dance?"

"Only if you consider it foreplay," Charlene retorted.

Lauren's eyebrows arched up to her scalp. Charlene winked at her, leered at Mark Watkins, and sashayed off with him arm in arm.

Well, that was the last she'd be seeing of Charlie until . . . oh, Monday morning.

Which meant she was left on her own, with midnight fast approaching. Swell.

New Year's Eve had always been her least favorite holiday. She hated the noise and the false cheer and the promiscuous kissing of everyone in sight, whether you knew them, or liked them, or not. This ballroom was the last place she wanted to be when the new millennium arrived.

But she couldn't leave until it *had* arrived. She had a good ten minutes of post-midnight schmoozing to do before she could legitimately claim to have accomplished her self-assigned task for the night. Perhaps the restaurant and disco on the top floor of the tower, where a good third of Montgomery Vance's guests were partying, would be a safer place in which to welcome in the new millennium.

Lauren handed her empty champagne glass to a passing waiter, and then walked to the bank of elevators in the marble-floored lobby just beyond the gilded ballroom.

Why, Griffin Sloan asked himself once again, am I standing in the middle of this loud, stupid party bored out of my mind? He longed to be home munching on popcorn—extra butter—and watching Humphrey Bogart and Peter Ustinov in *We're No Angels* on TV. It was one of his all-time favorite comedies.

Instead, here he stood, forcing himself to smile at the nattily attired Mayor, and the Deputy Mayor, despite her atrocious Cleopatra costume, and the District Attorney, his headline-loving boss.

Griffin loathed this kind of gathering. He was here because it was important for an up-and-coming Assistant District Attorney to be seen at a major civic function, and it was important to kiss up to the politicos for when he'd need their support on some dicey case later. He'd also come because he was lonely. His life was his work, and lately that hadn't been enough.

But then, neither was this party. He had nothing in common with the beautiful rich crowded into this opulent ballroom. The diamond necklace on the Celine Dion knock-off passing by on the arm of a garishly attired Rod Stewart clone would have fed everyone in his old neighborhood for a year. The trio of vestal virgins standing nearby—the shallow daughters of one of San Francisco's more important financiers—had never known what it was like to watch the reflection of police car lights on their bedroom ceiling night after night.

There were times when he felt trapped on an alien planet.

The noise level in the gilded ballroom had risen appreciably in the hour and a half he'd been playing politics. But then, the champagne *was* flowing freely. There were already several candidates for drunk driving charges later tonight, including a Caesar, an Abe Lincoln, and the Marilyn Monroe wannabe who had invested herself much too deeply in her role.

Griffin had never understood the supposed pleasures of getting drunk. Why would anyone want to lose control like that?

He grimaced at his glass of champagne, made a polite excuse, and escaped the District Attorney, the Mayor, and the fashion-obtuse Deputy Mayor. He had politicked enough. He'd stay until the new year, the new century, and the new millennium had been rung in, and then he'd get the hell out of here and go home to his TV. Even watching The Weather Channel would be more enjoyable than this stupid exercise in forced frivolity.

He wandered slowly through the beautiful throng, smiling at those he knew, and constantly checking his watch. Time was moving with all the speed of congealed sludge.

He should have brought a date to provide some relief from this tedium, but lately even that had been futile. In the last few years, his friends and colleagues had set him up with women who were intelligent and successful and attractive, which should have been enough. Except they were also either too driven, or spoiled, or boring.

He had once dreamt of finding a woman of passion—passionate opinions, passionate laughter, anger, love. Now, he'd happily settle for a woman who could laugh at herself and provide a little intelligent conversation now and then.

Griffin scowled at himself in the mirrored wall opposite him. Humphrey Bogart would not have given in to wishful thinking. Rick and Sam Spade and the rest of his cinematic gallery would see a woman with a good right cross and great gams, grab her, and help nature take its course.

Why couldn't he find someone like the hard-boiled dames who had breathed such life into the movies of the 1930's and 1940's? As a teenager hiding in old movies to escape his world, he'd fallen hard for Barbara Stanwyck, Bette Davis, and the young Joan Crawford. Why couldn't he find someone like that?

His gaze, of its own accord, gravitated to Lauren Alexander. The famous and voluptuous Piper Blake had left her slender daughter to return to Montgomery Vance, leaving Lauren and Charlene Tuttle laughing together.

Lauren Alexander laughing surprised Griffin because she actually looked human. In the year he had known her, he had only seen her in severe power suits which she wore like impenetrable armor, her shirt collar practically enfolding her chin, her skirt hem never rising above the knee. She had great gams, and a killer right cross, and a wall China couldn't touch.

Unlike so many at this party, she had chosen the perfect costume to wear: a white evening gown with a gold-striped bodice from *The Big Sleep* that, along with the 1940's hairstyle, made her look uncannily like a young Lauren Bacall. She looked . . . softer than he'd ever seen her, and it was disconcerting. Unlike the mostly naked Charlene Tuttle, as well as the banking heiress who had barely clothed herself as Jane from *Tarzan and His Mate*, and the obligatory Lady Godiva wannabe, Lauren Alexander hadn't exposed an inch of skin. She was the sexiest thing in the room, which only made Griffin madder.

She was everything that he despised: a rich golden girl who had had everything handed to her on a silver platter. Hollywood's crown princess had, according to the newspapers, a trust fund the size of Monte Carlo. *She* had gone to Stanford, while *he* had only been able to scrape enough money together to attend the law school at the city's Golden Gate University. She had led a privileged life. He had had to fight for everything he wanted. They had gone toe-to-toe in four very different cases, and each case had gone down to the wire. Right now they were tied, at two wins apiece, when he was used to winning eighty-five percent of his cases.

He had just never been able to catch Lauren unawares. Her court strategies were devious, her closing arguments spellbinding.

What infuriated him most of all was that she sold all of that talent to murderers, embezzlers, drug addicts, and thieves. She stood up in court on behalf of the kind of people he'd hated all of his life.

He'd lost his best friend in high school to a badly botched burglary that was supposed to feed his friend's new crack habit. The police weren't interested in the small-time dealer who'd hooked his friend on crack. But Griffin cared. He cared passionately about putting the small dealers and the big dealers behind bars for life. He cared passionately about using the law the way it was intended—to protect people who had no other defense against fear and poison and injustice.

Lauren Alexander, however, cared nothing for the people the law was supposed to protect. Day after day, she deliberately thwarted justice and that, as far as Griffin was concerned, was unforgivable.

He disliked criminal defense attorneys as a breed. He loathed Lauren Alexander, and he liked directing all of his animosity at the golden icon of all the things he'd been fighting his entire life.

Griffin set his empty champagne glass on a nearby table, and headed for the elevators beyond the ballroom. All of the New Year's noise and forced gaiety that he hated was almost upon him. If he was going to get any pleasure out of welcoming the new millennium, he'd better get as far away from Lauren Alexander as possible, and that meant the restaurant and disco on the top floor of this glitzy tower. He'd get a new glass of champagne, raise it to "Auld Lang Syne," and then get the hell out of here and go home to a cinematic world where good and evil were clear, and evil was always punished.

A thoroughly inebriated group of five people crowded onto an empty elevator ahead of him.

"Come on in!" a jovial man called to him, spilling champagne on his date.

"I'll catch the next one, thanks," Griffin said with a forced smile. He walked past two closed elevators and found a third one open and empty. He stepped inside to the Muzak rendition of "Santa Claus Is Coming to Town," and glanced at his watch. One minute to midnight. He was cutting it close, but the tower's press kit had boasted a forty-second elevator ride from the ground floor to the fiftieth floor, so he should make it.

"Come on in!" a drunken Lady Godiva slurred.

Lauren looked at the packed elevator in which Lady Godiva stood—actually, leaned—and forcibly held onto her smile. How could they breathe in there? "No, thanks. I'll wait for the next one."

"Suit yerself," the lady said, and the elevator doors closed.

Lauren sighed, both with relief and irritation. Why did men always have to build such towering monuments to their . . . egos? If this had been a reasonably sized building, say five stories tall, she could have walked to the top floor instead of having to take one of these cramped boxes on cables.

She looked up and down the long row of elevators and heard a *ding!* She turned and there, at the end of the row, of course, was an elevator in which just one man was entering. That was almost tolerable.

"Hold the elevator!" she cried on the run as the doors began to close.

A hand shot out to hold the doors open and Lauren dashed into the elevator. Her smile of thanks died in the next moment as she and Griffin Sloan stared at each other in horror.

"Ms. Bacall," he grimly greeted her as the elevator doors closed behind her.

"Mr. Bogart," she retorted. Stuck in an elevator with Griffin Sloan. Perfect.

Sloan leaned against the back wall of the elevator, folded his arms across his broad chest, and scowled at her as the elevator started upward. "Of all the gin mills in all the joints in all the world, *you* walk into mine."

"Wrong as usual, Sloan," Lauren said coldly. At least he provided the perfect means of ignoring her claustrophobia. "It was Ingrid Bergman, not Lauren Bacall, who co-starred in *Casablanca*."

"I know that! I just—Oh, forget it," he said disgustedly.

There was an awkward silence as the elevator gathered speed.

Lauren folded her arms across her chest—she always felt the need for shielding around Sloan—and watched the control panel. She could tough this out for one minute. She watched each passing floor light up on the panel: thirty-five, thirty-six, thirty-seven . . . This had to be the slowest elevator in the world.

The elevator suddenly jerked to a stop, throwing Lauren and Griffin against each other as everything went black.

Breast to breast, Lauren had an immediate impression of height and power and heat. She was too furious to be scared in the darkness as she pushed herself free of Griffin's accommodating chest and encircling arms. "Now look what you've done!"

2

"Me?" Griffin exclaimed. "I didn't do anything!" The elevator was pitch black. He couldn't see his nemesis, but he felt Lauren's presence and heard her sharp, rapid breaths.

"Why haven't the emergency lights come on?" she demanded.

"It's a new building, with new mechanical and electrical systems. There's bound to be some glitches," Griffin replied. Stuck in the dark with Lauren Alexander. It was a lousy way to ring in the new millennium.

An explosion of sound—blaring horns, loud music, cheers, and whistles—suddenly attacked them. He heard Lauren gasp and felt her jump. His own heart was pounding in his chest. It took a moment before he realized what had happened. "Happy New Year," he said grimly. He did not care what protocol demanded. He wasn't kissing Lauren Alexander.

"Ditto," she snapped. A narrow ray of white light suddenly hit the elevator doors and then swept to the control panel. "That's better," she said under her breath.

"You brought a penlight in your evening bag?" Griffin asked in disbelief.

"I carry a penlight in whatever purse I use," she said as she pressed the big red alarm button.

Nothing happened.

"That's odd," he said. "Try it again."

"I know how to push an alarm button! The damn thing doesn't work."

"Then we'll use the elevator phone to call for help," he said.

Lauren directed the penlight at the emergency telephone panel. Griffin opened the door and found nothing. The small enclosure was empty.

"Well, Vance said the contractors still had to add a few finishing touches to the building," Griffin said with a sigh. He suddenly brightened. "Wait a minute! I've got my cell phone with me."

He pulled the slim phone from his inside jacket pocket and pressed the power button. There was no dial tone. "That's odd. The power's on, but there's no connection."

"Geez, Sloan, that describes you to a tee."

"I don't understand what's wrong with this thing," Griffin said, ignoring her as he pocketed the phone.

"Why don't you just whistle for help, Sloan? You know how to whistle, don't you? You just put your lips together and *blow*."

Clearly, Lauren Alexander was not at her best in a crisis. "Use your penlight to scan the elevator for a security camera," he said. "Maybe we can signal the guards in the control room."

She actually followed his instructions. The thin beam of white light swept the top and sides of the elevator once, twice. "There!" she said, pointing to a glass circle about two inches in diameter, in the back left corner, just above his head.

A security camera all right. He pulled a slim notepad and pen from his jacket pocket, wrote "Help! Elevator stalled," and held the page up to the camera. "I'll give it a minute or two, just in case the guards are scanning other monitors or welcoming in the new year," he said.

Lauren was silent, which was amazing. She always had so much to say whenever they met. None of it pleasant, of course.

He finally lowered the note. Nothing had happened. They were still suspended in mid-air, not a pleasant thought. Griffin suffered from a touch of vertigo.

"It's hot in here," Lauren grumbled. She began directing the light around the elevator once again. "There has got to be some way to get out, or to at least catch someone's attention," she said in a tight voice he'd never heard before. The wood-paneled walls offered no hope. "Let's try pounding on the doors. Maybe someone will hear us," she said.

Griffin shrugged. Well, why not? Action was always preferable to standing around feeling helpless.

So, they pounded on the elevator doors and shouted nonstop for a good two minutes. He was just beginning to feel like a complete idiot when the elevator dropped from beneath his feet.

He gasped as Lauren shrieked. They both grabbed each other at the same time as the elevator plunged downward and then just as suddenly jerked to a stop, slamming them into the far back corner together.

They were both shaking, both gasping for breath. He could feel her heart pounding frenetically against his, and the tension that pulled her taut against his body. He didn't want to let go.

"I tell you what," he said, "let's *not* pound on the doors."

A startled gasp of laughter escaped Lauren as she pulled herself free of his arms. "Stop it, Sloan! Unlike so many others, I *don't* want to die laughing."

"We are not going to die, and I didn't even know you *could* laugh."

"What you don't know about me could fill the Westlaw computer. What the hell happened?"

"I guess the regular brakes gave way for a moment, and the emergency brakes kicked in," Griffin said, his toes digging into the soles of his shoes. An image of their elevator car hanging by a thread in a black bottomless shaft kept flashing into his mind. "We'll be fine. These things are built to withstand earthquakes that register up to eight on the Richter scale."

"Wonderful." There was a long moment of silence. "I don't hear anyone coming to our rescue."

"I guess we're stuck here for the duration, until someone in security realizes there's a problem with the elevator." He sighed heavily. "Welcome to the new millennium."

"Gee, thanks," Lauren said, slumping against the back wall of the elevator, her penlight fixed on the elevator doors. Silence once more stretched between them as her free hand fidgeted with her evening bag, opening and closing it again and again.

Fidgeting drove him up the wall. Griffin wanted to tell her to chill out, but he also didn't want to go three rounds with her just now. "We might as well get comfortable," he said instead, unbuttoning his white dinner jacket. "We may be here awhile."

"*Awhile*. This is my worst nightmare," Lauren muttered under her breath.

Griffin felt himself bristle. Somehow he could never control his temper around the woman. "Everything is always high drama with you, isn't it? You could take a simple jaywalking ticket and turn it into *The Grapes of Wrath*. There are worse things, Ms. Alexander, than being stuck in an elevator for a few minutes. Helping the scum of the earth escape justice, for one."

"I do not defend scum!" Lauren seethed as she turned on him. "I defend those people who are innocent or who've been trapped in the gray world between right and wrong."

"I suppose we could always blame Hollywood for destroying any sense of morality you might have been born with."

Lauren gasped. "You are the most arrogant man I've ever known, which is saying a lot, because *I've* met Don Johnson."

"*I'm* arrogant?"

"Yes. And that towering arrogance of yours, Sloan, blinds

you to some very basic human truths. I suppose that's why you can feel such satisfaction in sending an abused woman to prison for the rest of her life."

Okay. *Now* Griffin was beginning to get mad. "Jessica Kirby spent three weeks cold-bloodedly plotting to kill her husband, studying human anatomy, learning police procedures, and analyzing forensic techniques, all to get away with *murder*. She deserved everything she got."

"The world isn't black and white, Sloan!" Lauren snapped. "Twenty years of brutal emotional and physical abuse left Jessica Kirby incapable of judging right from wrong."

"This is San Francisco, Ms. Alexander, one of the most socially progressive cities on the planet," Griffin said angrily. "There are laws to shield abused women. There are police officers trained to handle domestic abuse. There are shelters and programs to help and protect abused women. Jessica Kirby chose instead to stab her husband as he walked from his mistress's apartment, and then make it look like a mugging gone bad. This is a capital punishment state, Ms. Alexander. Mrs. Kirby is lucky I only asked for life imprisonment."

"Oh!" Lauren said furiously, turning from him to stare again at the elevator doors. "You are the most arrogant, narrow-minded, judgmental—"

"And you are the greatest hypocrite I've ever known."

"*Hypocrite?*" Lauren gasped, whirling back to him.

"Yes, hypocrite," Griffin ruthlessly rolled over her. "How anyone who was kidnapped as a child can turn around and defend the same kind of scum who terrorized her years earlier, I do not know. After an experience like that, you should want to put criminals behind bars, not set them free. Yet here you are, glowing in the spotlight of your carefully staged legal successes—"

"*Staged!*" Lauren erupted. "Look, Sloan, I only work for clients I believe in, and I do whatever it takes to insure that they receive justice!"

"*Justice?* Ha! Is it *just* that, because of you, Darryl Winters has spent the last year walking around a free man while his former employer lies dead in his grave?"

"Yes! Because Darryl didn't kill his boss."

"Bullshit! He did it. Every piece of evidence pointed to him."

"That's because he was framed, you ignoramus! The jury got that, the papers got that, even the judge got that. Why can't you for once in your life admit that you were wrong and that you were trying to put an innocent man in jail for life?"

"If Darryl Winters was innocent, then *you* are the purest, most honorable woman since Snow White."

She gasped. "I hate to burst your bubble, Sloan, but I have very strong morals, and ethics, and a repugnance for all forms of violence, which is the only reason I haven't ripped your head off!"

Griffin felt free to grin at her fury since she couldn't see him. "It's good to know you have a little real passion in you, aside from your beautifully acted courtroom displays. Personally, I prefer presenting the facts to play-acting, but then, I'm not hampered by your genes."

"*Genes?* Did you just backhand my parents?"

"Not at all. I only meant that with actors for parents, it's only natural that you would act your way through life, and court."

"Are you calling me a fraud?" Lauren sputtered, the light from her penlight hitting him square in the eyes.

"I'm saying that having grown up in a world of fantasy and lies, you wouldn't know the truth if it was spelled out for you on a theater marquee."

Lauren surprised him by slowly shaking her head, almost wonderingly. "You're even more bigoted than you are arrogant, which would be frightening if it weren't so sad. You don't see people, or their homes, or their lives. You only see surface gloss or graffiti, and then make one assumption after another. You see my parents' faces on a movie screen, you hear rumors about my trust fund, and you think you know all about me. Well, here's a news flash, Mr. Assistant District Attorney: You know as much about me as you know about *brain surgery*."

The light left him and returned to the control panel. Silence stretched between them. The devil of it was, in his heart of hearts, Griffin knew Lauren was right, at least when it came to how much he really knew about her. But then, he didn't *want* to know her.

Lauren's fist suddenly slammed into the paneled elevator wall. "*Why* hasn't security discovered the problem with this stupid elevator?"

"They must all still be ringing in the new millennium," he wearily replied. "They'll realize we're stuck sooner or later."

"If only I wasn't so damned ambitious," Lauren muttered as she leaned back against the elevator wall, her fingers drumming rhythmically on the wood panels. "I could have spent the new year with the real Humphrey Bogart, or even Dick Clark, instead of with *you*. If this is a harbinger of the new millennium, I want a refund."

"Things could be worse."

"How?"

"The Muzak could still be playing."

A reluctant chuckle escaped Lauren.

Silence stretched between them again, which was ridiculous. They always had plenty to say in a courtroom. "So, think the Giants will finally go all the way to the World Series now that they've got a new millennium to work with?" he asked.

"Are you making conversation?"

"Yes. We can't just stand here rehashing every case and every legal principle we don't agree on while we wait to be rescued. There's got to be some way to pass the time without going for each other's jugulars. At this rate, it could be morning before anyone realizes there's something wrong with this thing."

The thin beam of light wobbled against the elevator doors. "That's it. I have to get out of here," Lauren announced. She shone her penlight up at the top of elevator. "There's the trap door."

"No way," Griffin said firmly.

"Look, Sloan, you know as well as I do that with the millennium celebrations going on in this tower, no one's going to be paying attention to anything except their drunken revels. Do you really want to be stuck in here with me for the next several hours?"

Risk his neck, or spend the first half of New Year's Day with Lauren Alexander? "I'll give you a boost up."

"Hold on." She held the penlight between her teeth, pulled a Swiss Army knife from her evening bag, and began to cut a good twelve inches off the hem of her obviously expensive dress, without wincing once.

"How did you get into this party with a weapon?" Griffin demanded.

Lauren took the penlight out of her mouth for a moment. "I promised the security guards I'd only use it on *you*." She went back to slicing away at her costume. When she was done, she slipped the Swiss Army knife back into her purse, handed the purse to him, and he tucked it into his jacket pocket. Then, she put the penlight into her left hand and said "Ready, Bogie."

He cupped his hands, she inserted an evening sandal, and he boosted her up, leaning against the back of the elevator for better support. Yep, she really did have great legs. They were long, and well-shaped by muscles she hadn't gotten sitting in her office day after day. Well, walking all over justice could be strenuous.

Wobbling only slightly, Lauren scanned the ceiling trap door with the penlight. "Looks pretty easy," she said.

"I guess it depends on where you're standing."

She shot him a quick grin, then she reached up and, with just a little shoving of a slim lever nearly flush with the ceiling, she managed to open the trap door.

"Careful," he cautioned, not that he expected her to pay any attention.

She pulled herself up through the trap door and sat on top of the roof, her feet dangling into the elevator. Griffin caught glimpses of the penlight swiveling through the dark elevator shaft. "Good news," she called down to him. "We're only about two feet from the door to what looks like the forty-seventh floor."

"That sounds like my cue. Can you move safely enough out of the way so I can join you?"

"Just a sec." Her feet disappeared, he heard slow, cautious movement on the roof of the elevator, and then she called down, "All clear."

"Shine the penlight on the trap door."

She obliged. With one jump, Griffin caught hold of the sides of the open trap door and pulled himself up and through until he was sitting on the roof, feet dangling into the elevator.

Lauren was pointing the penlight at the roof of the elevator, so he had a decent view of their position. She was standing no more than a foot away, one hand clutching the cables that were holding them up in mid-air. If ever there was a time to develop full-blown vertigo, this was it. Cautiously he rose to his feet and got both hands on the cable Lauren was holding.

Even in the pale reflected penlight, he could see her taut face. "This may not have been one of my better ideas," she said.

He whole-heartedly agreed. Images of the emergency brakes suddenly giving way kept his heart skittering in his breast. But they had gotten this far, and a hotel floor would feel so much safer than this elevator.

"Okay," he said, "let's see the next escape hatch."

Lauren shone the penlight on the door just about two feet above them.

"Scan the area immediately around the door," Griffin said. "There's got to be an emergency—there! Stop! There's the manual system for opening the doors."

The penlight shone on the word "Emergency" painted in red and a lever, also red, that was nearly flush with the shaft wall.

"Can you reach it?" Lauren asked.

"I think so. Don't move." Toes tingling, he carefully negotiated his way around the cables. He tried holding on with one hand and reaching for the lever with the other, but it was no good. *Damn it.*

Taking a breath to steady himself, Griffin let go of the cable, inched across the elevator roof, and then reached up with both hands for the penlit emergency lever. "Got it," he said. He pulled. Nothing happened. He pulled harder and the shaft doors began to inch open.

"Oh, to hell with it," he muttered and committed all of his strength to the lever. The doors slid quietly open.

"Thank you, God," Lauren said fervently.

He glanced at her. "I helped."

She smiled at him. "Thank you, too," she said without the slightest trace of sarcasm.

Balancing carefully, Griffin placed both hands on the carpeted floor of their newest escape hatch and pushed himself off the elevator roof and up onto safe harbor. He rolled quickly onto one knee and, using his other foot for support, reached down for Lauren.

"Grab hold of my wrists," he said. "I'll pull, and you use your feet against the shaft wall to climb up."

"Why do the guys always get to look like heroes and the girls always get to look clumsy and foolish?" Lauren said with a sigh, handing him the penlight.

"Testosterone has its uses. Come on up," he said, just before he popped the penlight into his mouth, directing the beam at his hands so Lauren could see what she was doing.

She reached up and caught his wrists with her hands, as he caught hers. He pulled, she climbed, and Lauren Alexander literally walked out of the elevator shaft to stand beside him.

"Thank God you work out," she said as he took the penlight from his mouth and rose to his feet.

"I knew that weight-lifting would come in handy some day."

"Was that a crack?"

He smiled. "No." His smile faded as he took in for the first time the complete blackness of the hallway in which they stood, except for the narrow beam of light from the penlight currently directed at the carpeted floor. "Looks like the entire building is blacked out."

"I could really use some *good* news just now," Lauren said in her tight voice.

"Wait a minute," Griffin said, gazing at the end of the hall. The tower had been constructed so that each hallway ended in a large window with a city view. He caught Lauren's elbow and tugged. "Come here," he said, pulling her with him.

He stopped at the end of the hall and, with Lauren, stared through the window out at complete and shocking darkness.

His heart went cold. "Where's San Francisco?"

3

San Francisco's famous skyline was blacked-out. Fog hid the moon and stars from view. Far, far below, car headlights provided the only reassurance that there were still streets, that the earth was still there.

Some children were afraid of monsters under the bed, or riding a bicycle down a steep hill, or facing the school bully. Ever since she had been kidnapped and held for ransom at the age of nine, Lauren had been terrified of pitch darkness and enclosed spaces, because they had been her world for three terrifying days.

She had managed to hold it together in the elevator, and on top of the elevator, because she had kept promising herself that, once she got onto an actual hotel floor, everything would be back to normal. There would be lights and space, and she would be safe.

But she'd merely exchanged one black enclosed place for pitch darkness. She had then fought off panic by telling herself that once she got out of the hotel and back into the city, there would be lights and space, and she would finally be safe.

Something had just stolen her life preserver.

The small corner of her brain that was still working told her it was nearly six hours before dawn. She couldn't survive six hours in darkness. She couldn't!

She grabbed Griffin's large warm hand, because in that moment she needed human contact more than she needed to breathe, which she couldn't do anyway. He squeezed her hand, and oxygen filled her lungs again.

"I am never leaving my home on New Year's Eve again," she said in a low voice. "Never, never, never."

"Dick Clark is looking pretty good right now, I admit," Griffin said, his hand tightening reassuringly around hers.

She could take another breath and hold fear at bay for another moment. "What the hell happened to the city?"

Griffin ran his free hand back through his hair. "It looks like all of those Millennium Bug doomsayers weren't off their rockers after all. My guess is the utility companies, including the phone company, have just suffered a system-wide crash."

"But this tower and the other buildings out there have emergency generators—"

"Which run systems controlled by computers. The generators are probably working fine. But the building systems no longer have the ability to use them."

Darkness was enveloping her. "We have to get out of here," she announced, grabbing the penlight from Griffin.

"Hey!"

She whirled around and began stalking down the hall. A heavy hand on her shoulder stopped her in her tracks. "Let go of me!" she said furiously, wiggling free.

"Why are you overreacting like this?" he said in surprise. "I agree we have to get out of here, but we can't go off half-cocked."

"You get out your way, I'll get out mine," she snapped, starting down the hall again.

He grabbed her arm and pulled her to a stop again. "No. Look, we're gonna have to work together on this one, just like we did in the elevator. We're in this together; we'll get out of it together."

"All right, all right. Just get me out of it now!"

"Will you just *chill*, Princess?"

Loathe though she was to admit it, that was just the slap Lauren needed. She forced herself to tamp down the panic surging within her, to pull oxygen into her lungs, to melt the ice clogging her brain, and to start thinking again. She was not locked in a crate in a windowless cellar. There was room to breathe all around her. There was the light from her penlight to hold the darkness at bay. She wasn't even trapped. There were ways to get out of the hotel. There had to be.

"Sorry," she said in her calmest voice. "I don't usually act like a spoiled brat, but then, I don't usually find myself in a blacked-out city. The reasonable thing to do, I think, is find the emergency stairs. We're only three floors below the top floor, where we should find a good third of Montgomery Vance's guests. Many heads are better than two."

"Agreed," Griffin said. "There should be a floor plan on a wall near the elevator. Let's go find it."

Lauren shone the penlight back down the hallway and walked at Griffin's side, refusing to reach for his hand which had offered such instant comfort before, even though the hall walls were closing in on her again, even though blackness surrounded her except for the narrow beam of her penlight pointing them down the hall. This was not a time to give way to weakness, let alone claustrophobia. This was a time to act like a rational, intelligent grown-up. She could become hysterical once she got out of this mess.

They found the floor plan easily, and the door to the emergency stairs thirty seconds after that. But the door wouldn't open.

"Try again," Lauren ordered.

Griffin put his full weight against the door. It didn't budge.

"The door to the emergency staircase isn't supposed to be locked. It's supposed to open for emergencies!" Lauren said, panic streaking up to her brain for a moment. She dug her fingernails into the palms of her hands and tried to get a grip.

"The door is probably wired into the security system, which makes sense, I suppose," Griffin said heavily. "Because the security system is down, the door's locking mechanism is jammed."

"My Swiss Army knife has a screwdriver. Can we take the door off the hinges?"

"Sure. But the hinges are on the other side of the door."

"Okay," Lauren's brain said, *"now you can panic."*

"We can't just stand here staring at this damn door!" Lauren said tightly. "Just because we're stuck on this floor doesn't mean we're helpless. Let's do *something.*"

"Let's get comfortable," Griffin said, catching her elbow and pulling her back down the hall. "When the Loma Prieta earthquake hit back in 1989, it took a few days for the utility company to restore power to the blacked-out neighborhoods. Tonight, emergency crews will be focusing on getting power and help to places like the hospitals first. A primarily empty luxury high-rise will be low on their priority list. So, we could be here for days and I, for one, want food and water and a comfortable bed to sleep in. We should be able to find all of those things in a guest room."

"How can we get through a guest room door if we can't get through the emergency door?" Lauren demanded.

"Well, first, they operate on two very different systems. And second, the guest room card-key lock gives me much more to work with, and *you've* got a Swiss Army knife." Griffin pulled her evening bag out of his jacket pocket, handed it to her and then spread his arms wide. "Pick a room, any room."

Having traveled the world with her mother from one movie location to the next, Lauren knew luxury hotels as well as she knew her own apartment. She checked a nearby floor plan and guided them to the southern hallway. "That one," she said, shining the penlight on the door to the corner guest room at the end of the hall. Southern exposure meant lots of natural light, and a corner room meant lots and lots of windows. Her claustrophobia wouldn't stand a chance—at least, come morning.

"You certainly know what you want," Griffin said in amusement.

"Yes," Lauren said grimly, "I do. Okay, Superman, open that door."

"It doesn't take brute strength. It takes finesse," he corrected her. "Your knife, please."

She opened her evening bag while he held the penlight for her, grabbed her Swiss Army knife, and handed it to him.

"Right," he said, squatting beside the door. "I'll need you to hold the light steady on the locking mechanism."

Lauren watched with growing admiration as Griffin methodically stripped away all of the technology that had been designed to keep intruders, like them, out of the guest room. She suddenly wanted to tell him how grateful she was that he knew what to do, how grateful she was not to be alone in this nightmare, but the words wouldn't come. After all, he *was* Griffin Sloan.

"Almost there," he said. "Angle the light a little to the—yes, that's it."

"Where did you learn to break and enter?" she asked.

"Assistant District Attorney's school. They wanted us to understand the criminal mind."

"No, really."

He shrugged, his brow furrowed in concentration as he continued to work. "I grew up on what used to be called the wrong side of the tracks. I knew people who did this sort of a thing for a living, and they enjoyed showing off their skills."

"I wish I'd grown up in an interesting neighborhood," Lauren said wistfully. "All my friends knew how to do was sign credit card receipts."

"My neighborhood was not *interesting*," Griffin said grimly. "It was ugly and poor and violent."

"Sorry," Lauren said in a small voice.

"I'm also grateful for all the things it taught me, including," Griffin said, suddenly standing up, "how to get a free room for the night." He pushed lightly on the door and it opened with a soft murmur of welcome. "Ta da!"

She shone the penlight on him. "I'd lavish you with praise, but your ego is big enough as it is."

He grinned at her, a first, and it had a remarkable effect on her. It warmed her and brought an answering grin to her own lips.

"Your boudoir awaits, my lady," he said with a slight bow.

"You'll find a little something extra in your Christmas stocking next year, Sloan," Lauren said as she walked into the room.

It turned out to be a large and lavish suite designed along Rococo lines, with a small marble entryway, a huge combination living room and dining room with—hallelujah—a wall of windows overlooking the city, and a single separate bedroom. Well, Griffin could sleep on the sofa.

Then Lauren's penlight began to pick out some of the details in the suite: the huge bouquet of roses resting on the glass coffee table with little Cupids and hearts festooned throughout the flowers, a champagne bucket with a magnum of champagne resting beside it, balloons with painted Cupids, unlit candles everywhere, and a banner strung up near the door that read CONGRATULATIONS CHUCK AND MARCY.

"Holy cats, we've broken into a honeymooners' suite!" she sputtered.

"Gee, and we haven't even kissed."

"Of all the gin mills in all the joints in all the world, *I* had to choose a love nest," Lauren said disgustedly as she turned on Griffin, who was leaning against the entry wall. She grimaced. "I will *not* start the new millennium stuck with *you* and a bunch of pudgy Cupids. Come on, Sloan, open yourself up another room."

"Nope," he said, catching her elbow and pulling her into the living room. "This suite is large enough for the both of us, it's late, I'm tired, and I've done my quota of breaking and entering for the night."

"Why is the universe choosing tonight to make every single one of my nightmares come true?" Lauren demanded.

"You have interesting dreams. Come on, let's find something to light these candles and then we can explore our new habitat."

He found a fire-starter by the gas log fireplace along the east wall and began lighting every candle he could find. It was remarkable, Lauren thought, the peace that candlelight could bring. Panic seeped out of her brain and heart and lungs. She could breathe again and think again and feel almost like her old self again. Life was good.

As Griffin continued lighting candles, Lauren took the penlight and began to explore the suite. The bar held over a dozen full-size bottles of wine, beer, and whiskey, along with a dozen more bottles of juice and mineral water. Displayed across the countertop of the built-in mini-refrigerator were baskets of complimentary chocolates, nuts, and fruit. There was even a gift basket of muffins. Life was looking better all the time.

Inside the refrigerator she found two more bottles of champagne, several bottles of mineral water, and a variety of sodas.

"Well, we won't have to worry about starvation or dehydration for a few days at least," she announced.

"You've got a knack for picking winners," Griffin said as he began checking out the cabinets and drawers in the living room and dining area, "even if it does have pudgy Cupids. Anything in the bedroom?"

"I'll see," Lauren said, walking into the large bedroom. The blackness closed in on her for a moment, but she quickly recovered. The king-size bed was festooned with pillows and a silver satin comforter that shimmered in the penlight. There were plush cranberry-colored armchairs that looked out the south-facing windows, and a second mini-refrigerator with more champagne, a pineapple, for some reason, and actual Russian caviar. Terrific. They had protein. The dresser drawers and mirrored closet were full of clothes. Chuck and Marcy were thoughtful hosts.

"Anything?"

Lauren shrieked and jumped about two feet in the air, whirling around to find Griffin standing behind her. "Don't *do* that!"

"Sorry," he said with a grin.

"I found more champagne," she said above the pounding of her heart, "and a bit more food." She wasn't about to mention the condoms she'd found in the bedside table drawer. "You?"

"A few extra candles, some magazines, and a hotel directory. Why don't you check out the bathroom while I light some candles in here?"

"Right," Lauren said, striding across the thick carpet and into a large bathroom with more marble than Versailles. She also found a wide assortment of mini shampoos, lotions, and mouthwashes. Well, at least they wouldn't reek.

A gentle rap on the door turned her around to find Griffin, fire-starter and candles in hand. "Anything?"

"Nothing edible, but at least we'll smell good."

"I'm afraid a sponge bath is all that either of us can hope for," he said, lighting the two candles he placed on the marble sink counter. "There's no telling how long the water will last. Electricity powers the water pumps, and the electricity is down. What's in the pipes now is all the water we can hope for until we get out of here. In fact, we'd better fill the bathtub and sinks."

"You're right," Lauren said. She watched the Discovery Channel. She knew what to do in an emergency, too.

"If need be," he said, "I can always break into another guest room to augment our food and water and lavatory facilities."

She raised her eyebrows hopefully.

"*Tomorrow,*" he countered before striding out of the bathroom.

Five minutes later they stood side by side in the living room. Lauren's head barely reached Griffin's shoulder as they stared out the wall of windows at a city they couldn't see. Except for the occasional headlights of a car driving down below, the city looked as if it had been swallowed by the Pacific Ocean, and she and Griffin had been marooned on an island.

So much for the fantasy list of Jimmy Stewart, Gary Cooper, and Alan Ladd she had drawn up for just this sort of emergency during one of the many study sessions with her girlfriends in college.

Still, it was a comfortable island. "We've got it a lot better than many of the people out there," she said into the silence.

"Yes," Griffin said in a rough voice.

She looked up at him. He had removed his jacket and bow tie and now wore just the white shirt and dark trousers. He stood tall and invulnerable, looking exactly like Humphrey Bogart facing down the Nazi police commander in *To Have and Have Not*. His beautiful face was grim in the candlelight, his sensual mouth a hard straight line.

She slipped her hand into his and squeezed. "We'll be all right. San Francisco has survived a lot worse than this."

"All right?" he said in disbelief, pulling his hand free. "Don't you know that there are always people who enjoy making the worst of a crisis? There was looting all over the city following the Loma Prieta earthquake. *This*," he said with a sweep of his arm that took in the city before them, "is an open invitation to mayhem. There are lots of people out there who like to loot and burn. Gangs can make reprisals on rival gangs. Petty thieves can break into homes whose security systems no longer work. Drug dealers can sell openly on the streets. It will be a goddamn free-for-all!"

"Why do you have to imagine the worst?" Lauren demanded. "The world isn't black and white, and neither are people. After the 1906 earthquake, *everyone* pulled together, good guys and bad guys and everyone in between, to help those who needed help and to start rebuilding the city."

"Unfortunately, Clark Gable, Spencer Tracy, and Jeanette MacDonald aren't on hand to help out now," he said witheringly. "The city has changed a lot since 1906, Ms. Alexander, and so has its people."

"Look, I know that a crisis brings out the worst in people. But it also brings out the best. Just watch. This city will surprise you."

"You can afford to be complacent," Griffin retorted. "Your mother is safe on the ground floor of this glitz palace with a good half of the city government. But *my* family is out there . . . and vulnerable."

Griffin Sloan had a family. She'd thought he'd sprung full-grown from one of those ultra right-wing John Wayne war films, like *The Green Berets*. "Your parents live in town?"

"My mother and sister do. Dad died when I was ten. Lung cancer."

It was a shock. "I'm so sorry." Lauren had never lost anyone she cared about.

He shrugged, as if putting memory aside. "I scraped enough money together two years ago to buy Mom a condo in one of those high-rise towers on Gough near the Roman Catholic cathedral. She's probably trapped—"

"And she probably has a lot of friends there, too," Lauren said firmly.

"Well, yes," Griffin conceded. "I suppose they'll see this thing through together."

"Of course they will. What about the rest of your family?"

He shoved his hands into the front pockets of his slacks. "My sister Emily is a junior at San Francisco State. She was going to a New Year's Eve party at a friend's house near the campus. I just hope she sticks with her friends and avoids obvious danger."

"Look, Sloan, if brains run in your family, then she's already found a way to be safer than we are."

He looked down at her. "Was that a backhanded compliment?"

"You weren't supposed to notice."

"Right. Sorry." He was silent a moment. "So, where's the famous Stephen Alexander?"

Lauren laughed. "Dad's camping out in the Australian outback, making a movie. They're living off generators and propane stoves and oil lamps. He probably won't know anything's wrong until he and the film crew get back to Sydney. Not that Dad ever had much talent for knowing when something was wrong. Now, my mother is probably downstairs leading everybody in patriotic songs from both world wars, to keep up their spirits while they wait to be rescued. She was born to make the most of a captive audience."

Griffin smiled, as she'd hoped he would, and she felt some of the tension leave his tall body.

"I'll lay you odds," she continued, "that before the night is over, she'll have turned herself into Jeanette MacDonald and will be leading everyone in a rousing rendition of 'San Francisco.' If she could find some rubble, she'd stand in it."

Griffin laughed, a low evocative chuckle that rumbled up and down her spine. "You love your mother very much, don't you?"

"She is a royal pain in the butt, but yeah, I do. I owe her a lot. She is probably the most self-absorbed person on the planet, but somehow she still taught me to grab my dreams by the throat."

"Strange."

"What?"

"That our very different mothers should be alike in that."

Lauren shrugged. "It could just be the maternal instinct acting out."

Griffin shook his head. "No," he said firmly. "Most of the mothers in my old neighborhood taught their kids how to give up and live off the welfare system, or to steal what they wanted from those who had as little as they did, or to escape the world in a drugged haze. It was a world without options, let alone dreams."

"Where on earth did you grow up?"

"Less than two miles from this newest towering homage to wealth and class privilege, on the edge of the Mission District. *Not* the safest place in the world in the late sixties and seventies."

Lauren gaped at the man. "Let me get this straight. As a child and teenager, you lived in a poor neighborhood colored by misery and despair, where all anyone could see were dead-ends all around them, and you grew up to become a prosecutor who makes no allowance for mitigating circumstances, or a life without dreams, or the complexities of human nature?" She was outraged. "I take it all back. You haven't got a brain in your thick head!"

She stalked across the living room, needing to put distance between them. When she thought of what a man with his background was putting Jessica Kirby through . . . She punched the top of the white-and-gold couch. She wished she could punch Griffin Sloan. Hard. Several times.

"I don't expect a Hollywood princess to understand," Griffin said bitterly.

Lauren whirled around to face him. "Understand what? That every day you go to work you betray the people you grew up with?"

"*Betray* . . . ?" The look in his dark eyes made her actually take a step back. "I am doing my *damnedest* to save them from violence, and drugs, and terror!" he said. "By convicting and jailing for a *very* long time the gangs and the drug dealers and all the others who feed off poverty, I am giving hope back to the people who matter. The people holding down two and sometimes three or four jobs at the same time just to barely scrape by. I am getting the poison off the streets so some real healing can begin." Arms akimbo, he glared at her. "But I don't expect a spoiled and pampered Hollywood *brat* to understand any of that!"

Well. Perhaps his costume tonight was more apt than she had at first thought. Like many of Bogart's characters, Griffin Sloan played hardball in the name of justice. Rough justice perhaps, but the kind the city needed just the same.

She didn't even mind the egg all over her face, because for the first time in the year she had known Griffin Sloan, she was finally beginning to understand him. It was surprising how important that was to her.

She took a deep breath, walked up to Griffin, grabbed his large hand, clasped it with her own, and shook it firmly. "I apologize," she said.

Seeing Griffin Sloan discombobulated was definitely worth the price of admission.

Dark eyes blinked at her.

"I was wrong," she said.

He stared at her.

She grinned up at him and shrugged. "It happens."

"Huh," he said, releasing her hand as he leaned back against the wall of windows and studied her. "Have I spent the last twelve months being wrong about you?"

"Anything's possible."

"*Did* you have everything handed to you on a silver platter?"

Lauren smiled. "Some things," she conceded. "Other things I had to work twice as hard for, just so people would take me seriously. Being the oft-photographed daughter of Piper Blake and Stephen Alexander has its drawbacks. I had to fight like hell so my law professors wouldn't discount me. I have to be twice as knowledgeable as every other lawyer in town just so the judges will actually give my arguments a hearing."

"Hm," Griffin said, his hand idly pulling on his right earlobe. "So why, despite being kidnapped as a child and making headlines around the world, *did* you become a criminal defense lawyer?"

She saw in his dark eyes that he really wanted to know. No angles, no secret agendas, just simple curiosity. It was so . . . nice. So, she told him. "Why, because I'd been kidnapped, of course."

"Oh, come on!"

"No, really! Being kidnapped changed everything for me. I learned at the age of nine that the world isn't black and white. See, there were two men who kidnapped me, and one innocent bystander: the nineteen-year-old girlfriend of the muscle man on the job. She had no knowledge of the kidnapping, until her boyfriend and his partner carried me into her house one night and locked me in a crate in her windowless cellar.

"But that didn't matter to the police, or the district attorney, or the judge, or the jury. It didn't matter that she did her best to take care of me during those three awful days. She still got sent to prison for life. I was just a kid. All the District Attorney's expert witness had to say was 'Stockholm Syndrome,' and the jury completely discounted my testimony on her behalf.

"Besides, she was Hispanic, she had a lousy public defender, it was a high-profile case with a lot of media attention, and the District Attorney planned to run for governor. No one cared about the truth. They were all out for the kill. I felt so sick and so enraged and so . . . helpless after the verdict, and I never wanted to feel like that again. So, I pretty much decided then and there I would do whatever I could to help the people no one else believed in."

"But those people can't afford you!"

Lauren stared at him, puzzled. "Sloan, three-quarters of my cases are pro bono."

She'd surprised him. "Like Melva Norris?"

"Case in point," Lauren said, leaning against the armchair behind her. "Woman deliberately drives her car into a crowd of tourists at the Ferry Building plaza, killing four and injuring five others. You could have had a field day with that one, but you didn't." Lauren's eyes met his. "I never thanked you for taking the insanity plea. It was . . . courageous of you. I know you were under a lot of pressure from the media and the bereaved families and your boss to fight it in court."

"Melva Norris was no criminal. She was a sick woman and she needed help, not the gas chamber."

"I know that, but however did you get our ambitious District Attorney to go along with you?"

A wry smile touched Griffin's mouth. "I argued him down with a combination of his Friend of the People platform and race politics. Going after an obviously sick black woman would have hurt him in the polls, and he was smart enough to know it."

"Interesting."

"What?"

"I'm just beginning to see how alike we are, at least in one thing. We both do whatever it takes to see that justice is done."

"Well," Griffin said, unfolding his arms. He took her hand in his and shook it. "In the name of justice, I apologize."

"For what?" Lauren asked, startled by how aware she was of the warm hand engulfing hers, and how much she liked it.

"For being wrong." His dark eyes crinkled into a smile. "It happens. I took the easy way out. Like you said, I made assumptions about you based on surface gloss, rather than making the effort to dig a little deeper to find the truth. You're a very different woman from the spoiled Hollywood princess I thought you were."

"Gee, sorry about that, Sloan."

He grinned at her. It was the most charming grin she'd ever had beamed at her. It warmed her all over.

"I'll live," he said. "My self-righteousness is only slightly dented."

Lauren laughed. "Griffin Sloan has a sense of humor! Who'd have thought it?"

"Sh! Keep it down, will you? I've got a tough-crimefighter image to uphold."

Lauren shook her head. "It's not fair. It's just not fair! I've worked so hard for over a year not to like you, and just one measly hour of being stuck with you blows it all to smithereens."

"Gee, sorry about that, Alexander."

Lauren laughed, feeling oddly liberated. "I'll live." Her laughter died as she heard the distant sound of sirens. Lots of them. She ran over to the windows and saw a stream of police cars and fire engines charging down Market Street toward Millennium Tower. "What's going on?"

"The cavalry has arrived," Griffin said as he joined her. Together, they stared down at the police cars and fire engines—lights flashing hysterically—as they parked around the base of the tower.

"We're being rescued?"

"Not us. The people in the ballroom. Don't forget, half the city government is down there, including the police commissioner. His troops need to make a good showing tonight if they want to be employed tomorrow."

"And *I* had to go for an elevator ride," Lauren said with a heavy sigh. "What about the people on the top floor? They've got equal clout."

"My guess is they'll be rescued by morning. Helicopters can land on the roof, don't forget. Unfortunately, it will probably be a couple of days before anyone realizes *we're* missing. In the meantime," Griffin said, turning back to face the suite, "we'll at least be marooned in comfort."

"I have always enjoyed luxury. But I prefer running water."

Griffin smiled at her. "Amazing. *Two* things we have in common."

Lauren chuckled and looped her arm through his. "Bonding

over plumbing. It's not quite the same as uniting against Edward G. Robinson and a hurricane."

Griffin looked around the candlelit suite. "It's a bit higher than Key Largo, but I definitely feel like I'm standing on a small island in the eye of a very big storm."

"For someone not raised in Hollywood, you sure do a good job of catching every movie reference I throw out." Lauren's eyes narrowed. "Griffin Sloan, is San Francisco's crusading Assistant District Attorney a secret *film buff*?"

"I have been known to wallow in American Movie Classics and the Turner Classic Movies until two in the morning."

"Me, too!" Lauren said in surprise. "I'll take Preston Sturges and Howard Hawks over Woody Allen and Sam Peckinpah any day. Why do *you* prefer the classics?"

He shrugged. "Modern films lack their romance and adventure. I'm not interested in realism. I watch movies to *escape* realism."

"Romance and adventure," Lauren murmured, gazing up at him. "You hide your peccadilloes very well."

"A courtroom is not an appropriate place to start quoting *To Have and To Have Not*," he retorted.

"I suppose not," she said, gnawing on her lower lip. "It's just . . . I don't think I've ever been so wrong about one human being in my life."

"That makes two of us," he said quietly.

Her eyes met his dark gaze and she was caught. She couldn't look away. She couldn't breathe. "So . . . we should call a truce?"

"Absolutely."

"Okay," she whispered.

"Do we need a white flag?"

"No."

A smile touched his lips as he reached out and slowly brushed his long fingers through her hair. "If I have to be marooned on a high-rise island with someone, I'm glad it's you," he said softly.

Griffin's dark eyes blazed into her, not with anger, but with something quite different.

From outside the window came the sudden throb of several helicopters buzzing past the Millennium Tower toward the Oakland Bay Bridge. Griffin took a hasty step back.

"It's late," he said, not looking at her. "We need to conserve the candles as much as possible. We've been through a lot tonight, and who knows what tomorrow will bring? We should probably try to get some sleep."

"I do feel like I've just been run over by a Packard," Lauren replied, not looking at him. She took a step back, putting more distance between them. But she could still feel his hand sliding through her hair and his heat enveloping her. Oh, God, what was *wrong* with her? "A shot of whiskey, a few hours' shut-eye, and I'll be ready to take on Mr. Robinson, in or out of a hurricane."

Griffin turned and stared out at the dark city beyond their windows. "We'll have a better idea of what kind of storm this is tomorrow."

And she'd be back to normal in the morning. "I'll take the bed and you take the couch. If we're still here tomorrow night, we'll switch. Deal?"

He hesitated a moment. Bogie would not have let Bacall sleep on the couch, even for one night. But Griffin Sloan was a practical man. "Deal."

"With all the building systems down, we don't have any heat either, which means it's going to get cold in here tonight," Lauren said. "There are some extra blankets and a pillow in the bedroom closet. I'll go get them."

"Right. Thanks."

Lauren put her thoughts on hold—a trick she'd taught herself in a crate in a windowless cellar. She grabbed the feather pillow and wool blankets from the closet, carried them out to the living room, and dumped them on the couch. Her heart was beating normally again. She could look at Griffin again without fear. He stood on the opposite side of the couch, his hands shoved into his slacks' pockets.

"We should probably try to find some form of pajamas, too," he said. "They'll be more comfortable than our costumes. Besides, if we're going to be stuck here for a few days, we sure don't want to wear the same clothes all the time."

"Marcy and Chuck unpacked."

"Let's see what they left us."

They walked into the bedroom together. Lauren refused to think about *that*. She took the right side of the long dresser, Griffin took the left.

"Now why would a newlywed pack these?" she demanded, holding up a pair of sweatpants.

"Maybe Marcy jogs."

"On her *honeymoon*?"

"Well, she probably thought it would be important to keep fit. Chuck seems like quite the lothario." Griffin held up a pair of boxer shorts festooned with hearts.

"Charming," Lauren said, struggling against a grin, "but I don't think they're quite you, Sloan."

"Darn."

Lauren laughed as she put Marcy's sweatpants back in the bottom drawer. She pulled open the middle drawer, and her fingers immediately connected with silk. She pulled out a skimpy black baby-doll nightgown.

"Marcy doesn't pull her punches," Griffin said appreciatively. "That is *definitely* you, Ms. Alexander."

She forgot to breathe for a moment. "It's not warm."

"You're missing the point."

Lauren was torn between laughter and heart-thumping pleasure. Holding the nightie in one hand, she pulled the pair of sweatpants back out of the bottom drawer and also held them aloft. "Let's see. Pneumonia," she said, looking at the nightie, "or toasty slumber," she said, looking at the sweats. "Pneumonia, warmth. Pneumonia, warmth." She put the nightgown back in its drawer and found a white cotton T-shirt to go with the sweatpants.

Griffin continued to rummage through Chuck's drawers. "Eureka!" he cried, pulling out dark blue flannel pajamas.

"I hope for Marcy's sake that Chuck had no intention of wearing those," Lauren said.

"The contrast of Chuck's romantic nature with his practicality is fascinating." He held the blue top up to his chest. "It looks like a decent fit."

Lauren's mind—which she had always relied upon to keep her on the safe, sane path—was suddenly filled with images of Griffin lying on the king-size bed in dark blue flannel pajamas, which her hands were quickly and methodically stripping off of him.

"I've got first dibs on the bathroom," she said hastily.

"Fine," he replied as she reached the bathroom doorway.

Lauren hadn't changed for bed in a bathroom since her fifth-grade class ski trip to Tahoe, but she did tonight. Even with the bathroom door locked, she still felt exposed as she stripped off her evening gown in the light of the two candles on the marble countertop and put on Marcy's slightly-too-large sweatpants and the loose white T-shirt. She pulled on a pair of Marcy's sweat socks to keep her feet warm, and then finally opened the bathroom door.

She walked to the bedroom doorway to tell Griffin the bathroom was his, but the words got stuck in her throat.

He stood by the couch in the light of just two candles, naked from the waist up. Lauren almost moaned. He was everything she'd just been fantasizing: tall and lean, with a broad, muscular chest that gleamed in the candlelight, a taut stomach, and narrow waist and hips.

"Your turn," she managed, as Griffin pulled on the blue pajama top and began buttoning it.

"Thanks," he said, coming around the couch, still buttoning the top. He already had on the pajama bottoms. His long, beautifully shaped feet were bare. In that moment, she thought they were the most erotic things she'd ever seen.

She hurriedly stepped out of the way as he reached the bedroom. His dark eyebrows, strong nose, and sensual mouth were mesmerizing. "Take your time. I'll . . . um . . ." *Stand around like an idiot.* "I'll put the fruit outside on the terrace to keep it fresh."

"Good idea," he said, walking into the bathroom.

Lauren grabbed the pineapple out of the bedroom refrigerator and stalked into the living room and away from Griffin, trying to get a grip, berating herself, ordering her emotions to chill out. It didn't help.

She collected the rest of the fruit, unlocked the sliding glass terrace door, and stepped outside into a freezing night that raised goose bumps all over her skin. She hurriedly set the fruit down and stepped back into the living room. The bottles of fruit juice and the caviar. They should probably go outside, too.

She loaded the jars of caviar and all of the juice bottles into her arms and carried them out onto the terrace. As she carefully set them down, a pinpoint of orange-red light caught her eyes. She stared out toward Hunter's Point, the struggling neighborhood near Candlestick Park. The pinpoint grew a little larger. A fire.

Whether it was caused by arson or a gas leak or something else, that fire meant tragedy for living, breathing human beings. Charlene had grown up in Hunter's Point. She still had family living there, family that had come to their office Christmas party just ten days ago. Were they anywhere near that growing fire now?

Equal parts of sadness and fear weighed down her heart as she turned and walked slowly back into the living room, her mind turning the dim light of two candles on the glass coffee table into the growing flames outside in another world. She stood over the candles and thought about lives coming apart tonight, while she and Griffin were safely nestled in this luxurious island suite.

"What's wrong?"

She looked up and saw Griffin walking toward her. "I saw a fire over near Hunter's Point."

"There'll probably be several more throughout the city in the next few days."

He was standing next to her now. She could feel his strength without touching him. She could breathe his scent into her lungs. Just standing there, he gave her comfort. That had never happened to her before. "I know," she said, hurriedly regrouping. "It's just that I have this morbid imagination. I always see the people that fire touches, the lives changed or ruined, the fear and despair they have to endure. I mean, I know people who live in Hunter's Point. I've even got a pro bono client from Hunter's Point."

"They have so little, and now even that's being taken from them."

"Exactly!" Lauren said, grateful that he understood, and then remembering that he understood because he had lived that life not so long ago.

"You care about people," he said. "That's not morbid. That's just a part of the goodness within you."

She smiled up at him, made radiantly happy by the simple compliment. She felt like Sally Field. He liked her, he really liked her! "You mean I'm no longer the Dragon Lady of criminal law?"

He smiled, his fingers brushing her hair back behind her left ear. "You never were." His thumb grazed her throat. She shivered as flames flickered through her body. "You're freezing," he said. "You should get to bed."

"Yes," Lauren said and made the mistake of meeting his dark gaze. Lightning streaked into her, eradicating sanity. She watched as her hands reached up to his broad shoulders. She felt herself rise up on tiptoe. "Griffin," she murmured just before her mouth met his.

With a moan, she pressed herself against his tall hard body, his mouth returning her kiss in the same moment. *Yes*. She arched into him, her arms wrapping around his strong back to pull him even closer as fire and insanity took hold.

She was devouring his mouth, pulling him into her heat, her skin, her body until she felt his arms crush her against the long, hard length of him and felt his heart pounding in her breast. She'd never had a first kiss like this. It was flame, and flood, and earthquake, and she wanted it to go on forever. She'd been wanting this kiss forever.

Suddenly, he pulled away from her. Their ragged breaths were the only sound in the suite as they stared at each other.

Lauren was stunned. *How could I have done that?*

"I'm sorry," they said at the same time.

"That should never have happened," Griffin said.

"It was a fluke," she said hastily.

"Yes," he said, rubbing the back of his neck. "Emotions get heightened, exaggerated, in a crisis. We're just reacting to everything that's happened to us tonight."

Staring up at him, Lauren had never felt more conflicted in her life: wanting him to be right, wanting him to be wrong.

"We can't let this situation get to us," Griffin continued. "Danger and survival and . . . and . . ." He was fumbling for what to say. In all the time she'd known him, she had never heard Griffin Sloan fumble for words. "And being forced together like this can raise all sorts of . . . of feelings and ideas that aren't real."

"You're right, of course," she said, struggling to hide the sadness overwhelming her. Their kiss hadn't meant anything to him. "We're both adults. We both know how to avoid succumbing to a situation, however bizarre. I'll just plead temporary insanity and leave it at that. Case closed. Court is adjourned. We'll both feel much more like ourselves tomorrow morning. Have you seen my penlight? If I wake up in the middle of the night, I might need it."

She began studiously searching the living room, not daring to look at Griffin, afraid of what she might see. Pity, embarrassment, distaste. None of it good, she was certain.

"I think I saw it on the bathroom counter," he said.

"Right. Thanks. Well, good night."

"Good night," he said as she walked into the bedroom.

She wanted to close the bedroom door and lock it and shove the dresser up against it and hide from the most awful embarrassment she had ever known. And pain. How could this hurt so much, when a few hours earlier she hadn't even *liked* the man?

She left the bedroom door open, walked into the dark bathroom, found her penlight on the counter, and walked back into the bedroom. She stared at the king-size bed. The silver comforter glowed in the light of the one candle Griffin had left her. She took a shuddering breath as she fantasized his arms encircling her, pulling her against his tall, delicious body, pulling her down onto the waiting bed and his hot embrace.

Damn her imagination! And damn Griffin Sloan!

Angry and scared and hurting, she tossed the throw pillows onto the armchairs, pulled back the comforter, and then glanced at the candle flickering so cheerfully at her from the bedside table. They could be stuck here for days. Practicality had to come before phobia. It had to.

She slid into bed, set the penlight beside the candle and then, closing her eyes, blew out the yellow flame. Still keeping her eyes closed, she slid down the cotton sheets, tucked the comforter under her chin, and let her head rest on a plump king-size pillow.

A profound silence assailed her ears. She knew if she opened her eyes, that she'd find a darkness just as profound and absolute, so she kept them closed.

Huddling in the huge bed, she'd never felt so alone.

4

For hours, Griffin lay on his back on the comfortable couch, his hands laced behind his head, trying to sleep. But it was impossible. All he could think about was Lauren.

Who would have thought that just a few hours could change every belief he'd self-righteously held about her this last year? Who'd have thought he'd ever see her as anything but a cold-blooded shark, using her clients to get her the headlines she craved?

What a difference a few hours could make. She was fire, not ice. Passion, not manipulation. Compassion, not calculation. It still amazed him that she had had the courage and strength to take a childhood nightmare and transform it into something . . . admirable.

She was smart and brave, loving and funny, and so much more that he'd never let himself see until tonight. Standing opposite her in court last week, he hadn't thought of her as being human, much less a woman. The truth was, she was more woman than he'd ever held in his arms before. Crushed in his arms.

Griffin muffled his groan.

He was such a fool.

He'd lied to himself for a year about who Lauren Alexander was, what she was, because if he'd let himself like her, he'd have wanted her, in his arms, in his bed. As he did now.

And that was dangerous. Too dangerous. Like Simon and Garfunkel's "I Am a Rock," Griffin had held himself apart from others from the day his father had died. He had prided himself on being a rock, self-sufficient, able to meet every trouble, every storm by himself, and survive. To lean on someone, or need them, or want them, meant devastation sooner or later.

So, he had been a rock, invulnerable, unfeeling.

Until tonight, when Lauren Alexander had made him flesh and blood again. Griffin wasn't sure he knew how to be flesh and blood. If these last few hours were any gauge, he sure as hell didn't know how to control it.

Every time he closed his eyes, he saw Lauren as she had stood over the candles on the coffee table. The cold from the outside terrace had hardened her pink nipples, the candlelight illuminating them as they pressed against her white T-shirt, knocking the rock from beneath his feet.

The slightly-too-large clothes she wore had made her seem younger than she was, softer and more vulnerable than he'd ever known her. And then he'd seen the anguish darkening her blue eyes, because somewhere in the city a fire was destroying the lives of people she didn't even know.

"*I will not kiss her. I will not kiss her,*" had been a litany in his head as they'd stood together talking. Then *she* had kissed *him*, and every vow, every scruple, every scrap of sanity had burst into flames, and him along with them. He could still feel her lithe body molding itself to him, her fierce arms wrapping around him, her hot mouth burning him, unraveling him, plunging him into all the truths he'd desperately ignored.

Feeling those truths in her warm body and incendiary kiss had rocketed him back into his old self and his old fears. From the moment Lauren had first stepped into his elevator a lifetime ago, he'd been feeling wildly out of control, a new and frightening experience. It went against everything he'd ever believed about himself.

He loved it. He hated it. He wouldn't let Lauren get caught in the middle of it.

"*No!*" Lauren's scream shocked him upright in the gray light of predawn. "There's no air in here!"

Griffin tore the tangled blanket from his legs.

"I can't breathe!" Lauren cried, her voice tinged with hysteria. "I can't . . . I can't . . ."

Griffin reached the large bed before he'd even realized he'd left the couch. The top sheet and comforter were twisted tightly around Lauren as she lay on her side in a fetal position, her hands pressing desperately against an invisible wall.

"*Please!*"

He sat beside her on the bed, hands trembling, heart thudding against his chest, as he shook her gently. "Lauren, wake up. You're having a nightmare." *A nightmare she had lived as a child.* "Lauren, wake up."

With a gasp, her eyes flew open. "I can't breathe! I can't—"

"Easy," Griffin said soothingly, his arms wrapping around her and pulling her against his chest. She felt so small as she clung to him. "There's plenty of oxygen, I promise. Take one slow breath. Come on, Lauren, you can do it. That's right. Now another."

Slowly, her sharp staccato gasps were replaced with calmer, deeper breaths, and she relaxed a little against him. "Sorry," she said in a low voice, not looking up at him. Her arms fell from him. "I don't know what happened. I haven't had that dream in years."

In the elevator, she had said, "This is my worst nightmare." He'd thought she meant being stuck with him. She had said, "I have to get out of here," and he'd thought she meant she had to get away from him. Her hand had clung to his when they'd first looked out the hall window at the blacked-out city. He'd felt panic rising within her as they'd searched for a way off the hotel floor. She always carried a penlight, and there wasn't enough oxygen in the room.

He had to be the stupidest, most obtuse man in the universe.

"You're claustrophobic!" He grabbed her shoulders and

turned Lauren so she had to look at him. "Why didn't you tell me?" he demanded.

"Expose my greatest weakness to my greatest adversary?" she scoffed. "Oh, sure, that makes sense."

"Lauren, if I'd known, I could have made things easier for you."

She took a ragged breath. "You did fine."

"I could have left a few candles burning for you. I—"

"No," she said firmly. "We have to conserve the candles as much as possible. Who knows how long we'll be stuck here? Practicality before phobia—it's my new motto."

"You're a brave woman. Stupid, but brave."

That made her smile. "Gee, thanks."

His own smile faded. "This whole night must have been hell for you."

She shrugged. "It wasn't so bad. I had company." She looked up at him, a gentle smile on her lips. "Good company."

He felt himself slipping into her warm blue gaze and hastily hauled himself back. He made himself let go of her shoulders. "You hide your claustrophobia well. I've known you a year, and I never guessed."

"I've got it pretty well managed. I've done therapy and hypnosis, the works. If it hadn't been for the damn Millennium Bug, you'd never have known."

"But why keep it a secret? Are you ashamed of it?"

She bit a corner of her lower lip. "Not ashamed, just . . . leery of spreading the word around. There are a lot of people in this world who enjoy exploiting others' weaknesses." She took a shaky breath. "I was exploited once. I don't want to go through it again."

"You thought I'd use your claustrophobia against you in our trials together."

She surprised him by wrapping her slim hand around his. "I told myself that you'd think less of me for such weakness, that you'd taunt me, try to push my buttons in court. But truly, Griffin, I knew you'd never do anything so manipulative. You're a good man. It isn't in you to deliberately hurt someone else."

Her lack of judgment, her complete trust, felt like profound gifts. "Thank you."

Her warm blue gaze enfolded him. Resistance slid away, along with his sanity. He felt his free hand moving in slow motion, sliding through silky blond hair to cup the back of Lauren's head. She whispered his name and the world fell away.

"This isn't real," he said, even as he drew her closer, closer. *Yes.* A sigh of gratitude escaped him as he brushed his mouth against hers. Warm and sweet and intoxicating, like apricot brandy. He brushed her mouth again and heard her sigh, setting the brandy aglow within him.

He kissed her languorously, taking his time, savoring every sensation as he pulled her closer, her hard nipples pressing into his chest, her arms twining around him. Their kiss went on and on as he explored her soft lips, learning them thoroughly until he felt them imprinted on every cell of his body.

He moaned as her lips parted, inviting him, welcoming him. His tongue slipped in, stroking her tongue, his body absorbing her shuddering response as her body absorbed his. He'd never known anything this wonderful.

Her hand behind his head pressed him closer, deepening the kiss as she caressed the sensitive nape of his neck, raising goose bumps all over his flesh. His right hand cradled her small, soft breast, his thumb stroking across the hard nipple through her T-shirt. She undulated against him, arching into his hand, setting hunger aflame within him.

He would have laid her back against the broad bed. He would have stripped off her clothes and then his own. He would have taken her again and again until neither of them had the strength to continue.

But her hand clasped in his, palm against palm, fingers twining with his, tightened just then, bringing back the memory of her hand clinging to his in the black outer hallway.

He pulled back from Lauren, staring through the gray light at her swollen lips.

"I'm sorry!" he said roughly as he rose to his feet beside the bed. What the hell was wrong with him? There were *rules*!

"Don't be sorry," she softly replied. "It was lovely."

"I can't believe I'm taking advantage of your nightmare and your . . . your vulnerability like this! You've had a hellish night, and I'm only making it worse."

"Actually, you were making it a whole lot better. I never felt so good in my life."

"Look," he said grimly, "we are trapped together in this completely weird situation, and I don't want to take advantage of you."

"Has it never occurred to you that I *want* you to take advantage of me? Hell, I'll take advantage of *you* if you'll let me."

She was clearly under the influence of her mother's genes. It was the only explanation. He pointed a desperate finger at her. "Just . . . just lie down and go back to sleep, and in the morning you'll be grateful that *one* of us managed to cling to sanity!"

"No, I don't think I will."

"Good night, Lauren!"

"Don't go, please."

"*Lauren—*"

"Please!"

That stopped him just as he was turning to the safety of the door. There had been panic in her voice.

He stared at her in the gray light of the room. There wasn't a wall in her. She sat on the bed, completely open to him, and frightened.

She took a ragged breath. "Would you please stay and help me get through the rest of the night? If I go back to sleep, I'll just have another nightmare. I always do. And I don't think I can stand another one tonight. If you'll just help me get through tonight—"

"Lauren—"

She held up her hands, which shook slightly. "Perfectly platonic. I promise. I just can't sleep alone tonight."

What was a man supposed to do when the woman who was driving him out of his mind looked up at him with pleading blue eyes?

"Where's John Wayne when you really need him?" he

muttered as he turned back toward the bed. And Lauren. "Choose a side. Any side."

"Left," she said, hurriedly scooting across the bed.

He stared at the rumpled sheets and comforter. He was certifiable.

He straightened the sheets and comforter and covered Lauren. "Comfy?" he inquired acidly.

"Yes, thank you," she replied.

Sighing heavily, Griffin slid into bed, reminding himself that they were both wearing clothes, reminding himself that he was safe if he wanted to be. He pulled the sheet and comforter up to his chin.

He lay stiff and silent, a good two feet away from Lauren Alexander.

"Thank you, Griffin," she said softly.

He swore, slowly, thoroughly, and then he rolled onto his side, facing her. "Come here," he said, holding out an arm.

She slid across the bed and he tucked her into the curve of his body, pulling her slim back against his chest, encircling her waist with one arm. He'd never felt anything more perfect in his life.

"Good night, Lauren."

"Good night, Griffin."

He lay in bed, holding her close, and listened to her even breathing slowly deepen as her body relaxed against him. She couldn't have come up with a better torture if she'd planned it for a year.

It took another two hours before exhaustion finally numbed his brain and pulled him down into a deep and dreamless sleep.

Griffin woke slowly. His closed eyes felt the brightness and warmth of sunlight; his ears heard only silence. His arms were empty. He was alone.

He lunged out of bed, and was halfway into the living room when he saw Lauren standing in front of the west-facing windows, her back to him. She wore slightly baggy powder blue track pants and a matching sweatshirt. There were sweat socks on her feet. She'd pulled her blond hair back into a ponytail. She was even more beautiful this morning than she'd been last night in the gilded ballroom downstairs.

She suddenly turned and smiled at him. "Good morning, Steve."

"Morning, Slim," he replied automatically. After all, *To Have and To Have Not* was one of his favorite films.

"Thank you for last night," she said, clear blue eyes engulfing him. "Usually, one nightmare just follows another until morning. But not last night. I had the nicest dreams sleeping with you."

There were so many aspects of that statement he didn't want to touch. Yes, his earlier panic was gone. But in its place was the realization that waking up to find Lauren smiling at him fulfilled way too many of last night's fantasies. "Glad I could help," he replied with feigned Bogie calm. "What time is it?"

"Just a few minutes before eleven. I made brunch. Why don't you go scrape the morning lint off your tongue and I'll set everything up."

"Good plan," Griffin said.

He walked into the bedroom and faltered to a stop in front of the bed where they had slept together. His senses were inundated with Lauren curled against him, breathing softly, her warmth and her scent permeating his pores. It had been the best night he'd ever known. Griffin swore bitterly and stalked into the bathroom.

He returned to the living room ten minutes later, the morning lint removed from his tongue and the sleep from his eyes. Fortunately, Chuck eschewed the electric razor in favor of Gillette, and he'd been able to shave. He wore Chuck's forest green sweatpants and sweatshirt, sweat socks on his feet, and a ruthlessly imposed innocuous smile on his face.

"I've been slaving away over a hot stove," Lauren said, as she finished filling a wine glass with juice. She sat in the chair at the foot of the dining table. "Come eat."

He couldn't help but smile at the muffins and the apple and pineapple slices she had arranged on his plate. "You're a master chef, I see," he said, sitting in the chair at the head of the table.

"It never hurts to be handy in the kitchen," Lauren quipped. "I spent many an hour after school learning the necessities of life from Mom's chef. Dig in."

Grateful that Lauren was avoiding what had happened last night, Griffin took a sip of orange juice, and then broke apart a blueberry streusel muffin.

"Did you sleep well?" she inquired brightly.

The muffin crumbled onto his plate. "Very well, thank you," he grimly retorted.

"I don't think I've slept so well in years," Lauren said, stretching languorously, the blue sweatshirt rising up and exposing her navel.

"You chose a good place to camp out," he said tightly. "The sunlight is already warming up the suite."

"Funny, I hadn't thought about how cool it is in here. Afterglow, I suppose."

"*What?*"

She smiled innocently at him. "You did a wonderful job of keeping me warm all night long."

Griffin stared at her. "Glad I could help," he snapped. "Anything happening outside?"

"I've seen some National Guard and police patrols, a few brave souls walking along the streets, and a couple of small fires. Aside from that, the skies are clear, the air is frigid, and the city is still standing, for which I am intensely grateful."

"Ditto," Griffin said, glancing out the wall of windows beside the dining table. SOS had been scrawled, backward, across the top of the south and west-facing windows. "Very clever," he said. "What did you use? Berry juice?"

Lauren laughed, raising goose bumps on his chest. "Shoe polish," she said. "Chuck had some tucked away in the closet. I figure there are bound to be police and National Guard helicopter patrols some time and they'll notice our SOS sooner or later." She slowly sucked an apple slice into her mouth, mesmerizing him.

"Let's hope sooner," he said fervently. January sunshine was flooding the suite. Sanity was supposed to have returned to him in the clear light of day. Clearly, *that* had been a pipe dream.

Lauren considered him a moment. "Why haven't you married?" she asked.

Griffin choked on a bite of muffin. "I've been busy," he grimly replied.

"So have I." She propped her elbows on the table, clasped her hands, and rested her chin on her thumbs. "It's not enough, is it?"

He took a sip of orange juice. It felt impossible to lie. "No, it's not."

"Why do you suppose you and I chose loneliness over the alternative?"

"Maybe because you and I are used to loneliness, and leery of the unknown."

She cocked her head. "Leery is such an interesting word. It hides much more than it reveals. Like all those Bogart films, where it was clear that he was crazy for Bacall, but he would never come right out and *say* it. Have you noticed that, whenever you and I stop talking, life becomes much more interesting?"

"Stop it, Lauren."

She smiled at him. "You don't snore."

"What?" he said, a slice of pineapple arrested halfway to his mouth.

"You don't snore. It was a very pleasant discovery." She ate a bite of her muffin. "Mom's third husband snored so loudly, the house shook. It was one of the reasons she divorced him. That and the fact that he wanted to invest her money in a movie based on the pretentious, misogynistic tripe of D.H. Lawrence."

"She did the world an enormous favor."

Lauren's smile grew, warming him all over. "It's odd to think of you and Mom getting along, but I think you'll be each other's biggest fans."

Griffin carefully set down his fork. "Are you planning for me to meet your mother?"

Blue eyes bored into him as a soft smile played upon Lauren's lips. "Oh, yes."

"Why?"

Her chuckle was low and evocative. "Because I'm an old-fashioned kind of girl, and I think my mother should meet the man I slept with."

For the life of him, Griffin couldn't summon a single word to say.

"Try the banana nut muffin," Lauren cheerfully advised. "It's great."

"You do realize that you are completely out of your mind, don't you?"

"You don't like banana nut muffins?"

"*Lauren!*"

She laughed and laughed. Then she stood up, walked around the table and, to his utter surprise, sat down on his lap, twining her arms around his neck. "I had a couple epiphanies last night," she said, her blue eyes looking right into him, "about you, about me. I don't want to spend the rest of today tap-dancing around them. I want to spend it with *you.*"

Her mouth scorched his, spiking a fever in his brain, as he crushed her in his arms. He was only human. Lauren had made him flesh and blood. There was only so much a man could take, and Griffin had passed his limit long ago.

"This isn't real," he groaned, against her arched throat. "This is just some fantastic moment in time that will end the minute we walk back into the city."

"Maybe," she whispered into his ear, her hot breath sending shivers through his taut body. "We're both adults, Griffin. The sun is shining and we know exactly what we're doing. Let's enjoy this moment for as long as it lasts." She sucked on his earlobe, and his whole body shuddered.

"I'm willing to risk it if you are." In this insane moment, he was willing to risk anything to keep her in his arms. His mouth slanted across hers hard and she arched eagerly into him. His tongue met hers, their shudders rippling into each other, as his hands roved frantically over her lithe body. There was so much he wanted to touch, to taste, to feel.

He took her swollen mouth with all the fire she had ignited in his soul. He wanted that fire to meld her into his body. He wanted to throw himself into her flames. He wanted, needed, hungered, and he told her with his hard kisses and even harder body.

She replied with her own want, and need, and hunger, stirring something savage within him.

"I want you, Griffin. *Now.*"

She had just shredded the last of his self-control.

"Now's good for me," he said as he lifted Lauren up into his arms and headed for the bedroom.

5

Lauren loved how easily Griffin carried her into the bedroom. She hadn't known physical strength could be erotic.

Just as he stopped beside the bed, her mouth claimed his hungrily. She'd gone too long without his kiss. He moaned into her as he answered her kiss, and then moaned again as she twisted in his arms and slid down his long, hard body until she was standing once again. She grabbed his sweatshirt and pulled it over his head and tossed it across the room.

"Oh, yes!" she breathed as her fingers eagerly explored the warm skin and rippling muscles she had only glimpsed—and dreamt about—last night. Her tongue was just as eager. Starting at Griffin's shallow navel, she dragged it slowly up his rigid torso, his breath becoming harsher with each inch she traveled. "I've been wondering how you'd taste." She sucked at his Adam's apple. "You're delicious."

He gasped as her mouth left his throat to lave one of his dark nipples. "You're killing me, Lauren," he groaned.

She smiled just before her teeth sank into the flesh around his other nipple. She sucked it into her mouth, feeling the jump of his heart against her lips, loving his harsh gasp of pleasure, wanting to taste more of him, so much more.

She pushed his green sweatpants off his hips and down, her hands loving his dark, crinkly leg hair. Loving even more the column of flesh she had freed.

"Lauren," he groaned, fingers pulling off the ribbon she had used, his hands burying themselves in her hair, pulling her mouth to his, devouring it. His tongue began thrusting into her mouth. She felt it in her entire body, as if the flesh she caressed was already driving into her.

Her heartbeat was deafening. Her knees began to buckle and she sank down onto the side of the bed. She pulled her mouth free from his and lapped her way down Griffin's chest, swirling her tongue in his navel, before going lower. Her tongue swirled around smooth silk, then stroked up and down the length of him.

"Lauren, you can't," he said raggedly. "You don't know—I have no—I can't control—"

"Good," she said, and began to suck at him, feeling wildly out of control herself and loving it.

With a cry at once agonized and exultant, he thrust into her and she opened herself to this invasion she had never wanted or allowed any other man to make. But she wanted it now. She wanted Griffin. She wanted to hold and caress and suck this heady combination of vulnerability and power.

She heard more than felt the ripping of fabric. There was a sudden, disorienting disconnection and flight. In the next moment, she found herself lying half naked in the middle of the bed. Griffin was tearing off her track pants and panties and socks.

"But—" she said.

"My turn," he said, the blaze in his dark eyes making her heart leap and her whole body reach for him as he stretched himself over her.

Her hands clutched at his shoulders as waves of pleasure cascaded through her. Griffin's naked body resting against her naked body. Nothing could ever feel better than this.

But she was wrong.

Slowly he worked his way down her body, his sensual mouth nuzzling and sucking at one swollen breast, before his tongue began swirling across a nipple that was so engorged it ached. Sounds were coming from her throat that she'd never heard herself make before: whimpers and moans, purrs, and a strangled cry as he sucked her nipple into his hot, hot mouth.

He suckled her other breast until she felt as if he was drinking her into his soul, a soul lit with brilliant sunshine that blinded and dazed her. She could only feel, as Griffin's wet tongue stroked across her ribs, swirled over her belly, dipped into her navel, making her gasp at the shock of that pleasure.

"Mm, you're delicious," Griffin murmured just before his teeth fastened on her hip.

Lauren cried out, taken unawares by the electricity that jolted through her.

His tongue soothed her sensitive hip. "Go ahead," he said, looking up at her with a smile, "fulfill all of my fantasies. I can take it."

"I-I-I don't know if *I* can," she said, as his tongue laved her other hip and his large hands gently stroked her thighs.

"It'll be fun finding out," he murmured against her thigh, bypassing completely the nucleus of her desire.

"No fair!" she complained, which made him laugh.

"I always thought that calm exterior of yours masked a secret impatience," he said, sitting up between her legs. "You have great gams, and they need attention, too."

"They can wait," Lauren informed him.

Griffin laughed again as he lifted her right leg and bent it at the knee. "But they're so damned succulent," he said, biting into her calf and sucking.

"I am not normal," she gasped. She had never suspected that her calf had erotic potential.

"I don't want normal," Griffin said as he nibbled on her tingling toes. "I want you."

Lauren moaned, those three words acting as an aphrodisiac.

"How did I keep myself from touching you all last night?" Griffin marveled as he stroked her other leg, his mouth following his hands back up her body. They slid slowly beneath her, cupping her buttocks, raising her slightly. "How did I keep myself from this?"

His hot mouth sank into her tender, drenched, folds of flesh. She arched off the bed with a startled cry. His tongue began slowly, thoroughly, exploring her, and she couldn't stay still. Her legs writhed against his, her hands stroked through his black hair and over his shoulders, her head turned and twisted on the pillow.

She didn't know what to do. No man had ever licked, and stroked, and sucked her there. The effect was too intense. She couldn't bear it. She wanted more. She wanted to beg him to stop. She wanted to beg him to suckle her there—"Yes!"—and to stroke her there—"Oh God, yes!"

Slowly she became aware that, for all the stunning sensations wreaking havoc in her body and her brain, the core of her was burning, aching, starving.

She raised partially up just as he left his feasting to look up at her. "Griffin," she whispered at the same moment that he said "Lauren."

She reached down for him. "Please."

"Are you on the pill?"

"No. But Chuck and Marcy brought condoms." She rolled on her side and opened the bedside table drawer. She drew out a string of red foil squares. "See?"

"How very considerate of them," Griffin said with a sexy smile that curled her toes.

"Let me help," she said, tearing open one of the foil packets.

"By all means."

Her hands were shaking, not with nerves but with eagerness, her concentration focused entirely on the job at hand. When she looked up, his sensual mouth was a breath from hers. "*Griffin.*"

He kissed her hungrily, as he lowered her back down onto the bed and followed her down, crushing her. She loved it. Loved it!

She slid her hands down the taut muscles on either side of his spine as she raised her knees, her legs cradling his hips, her feet stroking his calves, as her hands grasped throbbing flesh and he groaned against her throat. "Please," she whispered.

He raised his head, dark brown eyes burning into her. She could see and feel nothing else. "Take me," he said, just before he slid into her in one smooth stroke that made them both cry out.

She climaxed with his second stroke, the orgasm pounding through her, but he gave her no chance to recover. He was driving into her, eradicating every wall until she had no defense left. He was in her, part of her, part of her heart and blood and breath, and it was glorious! It was nothing she had ever known, this connection, this convergence, this fusion of body and soul.

She wrapped herself around him, wanting to merge herself into his body as he had become a vital part of hers.

His hands cupped her face as he covered her with kisses. Her body was moving of its own accord, in perfect rhythm with his, as if they had always made love. There were lightning, and tidal waves, and nitroglycerin within her—streaking, engulfing, exploding—as he called her name with every pitiless stroke, luminous eyes the only world she saw, the only world she wanted.

He was consuming her, the pleasure intensifying until she was swearing, shouting, pleading for release.

He drove into her again, his eyes darkening, the force of his orgasm slamming into her, igniting her own.

"Griffin, Griffin, Griffin," she cried, clinging to him.

The world dissolved around her as she melted into his heat, hearing his murmured words of gratitude and awe as she slipped into a profound sleep.

6

When Griffin woke, for the third time that day, it was mid-afternoon, judging by the quality of sunlight in the bedroom. Making love with Lauren again and again was a wonderful way to pass the day. He opened his eyes to find her leaning on one elbow beside him, her index finger languidly tracing designs on his chest.

"Hi, Steve," she said with a smile.

"Hello, Slim," he replied with his own smile. The most intense happiness suffused him. He felt as if he could lift up Coit Tower with one hand tied behind his back. He was lying beside the most spectacular woman in the universe, and he just had to kiss her. So he did.

"Mm," she purred against his mouth. "It's even better when you help."

He chuckled. "Who needs a video library when I've got you?"

She pulled slightly back, grave blue eyes fixed on his face. "There's something you should know."

"Yes?" he said, his hand sliding up and down her slender back.

She sat up beside him. "It came to me last night, as I lay so platonically in your arms, that there was a reason we had both assumed the worst about each other and hated each other so passionately this last year. It was all a tremendous defense against the truth."

"What truth?"

She rose onto her knees and twined her arms around his neck. "We belong together, Griffin. We always have. We just couldn't admit it until now."

"I've admitted nothing—"

"Oh yes you have, every time you kissed me, touched me, spoke my name."

He closed his eyes.

They weren't playing in a moment in time. This was no fantasy he was living. This was real. The most real thing he'd ever known. It always had been. He had told Lauren he was willing to risk it, but he hadn't told himself how much he was risking, until now.

He opened his eyes to Lauren's luminous blue gaze and felt again every moment of their lovemaking, and the trust she had given him so freely, and the heart that had welcomed him as eagerly as her body had welcomed his.

"You pack a helluva right cross for a dame," he said.

Her smile was blinding. "A girl growing up on the mean streets of Hollywood has got to know how to take care of herself."

"You're scaring me to death, Lauren Alexander. I've never had anything I wanted handed to me on a silver platter, and here you are *throwing* yourself at me."

"I'm shameless," she agreed.

"But dammit, Lauren," he said, his fingers trembling slightly as they stroked through her silky blond hair and then slid slowly down her warm back, "we're so *different*."

"Are we?"

"Yes! We come from completely different backgrounds, with very different families. That's bound to have created wildly different expectations, and beliefs, and needs, and—"

"And *I've* never seen a marriage last more than five years, and you're used to fighting for everything you have—"

"Exactly!"

"You think too much," she said, pushing him down onto the bed. "Sometimes you just need to *act*. I love you, Griffin. Deal with it," she whispered, and then she kissed him, her mouth soft and lush against his, her hands sensuously stroking him, her nipples hardening against his chest.

She loved him. My God, *she loved him*.

He crushed her in his arms, hunger and need and *joy* surging within him. He rolled her to the middle of the bed, his body covering hers. "I love you, *I love you*," he said over and over, as he covered her face with kisses.

"So," she gasped, "you seem to be handling this well."

Griffin laughed. "Lauren, honey, you closed the sale in the elevator when you pulled that Swiss Army knife out of your purse."

She was glowing. "He loves me! Say it again, Sam. And again, and again, and—"

His mouth claimed hers, stopping her words and ending all further coherent conversation for the next hour.

During the first sunset of the new millennium, Griffin dragged himself out of sleep because something was wrong. He heard laughter. *Masculine* laughter.

Blearily, he opened his eyes to find half a dozen firefighters arrayed at the foot of the bed. Lauren woke at the same moment and apparently had the same vision, because she shrieked in his ear and pulled the comforter up to her nose.

"Um, hi, guys," he said.

"I'm glad to see you two made the best use of your time and the situation," a brawny, freckle-faced fireman in the center of the pack said with a broad grin. "We saw your SOS. You don't exactly look like you need help, but consider yourselves rescued. We've got the emergency stairway doors open. The next chopper leaves the roof in fifteen minutes. You might want to put on some socks. It's cold outside."

"Thanks," Griffin managed as Lauren pulled the covers completely over her head.

Griffin had never heard firefighters chortle before, but this pack did as it left the suite. "A fun group of guys," he commented. He glanced down at Lauren, who was still hiding under the covers. "Come on, dearest. We've been rescued."

"Naked, in bed, in your arms!" Lauren fumed under the covers. "Not even my mother has been caught like this. The press will have a field day."

"The press isn't printing, my love. The city's still blacked out. And those firefighters didn't have cameras. I think you're safe."

Lauren pulled the covers off her head and glared up at him. "You'd damn well *better* love me after putting me through this!"

"*Me?*" Griffin gasped. "I didn't do anything!"

A slow, sexy grin spread across her face. "Well, I wouldn't say *that*."

Griffin laughed and pulled her into his arms. "Come on. Let's get dressed, and leave a thank-you note for Chuck and Marcy, and go to my apartment. With any luck, we won't be bothered for days."

Lauren's blue eyes widened. "Mr. Sloan, I think this is the start of a beautiful friendship."

About the Author

Michelle Martin is the author of eight other novels. She lives and writes in Albuquerque, New Mexico.

Close Quarters

Donna Kauffman

1

Committing a felony was not on Veronica Rourke's schedule for New Year's Eve, but here she was, freezing her ass off trying to jimmy the damn door open.

She should be in the house, sipping mulled wine with her father and his fishing buddy, Ronald Henry, though she doubted the former British prime minister had ever been thought of as a "fishing buddy." But that was only one of the changes she'd dedicated herself to making in her father's life. Former United States President Lawrence Harrison Rourke had been out of office now for five years. At seventy-two, he deserved to relax and enjoy his senior years, knowing his contribution to mankind was well done.

She swore as she busted a fingernail. Kid leather was worthless for breaking and entering. She aimed the Maglite clenched between her teeth at the keyhole. She'd spent her formative years making a game out of getting around the succession of nannies who'd raised her from infancy, and then the Secret Service agents, whose mission in life had been to keep her from having one.

One lock should not be this impossible.

She slid another pick out of the case. Her father would be most unhappy if he knew she still had this thing.

But the RV she'd discovered while out riding earlier, hidden amongst the spruce trees, was on Timber Springs property. The person inside was a trespasser. Not the first one to try such a bold stunt, but by damn he'd be the last one.

Her father had promised that for one weekend, they'd be a normal family celebrating a holiday. Christmastime had been an endless round of political parties and speeches given for this cause or that, with flights to somewhere every day for a week, sometimes more than once a day. Well, nothing was going to get in the way of their quiet and peaceful New Year's.

Tonight there were no Secret Service agents, no extra guards, just regular electronic security and old Jamie at the front gate. Everyone else was home with their families, as they should be.

Everyone but the muckraking slime who'd somehow managed to sneak this sleek little bullet past their defenses. *Hoping to get some candid photos of me or my dad to spruce up your bank account, were you?* The tumblers fell into place. *Well, you didn't make Santa's list this year, little boy.*

Veronica slipped inside. She'd seen what she hoped was the sole occupant leave twenty minutes ago. He crept along the trees toward the house, then began to climb uphill, staying close to the trees so his tracks in the snow would be less obvious. It also kept him just outside the security field that surrounded the main house. Someone knew his business.

Well, she wasn't stupid enough to take the stranger on in a one-on-one confrontation, but some behind-the-scenes sabotage was right up her alley.

The main area of the RV held a bank of monitors, keyboards, consoles, and what all else she didn't know. There was a closed accordion door to the rear. Probably a bed and bathroom. She heard the low thrumming of the generator she'd spied from her earlier surveillance. That hum, and the two minidishes mounted to the top of the truck, were what had originally caught her attention yesterday.

She traced the wires from the minidishes coming in from the roof to where they plugged into a flat black box. She unscrewed them, then jammed pieces of her gum into the fixture on the end of each wire. She smiled and bent the little prong that stuck out of the fixture for good measure.

A few clicks on the keyboard brought the main monitor blaring to life. The six others remained black, but she had a pretty good idea they would all show various angles of the house and property around it.

She knew next to nothing about surveillance electronics, but ever since personal computers became the rage, intriguing gadgets had become a hobby. She hadn't had much formal training, but she did know a little something about programming. Okay, maybe more than a little.

The muckraking geek probably had spare parts lying around to fix the minidish connections, but it was going to take some time to deprogram the mess she'd just made out of the operating system.

Job done, she spun around—and swallowed a scream.

"Hi, Nicki. Long time."

She flashed the beam of light on the man she'd seen leaving a short while ago. He was dressed all in black. Black parka, tight black ski pants, black boots, black knit ski mask. She only saw two bright blue eyes, staring back at her. Heart pounding, she tried to figure out who he was. That voice . . . those eyes . . .

No one, absolutely no one, called her Nicki. Except . . .

"Agent McTaggert?" She started to stand, but a black-gloved hand pinned her back to the seat. "Oh, my God," she whispered. "You're working for a tabloid now?" He had been one of the youngest Secret Service agents ever to have private family detail. At twenty-two, he'd been assigned to protect her thirteen-year-old rebellious hide. She'd thought of him as The Saint back then, a man with a moral code so strict it would snap at the very idea of bending a principle, much less a law.

And then when she was nineteen, he'd abruptly left the Service during the last year of her father's second term.

She sat up straighter and crossed her legs. "I heard you went into the private sector. I figured security, not sleaze. What did they offer you to do this? My father will be outraged." And deeply hurt. He'd admired the young agent immensely and had personally asked him to be assigned to the family, correctly assuming that his young age would make him wise to the thinking patterns of a teenager.

Veronica never did know what had triggered McTaggert's sudden transfer. She'd simply sighed in relief.

"What are you doing out here, Nicki?"

His voice was a low, cool drawl that had given her chills as an adolescent, and, though she was loath to admit it, a few private thrills as a teenager.

"Don't call me that. And I asked you first. I can't believe you, of all people, would stoop this low. What happened? Did you go broke? Drug habit? Something had to snap to make The Saint do something so . . . unsaintly."

"The Saint?" That dark, dreamy voice of his had never uttered so much as one nonmonotone syllable the entire time she'd known him. Except when he'd called her Nicki. He'd been sardonic then. Amusement was something new.

"Is that how you thought of me, Nic?"

"Please, I hate that name."

"I know."

Yes, he did. And he'd very specifically used it to piss her off. Every time he caught her, which was most every time she tried to sneak out without protection. "Will you take that damn ski mask off? I feel like I'm talking to a cat burglar." Besides which, those blue eyes of his were disturbing enough without being spotlighted. And those lips . . .

"Perhaps you'd feel more at home in it, seeing as you're the burglar here."

"Oh, I don't think you want to quibble over something that trivial when you have no right to be on this property."

He folded his arms. "It's interesting that you'd assume I'm working for a tabloid. Tired of your love life being the source of so many photographers' incomes?"

"My love life, or lack thereof, is no one's business but my own. I'm appalled that you would do this."

"It never occurred to you that I might be here for another reason?"

That sat her back for a moment. "What other reason could you possibly have for skulking around Timber Springs? I mean, even someone like you can't be that desperate for a date."

"Someone like me?" There was a warning somewhere beneath that deceptively laid back drawl. Typically, she ignored it.

"Mechanical. Cold. Reserved. You know. A cold fish."

He stepped closer. "Is that how you see me, Nicki?"

For the first time, his use of that nickname sent a buzz through her that she couldn't quite describe as unpleasurable, much as she'd like to.

"It doesn't matter how I see you. But I can guarantee my father won't be happy to see you under these circumstances." Anger crept back in, with a healthy dollop of righteous indignation. "I still can't believe you'd do this to him. After all he did for you."

"And I still can't believe you think you have any idea what you're talking about."

She'd seen Dylan McTaggert riled up before. It took an expert to notice the fine tic in the cheek, the icy look in those eyes. She'd become an expert.

It didn't take one to see he was riled up now.

"You've changed, McTaggert."

"People have a way of doing that." He tugged off his gloves, then pulled the mask over his head. He raked back his dark hair with his fingers. It was no longer military short, but thick, wavy, shaggy even. Uncontrolled.

My God, *when did he become such a hunk?* Veronica's face grew hot, and she damned her pale skin. He might have changed, but she bet McTaggert still missed nothing.

"Warm in here for you?" He slipped off his jacket.

She stood and pushed past him. "It's time we go have a talk with my father."

"Oh, I don't think we're going anywhere just yet." He snagged her arm and spun her smoothly back toward the chair.

She was so stunned by the physical contact she let him do it. Just as she opened her mouth to demand he unhand her, he did so, sending her butt back into the seat. Hard.

Things had changed. As a kid, she'd made a game of eluding his protection. But she wasn't a kid anymore.

And Dylan McTaggert was no longer trying to protect her.

2

The balance of power was shifting. Veronica moved to correct that little error immediately. "Tell me what's going on here, McTaggert."

"I don't work for you."

"Fine. Who do you work for? We'll start there."

"None of your goddamn business."

She'd heard that emotionless tone a thousand times before. But she'd never once heard him swear.

"I thought I knew you."

He laughed. "You don't know the first thing about me. Now or then."

"Then enlighten me. Since I'm in no apparent hurry to leave."

"What did you touch while you were in here?" He pressed a few buttons on the keyboard. His face went taut as he stabbed the keys harder, more rapidly. "Goddamn it, Nicki, what have you done?"

Veronica rolled the chair back when he turned on her. There was nothing remote or unemotional about him now.

He grabbed the arms of the chair. "Tell me what you did. Exactly."

Her heart rate jacked up so fast she thought she'd faint.

"Now, Veronica. I don't have time for games."

Why was it she suddenly wished he'd call her Nicki again?

She shoved his hands off the chair, then sat back and folded her arms. She forced a cool smile, when she was still anything but. "Before the gum or after?"

"Gum? What are you talking about now?" He turned his attention back to the monitor. Lines of text scrolled past.

"Your satellite receivers don't work well with gum stuck in their plugs." She shrugged. "Go figure."

He shot her a murderous look, then looked for the wires that had been plugged into that black box. He yanked them from the floor, then swore some more when he saw the red gum shoved into each end.

"The prongs were harder to bend." She examined her hand. "Broke another nail. I hate that."

She glanced up in time to see the glint harden in his eyes. She was just beginning to think she'd played her hand entirely wrong when he spun back to the computer. She watched him fiddle and swear, and breathed a sigh of relief. Narrow escape? Or biding time?

This was not the man she knew. Not even a close approximation. What had happened to him over the last six years anyway?

She jumped when his palm slapped the counter. "Give me some answers. Every second counts." His attention remained focused on the monitor.

Veronica looked at her watch. It was closing in on midnight. It would take her a good ten minutes to walk back to the house. Her father and Ronald were probably well into their reminiscences at this point, but she would be missed if she weren't around when the clock struck twelve. This was not how she planned to ring in the New Year.

"I doubt you'll have it up and running anytime soon," she said. "Your publisher will just have to get by without your photos."

"If I don't get these monitors up and running again, you'll have more to worry about than a tabloid story."

Veronica frowned and stood. She looked over his shoulder, but he clicked off the screen before she could read the code he was typing.

"You screwed this up, you fix it." He turned to look at her. "Or do you even know what you did?"

She smiled at the taunt. "Yes, I know exactly what I did to the program."

"Since when do socialites know computer programming?"

"Since we stopped letting ourselves be clubbed on the head and dragged around by our hair. And I take offense to the term socialite."

"If the shoe fits." He yanked a box off the shelf and began digging around.

"Well, the shoe doesn't fit. I head the board of directors for three national charitable foundations."

"You throw parties."

"Damn good ones," she agreed. "And I make a lot of money for those foundations. A lifetime spent in the public spotlight has to have advantages. Making valuable contacts is one of the few. I use them."

He held up one cord, examined the connector, then swore and tossed it back in the box. "Exploit them, you mean."

She bristled, which was precisely what he intended, so she smiled sweetly. "I haven't heard anyone grumbling as they signed their check."

"It takes money to know money."

She paused. "I take no salary for any of the positions I hold."

"And why should you? Your mother's estate left you enough to fund those charities single-handedly. It's just a way to stay in the spotlight."

She grabbed his shoulder and turned him to her. "Say what you will about my profession, but I'll thank you to leave my mother out of it. You know nothing about her." Her voice was vibrating as she finished and she let him go and stepped away.

"I know what every American knows. She died when you were two and left you a truckload of money. Money she made with her own sweat and blood, running her investment firm, all of which got handed to you on a silver platter for doing nothing. What you do with it is none of my business, and I don't really give a good goddamn. I was merely making a point. She worked. You play." He jammed the box back on the shelf and picked up the gummy wires instead. "Jesus Christ. I should have known better than to take on this assignment. Six years, and you can still screw up an operation without hardly trying."

Veronica merely stood there, speechless. Hurt far more by his harsh summation of her than she should be.

No, this was not how she planned to ring in the new year. She headed for the door.

"Don't even think about it."

"Too late. Although I'm sure you find it hard to believe, I can actually have thoughts. But, hey, I have to fill up this big, empty head of mine with something."

"Sarcasm doesn't suit you."

"On the contrary, I nailed sarcasm by the age of eight. Before Big Bad Agent McTaggert even existed in my world. Now, unless you plan to strap me to a chair, I'm out of here. When the clock strikes twelve, I will be inside, sipping champagne with two former heads of state, and you'll be on the road back to whatever rock it is you crawled out from under. I'll even be nice and leave our little rendezvous out of my next chat with my father."

He closed the distance between them so fast she didn't have time to move. "Tying you up sounds like a fine idea. Along with a nice thick gag."

"Computers aren't my only hobby, you know."

He smiled then, and it was a powerful strike to her defenses. "If this is where you tell me you have a black belt, save it. The only black belt you have comes with a garter attached to it. And, frankly, I'm not interested." He pulled her back to the console, parking her in the chair facing the keyboard. He stood behind her, his mouth disturbingly close to her ear.

"Now, if you want that bubbly passing your lips anytime soon, I suggest you deprogram whatever the hell you put in here and do it now."

Veronica had no idea where the trembling came from, but

she couldn't make it stop. She kept her hands balled in her lap so he wouldn't see. He was so close to her, she wondered if he sensed it. She willed her voice to be calm. "You're right. Some things don't change. You're still just as overbearing and pompous as ever."

"Start typing, Nicki. The clock is ticking."

"I'm not fixing anything until you tell me what you're doing here."

She thought she heard his teeth grinding. "I'm working for your father."

That brought her head around . . . and positioned her mouth dangerously close to his. Veronica didn't at all like it that the trembling sensation increased. "I don't believe you. He promised me we were going to have a quiet family New Year. There is no reason for you to be skulking up here."

"A quiet New Year? With a former prime minister? Just what kind of degree did you earn at that fancy college anyway?"

She feigned surprise. "Why, a master's in socializing. First in my class, of course. And Ronald Henry happens to be a close personal friend of my father's. They are going to spend the weekend fishing. In private."

It was only when he didn't come right back with a smart-ass response that she began to wonder. Could it be possible he was telling the truth? "If what you're saying is true, then exactly why did my father have to hire you to spy on him? Expecting an alien landing? A missile attack from some unknown threat?"

"You just keep running that smart mouth of yours and put your dad square in the middle of a mess he's trying not to be in. Fix the program and I'll explain it all later."

Veronica hated feeling indecisive. If she stayed out here to unscramble what she'd done, she'd miss midnight for certain. Her father would worry and probably send poor Jamie on a manhunt or call in the troops or something. Then no argument would ever be good enough to convince him that he could sit back and enjoy the quiet life.

On the other hand, if McTaggert was telling the truth and

her father really had cooked something up—which, frankly, she wouldn't put past him—she'd never forgive herself for putting him in any undue danger.

"Have I ever lied to you, Veronica?"

The quietly spoken words pulled her out of her thoughts. "You've never had reason to."

"A lot of things have changed since I last saw you, but my belief in honesty isn't one of them."

Now this sounded like the old McTaggert. She blew out a long breath. "Okay. But when I'm not inside at midnight, I take no responsibility for whatever action my father takes."

"Fine."

The edginess was back, the quiet moment over. Veronica tried to shut out the odd emotions he roused in her. And the questions.

She clamped down on the urge to ask them anyway, and began punching in codes.

Seventeen minutes later, the clock struck twelve. There were sounds of metal sliding, whirring, clamping, and locking. The monitor screen went haywire.

Then everything went dark.

3

"Damn it all to hell!" Dylan smacked the backrest of her chair, making Nicki jump.

"What? What just happened?"

He pushed the button on his watch. He should have known having her anywhere in the vicinity was going to be trouble. "Midnight."

"Not my idea of a perfect New Year's, either," she said dryly. "But what does that have to do with the power shutting down?"

"The damn bug got us."

"You mean to tell me you came out here with all this sophisticated equipment, and you didn't bother to update it against the Y2K thing?"

A small sliver of moonlight filtered in from the slit in the overhead panel and washed over his face. "Everything in here was secure. Apparently your little program overrode the fixes I had."

"Oh." She smiled weakly. "Oops?"

"Oops, hell." Her warm breath fanned his cheek. Her hair was loose over her shoulders, and perfect. She smelled good, too. He pushed her chair to the side and felt for the keyboard, then began punching keys. He gave up quickly. "It's dead."

She stood up. "Fine, then we can go to the house, tell my father that your mission has been aborted, and we'll all down some champagne. Maybe we can salvage the evening yet."

He clamped down on her arm before she could move to the door.

"Stop grabbing me every other minute." She shrugged free of his grasp.

"Don't bother with the door."

"Are you threatening me? Because there is nothing else I can do for you out here."

"For Christ's sake, I'm not going to do anything to you." Although the fingers curled into his palms said otherwise. He couldn't decide if he wanted to hold her, or strangle her. Christ, what a hell of a mess.

"A few minutes ago you were willing to bind and gag me."

"Don't tempt me," he said darkly. "We're going to be in here for a while."

Her alarm grew. "How long a while?"

"Until someone comes along who can unseal this truck. When the computers fritzed, it triggered the security system. We're stuck in here."

She snorted. "Good try. I picked my way in here in under ten minutes. I'm sure we can manually bypass any locks you have."

"I didn't have full security engaged when I left earlier, since I was only gone long enough to adjust a monitoring device."

"So, we'll bypass full security then. How much harder can that be?"

"Look around you. What do you see?"

"Very funny. I can't see much of anything."

"Precisely. No light coming in from the front windshield, or from the side window panels." He pointed to the thin light coming in from overhead. "That's it, and that slit is built into the plate. You might be bony, but even you aren't squeezing through there."

"I am not bony!" She dug in her pocket and took out a thin flashlight and a flat leather pouch. "You might be content to sit in here and wait for rescue, but I have other plans. So, if you don't mind." She yanked the chair over to the door and sat down. She gripped the flashlight between her knees, directing the beam of light at the door.

"Nice tools. Come in handy for fund-raising, do they?" He frowned as he watched her work the locks. She'd done this before. In fact . . . "Just when did you take up lock-picking?"

She looked over her shoulder, the pool of moonlight highlighting her saccharine-sweet smile. "Whatever could you be getting at? Oh, yes, you must be thinking about that night in New York City when Dad was giving that speech at the U.N. I spent that night dancing, as I recall. When I was supposed to be locked in my room." She laughed. "Memories, memories."

Dylan scowled.

Twenty minutes later, it was Nicki's turn to scowl.

"Having problems?"

She tossed the pouch on the console. "Useless." She wedged the flashlight on the shelf so it illuminated the small space somewhat better.

He stood in shadows, just beyond the light. "In case you were wondering, full security for this vehicle means armored plates. No entry, no exit."

"Well, there has to be a bypass code."

"Sure, there is. Just punch it into the computer there. You know, the one that jammed up at midnight and is no longer working." His cool began to unravel on that last part. If anyone could put his control to the test, it was Nicki Rourke.

She edged back to the door.

"You're sealed in here." With me. He didn't even want to go there. But there he was. The last place he'd ever planned on being.

"What do you need all that armor for, anyway?" she demanded. Frustration gave way to the first note of real fear. "What is going on with my father, McTaggert?"

Now she was worried. Disgusted, he said, "There's nothing I can do about it, now. No way I can protect him inside this."

"Then there's no problem in telling me, is there?" She moved toward him. "What trouble is he in, Dylan? What have I done?"

He stilled. She'd never called him that before. Her voice was more deeply pitched than most women's, had been even when she was a kid. However, as a kid's voice, it had only annoyed him. Now . . . Now he didn't want to think about what it did to him. "Ronald Henry isn't here to fish."

"So what is he really here for?"

"What do you know about his visit?"

"I know he brought fishing poles." Her patience snapped. "Just tell me, already. I'm sorry I doubted you; does that assuage your ego?"

"My ego was never in question."

"Yeah, didn't threaten you a bit that I got in here and thwarted your mission with only a set of lock picks and a few programming textbooks under my belt."

"I'd say you've read more than a few. When did you get into computers?"

"Don't sound so surprised. Like I said, it's a hobby."

"You didn't take college courses in it."

She raised an eyebrow. "Since when do you know my college curriculum?"

Dammit, how did she always manage to get him running his mouth? "Every American—"

"Spare me the 'every American' speech. Every American didn't know my course load. In fact, the media backed off fairly well for the four years I was in college. So what, were you checking up on me or something?"

He silently took the Fifth.

The silence deepened and the tension grew. But there was nothing personal between them. He'd made damn sure of that. Sure, he'd woken up after a sweaty dream or two. But Christ, the way she used to look at him . . . She was barely legal and she twisted him up like a seasoned pro. Only she wasn't seasoned. She hadn't skipped out on her guard that often that he didn't know just how sheltered she'd truly been.

And he couldn't very well help where his mind went when he was unconscious, could he? He'd never let it creep into the job. A job he'd had to forfeit shortly thereafter anyway.

"What is Ronald Henry doing here?" she asked again.

What the hell. It was all gone to shit now, anyway. "Your father and Henry have been involved in some talks regarding a new missile testing site. I don't know much more about it, other than that your father owns the test site property and he and Henry organized a good deal of the setup. They are set to deliver the final plans tomorrow. There will be no public announcement of this joint venture. Their plan will join the United States and Britain in a new phase of military operations."

She stared at him, and he saw she wanted badly to disbelieve him.

"Well, that explains the travel schedule recently." She dropped into the seat again. "He never had any intention of cutting back." There was no missing the hurt in her voice. "Just how much danger have I put him in? He and Ronald are finalizing plans for a missile site. So, you're here because—why?"

"Because your father has intelligence that tells him there is a threat to the plan. Right now your father and Henry have the only full set of plans and documentation available. If it were to fall into the wrong hands—"

She waved a hand. "You don't have to spell it out. Why would he do this without high-level security?"

His voice took on a harder edge. "Because he promised his daughter they'd have a regular family holiday and, at her insistence, he let the security team have the evening off."

Guilt colored her expression. He'd expected her to get angry. She didn't, but her defenses seemed to crumble.

"I just wanted us to escape the spotlight. For one night. With no one skulking about in doorways, no walkie-talkie conversations, no steady hum of the ghosts."

"Ghosts?"

"The men who shadowed our every breathing minute. You were one of them, but you still have no idea what it is to have a life like that."

She stood. He closed the space between them, making her

back up against the door. "And you should know by now that they are there to make sure your father continues to have a life at all. And when push comes to shove and it's his life or theirs, they'd give up theirs like that." His fingers snapped in front of her face, making her flinch.

She shoved his hand out of the way. "I know that, dammit. And don't think I don't appreciate what they do."

He snorted. "I only recall a girl who did everything in her power to escape the safety we provided, causing her father endless hours of worry and her security detail endless hours of headaches."

"Well, I'm not a little girl anymore!"

"No, you're not. So stop acting like one."

She went to slap him, but he grabbed her hand and held it tight, his body trapping her against the door. It was a tactical error, the magnitude of which hit home the instant her breasts pressed against his chest.

"Let me go," she ground out.

He struggled to maintain his control. "I know you didn't sign on to run this country," he said quietly. "I know you didn't sign on to have your life constantly monitored. But you can't make that kind of decision for your father. Any more than you can ask him to give up the one thing that has been the focus of his entire life."

"How do you know what my father wants? You left his detail over six years ago."

"Your father and I have had many long conversations."

She opened her mouth, then shut it again. "You make me sound like a spoiled brat." She raised her free hand and covered his mouth. "Don't."

A slight shift and he could pull one fingertip into his mouth, and—

She dropped her hand to her side. His grip on her other hand tightened instinctively.

"I . . . I assure you I wasn't being selfish asking him to slow down."

"Weren't you?"

She shook her head, then paused. "Maybe a little. I always thought that once he was out of office, he'd make more time for us. I thought, this was all he could do. He's done. He deserves to rest. He deserves, we both do, to just be a quiet family, enjoying some peace and quiet out of the public eye."

"And yet what you do puts you very much in the public eye. Maybe you aren't cut out for the quiet life, any more than he is."

"I do what I do because I can. Because I believe in those causes."

"But?" His grip on her hand gentled, but he didn't release it. Suddenly the tension between them shifted again. Careened.

He didn't know what to make of it. Well, that wasn't true. He knew exactly what to make of it. It was sexual tension. Screaming sexual tension. He was vibrating with it. And if he wasn't mistaken, so was she. It made no sense.

She swallowed hard. "I'd give it up in a heartbeat if I thought it meant settling down into a nice, normal, routine life."

He laughed then, but it only served to jack the tension up higher.

"What's so funny?"

"The thought of you, settling for anything." His hand slid down her arm, then dropped away. "Your star will always burn bright. You're your father's daughter."

4

Burning. Yes, she knew something about that right now. She wanted to slide out of the space he'd boxed her into and get some air. Great gulps of it.

She wanted to slide her hands up his chest and pull those lips down to hers, to feel what that strong mouth could do to her if she let them.

She swallowed a groan of frustration.

"How real is the threat to my father and Henry?"

"I'm not sure. I don't know much more than I've told you. I'm here to make sure the grounds aren't penetrated by any persons unknown, or any kind of signal."

Hence the network of monitors and the minidishes. "And what if someone were to breach the security?" She brightened. "Don't you have a cell phone or radio to signal the rest of your team?"

"There is no team."

"Just you?"

"Just me."

"What in the hell good will that do if someone does threaten my father?"

"He has additional security measures within the house.

All I'd have to do is alert him, and he'd take care of it from there." He paused, then said, "He really was trying to make this the holiday you wanted. No extra people."

Guilt warred with anger. She wished she'd never attempted to get her father to do anything other than what he obviously wanted to do. But at the same time it made her angry, and hurt, that he hadn't trusted her enough to confide in her. Something that was this important to him, she would have understood. Or at least, she told herself she would have. She leaned back against the door. Had she really been that selfish after all?

"I know your life hasn't been anything close to normal, Veronica. But he does love you, and he's very proud of you."

She raised her eyebrows. "Just how often do you two talk anyway?" And she was really beginning to hate being called Veronica.

"We've kept in touch."

"I suppose I'm not surprised he didn't mention it. You weren't exactly my favorite person. Why did you leave the Service, anyway?"

"Why do you want to know?"

"You seemed so dedicated. Much to my dismay."

"Yeah, well, I had no choice. It was a family matter."

Funny, but she'd never thought of McTaggert in terms of family. He'd been so young she'd never thought of him as being possibly married.

She almost smiled at the idea that, after all this, she might have been having lascivious thoughts about a married man. But something about the idea of him belonging to someone else bothered her.

"You were awfully young to be married," she said. "But then you *were* an overachiever."

"I wasn't married when I resigned."

"And now?" The question came out before she could stop it. Pushing, always pushing. One of these days she was going to learn.

"What difference does that make?"

"None," she lied. "Just wondering if there's a family somewhere wondering where you are when you don't show up on time."

"No. No family out there waiting."

"I'm sorry for that," she said sincerely. "I don't know what I'd do without my dad. Maybe that's why it's so important to me to spend more time with him. I know we probably don't have that many more years left together." She felt foolish for treading on sentimental ground around someone as unsentimental as McTaggert. "So how come you never married?"

He laughed. It made that itch come back. Hot and achy.

"I'd think you, of all people, would have the answer to that. I'm too controlled to cut loose and fall in love."

She smiled. "You're nothing like that anymore. At least, not all the time."

"Maybe so. Maybe I'm not the same man who worked for your dad. But I'd like to be."

"Are you sure that's such a great idea?"

"I suppose I should have expected that from you."

"Actually, this time I wasn't being a smart-ass. Hard to tell, I know."

"Hard to believe you charm so many people out of their money with that mouth of yours."

"Oh, I can be very charming with people I like."

"Or people you need to like you."

"I suppose I should have expected that from you," she tossed back. "Can we call a truce on blasting my occupation?"

"Sorry."

"No, you're not. But do you honestly hold the harmless shenanigans of a kid in such contempt that you can find nothing positive in the person I became?"

"Hardly harmless. You routinely tied your detail in knots. We wasted time, manpower, and taxpayers' money keeping up with you."

She raised her hands. "Okay, okay. What do you want me to do now? Community service? I think I do that in spades already. I make a ton of money for very needy charities. Charities, I might add, that I don't just look up in a phone book. When was the last time you sat and held an AIDS patient's hand, or rocked a crack-addicted newborn? When was the last time you walked the streets of Washington, D.C., trying to find a house that fit the zoning code so you could renovate it and turn it into a halfway house, or a shelter?" She stopped and took a breath and calmed down. "Forget it. Believe whatever the hell you want about me. I don't know why I give a damn."

Dylan blew out a long sigh. He'd spent so much energy trying to make her into something he wasn't attracted to. "Maybe you give a damn because you believe in what you do and hate to have that work slammed. I'm sorry. I didn't know."

"And you're such buddies with my father, huh?"

"We don't talk much about you." Her father had, but Dylan always managed to change the topic. Honesty prodded him to add, "I might have made a few comments about your charity work." None of them overwhelmingly sincere. "He didn't defend you, just said he was very proud of the work you do."

"Those parties I put together require enormous work and campaigning to get the right people to show up—people who have money but would never sit in that AIDS ward."

"Then why do *you* do it? The rest of it? Why?"

She hesitated.

"I want to know. I was ignorant. I admit it, and apologize." He'd spent so much time closing his mind to her, and yet he'd never been able to look away when she was on television, never could pass up a story about her. Maybe it was time he was honest with himself and admitted his interest had only increased the more he'd tried to deny it.

"My mother died of cervical cancer. I was too young to really remember her, much less what she suffered through. I've read many of the newspaper and magazine stories and I've talked to my dad, although he really doesn't like to talk about it." She rolled her shoulders and he had to curl his fingers again to keep from reaching for her.

"I went to school, but I never found my path."

"You obviously liked programming."

She smiled dryly. "As a hobby. Doing it nine-to-five for some faceless corporation didn't excite me too much."

"President's daughter as just another computer geek. I can see why that didn't suit." He said it with a smile, and earned one in return. Why wasn't it always this easy?

"It's not about suitability. If I never had to put on another gown, so the media can analyze my choice of designer instead of the cause I'm trying to support—" She shook her head. "No, I wouldn't miss that. But there is no other way. Yes, I've lived a more privileged life than most could imagine. But I've seen more suffering than most could imagine as well. Yes, I bitch about the restrictions, and probably always will. But that was my life, it's who I am, and I knew it had to be good for something. And it was. In the absence of a First Lady, I made a damn fine hostess. So I put those skills, my luck of birth placement, and my interest in the disease that killed my mother together into a common goal. It was a start. I worked from there."

Her eyes were glowing, her face animated, her body taut. She was magnificent, and he understood exactly why people handed their money to her. "You don't publicize the other stuff."

"It's not glamorous. It doesn't draw the funds. I try to educate people about the charities, but frankly, most of them just want to be seen at the right function. So I give them a guest list to drool over. The other part I do myself."

"I misjudged you." More than even she knew.

She shrugged. "Happens all the time. I don't let it get to me."

He laughed. "Yeah, I noticed that."

She smiled then, too. "Yeah, well, you always did have a way of getting under my skin."

He stepped closer; he had to. "Hard to believe the girl who gave hellion a new definition could grow up to be such a saint."

She grinned. "I sweet-talk money from the rich and give it to those in need. Hardly a saint."

"Robin Hood of the nineties, huh?"

He watched her throat work, then his gaze landed on her lips. He looked up, and fell into those golden-brown eyes. And he saw it there, saw that she knew exactly what he was going to do. Maybe before he really did himself. Some things never changed.

Her lips were warm, and incredibly soft. She tasted even better than she smelled. Even better than he'd dreamed all those years ago. All he did was kiss her. So why had his whole world suddenly gone sideways?

"What—" She broke off and brushed the hair from her face, then touched her lips. "Why did you do that?"

"I have no idea." He lied. He looked at those lips, and he knew exactly why he'd kissed her.

5

He stepped out of the light. Veronica turned around and covered her mouth with one hand, and placed her other hand on her chest. Whoa, she had definitely moved into dangerous territory by letting him get away with that little maneuver.

Of course, he wasn't exactly groping her for more, either. She straightened.

"You just felt this sudden urge?"

"Yeah. I'm over it now, okay? I can control my urges, you're not in any danger."

"I never felt I was," she lied.

"Well, I did," he muttered.

"What was that?"

"I said we should be thinking about the mission here, not running our mouths."

She smiled, more comfortable now that she knew he wasn't. "Was that what that was? Your mouth running?"

"In a manner of speaking." She heard the smile in his voice.

"Was it so awful as all that, then?"

He raked his fingers through his hair. "Do you ever know when to stop pushing?"

"That's one skill I'm still working on. I'm taking a remedial class for it in saint school."

He laughed then. "It's not helping."

He'd stepped into the shadows again, but she didn't need bright light to recall just how those tight ski pants fit his legs, how his shoulders and chest filled out that sweatshirt. How his hair was a sexy tumble, and his eyes . . . his eyes were still a mystery.

And those lips . . . Yes, she knew all about those lips now.

She smoothed her hand over her jittery stomach and rubbed her arms. "It's getting cold in here. Isn't the generator still operating?"

"I wired everything into the system and ran it all from a computer program. It was more efficient."

"Unless the computer crashes."

"Had it been a regular system crash, I could go outside and operate the generator manually. A regular system crash would not have triggered a security lockdown."

She raised a hand. "Okay, okay, no need to bludgeon me with my stupidity." She paced the tight space. "Did you have any indication that anyone was going to try and stop what was happening tonight?"

"No. But based on the intelligence your father gathered, I expected some activity."

"What about the device you went to check on? Could it have been sabotaged to lure you from your post?"

He leveled a look at her. "Had I known your agenda, I might have been concerned, but no. The wind knocked it down. And your father knew I was out of the truck."

"You had no alternative means of communication? No digital phone, radio, anything?"

He shook his head. "Didn't trust them. The signal was set up via computer satellite link."

"I'll never forgive myself if I've put him in danger."

The edge left his voice. "When he tries to check in here and doesn't get a response, he'll take every precaution and use the security measures we put in place—"

"Or come out here looking for you."

He shook his head. "No. That's not part of the plan. I'll take care of myself, and he knows that."

"But what about when he realizes I'm not there?"

There was silence, then a soft swearing. "Then I don't know what he'll do."

She was heartened by the fact that her father did have some in-house safety backup. He wouldn't do anything reckless if national security were at stake.

Unless, of course, he felt her safety was at risk. "We've got to let him know I'm okay so he doesn't do anything foolish."

"You've got an idea how?"

"You have no other backup plan?"

"I've been trying to think of someway to boot the system, but I need a patch to fix the BIOS clock, and the only way I can get that is to go online."

She placed her hands on her hips. "So, if the worst had happened, and you'd had to go into full security mode, how in the hell did you plan on getting out of here? I mean, what if the invaders had sabotaged your computer system, then what?"

"The only way they could have done that would be from inside. If they got inside, then it didn't much matter how I would get out of here."

"If this really was a matter of such high-level security, then why was it so easy for me to get in?"

"I told you. I didn't engage full security because there were no trespassers on the grounds at any time."

"You knew I was out riding yesterday?"

"Yes. And I knew you were out on the terrace when I left to go up the hill. It didn't occur to me that you were on your way up the trail. I thought you were just getting some night air."

"And yesterday, you weren't worried that I'd spotted you?"

"I didn't think you had, but I wasn't particularly worried about it. I figured if your father let you come up here he wasn't too concerned. I'm set up where he told me to set up. This is his gig, his equipment."

"I had binoculars. I like to watch the hawks. I spied on you after I caught sight of the minidishes from farther up the trail."

"If you're trying to make me feel inept at my job, trust me, I've already gone there. I should have engaged security when I left yesterday; it was an inexcusable lapse and one I expect to hear about from your father. I don't, however, need to hear anymore about it from you."

"Fine, fine." She sat down again, then rose and paced again. "So, you really think he's okay inside the house?"

"If he's followed the plan, then yes, I do."

She didn't have to ask if not. And she had no one else to blame but herself. She swore under her breath.

"I didn't know they taught that kind of language in saint school."

"They don't. I learned it from you."

"Very funny."

She pushed her hair off her forehead. "Do you have anything to drink?"

"Spring water."

"Ooh, you sure know how to live on the edge."

He opened the small fridge she hadn't noticed tucked in between the front seats and handed her a plastic bottle. He pulled another one out for himself.

Then there was a rustling of paper, followed by the unmistakable smell of chocolate.

Her stomach leapt to attention. "What are you eating?"

"Staple of life."

She grinned. "Maybe you live better than I credited you for. Dark or light?"

"There is only one kind. Milk."

She sighed in agreement. "Nuts or plain?"

"You never adulterate chocolate with foreign objects."

"Man after my own heart." She stood and walked closer. "How much will it cost me?"

He said nothing and after a moment, the light air between them deepened into something . . . not so light.

"What, you don't believe in sharing?"

She heard another rustling sound, then felt a piece of chocolate press against her lips. She opened her mouth. A

Kiss. Why this one should be more erotic than the real one he'd given her earlier was a mystery. She had to stop standing so close to him.

"Thanks."

"Want another one?"

"Another Kiss?"

"Whatever."

The tension was enough to make a girl dizzy. "Why did you kiss me, Dylan?"

"I wanted to see what that smart mouth tasted like."

"And?"

"Surprisingly sweet."

"I don't think I have a comeback for that one."

He grinned. "Will wonders never cease."

"Why kiss me when it's obvious you don't like me very much?"

The smile disappeared. "I like you. I just didn't expect to. Maybe I didn't want to."

"Why?"

He shifted his weight. "Let's just say that it was probably just as well my family emergency happened when it did."

"I have no idea what you're talking about."

He slid his hand around the back of her neck and drew his thumb along the skin below her ear. "Don't you, Nic?"

She couldn't swallow, much less speak.

"While I worked in the Service you grew up into a beautiful young woman. You were smart, sharp, and didn't have a phony bone in your body. I respected that a great deal."

"Could have fooled me. Every time you caught me looking at you, you glared."

"Why were you looking?"

She'd trapped herself with that one. "No particular reason."

"That's not how I interpreted it."

"Oh? Is the ego talking again?"

"I don't think so." He moved closer. "Tell me I was wrong about those looks you were sending my way."

"I couldn't possibly have sent you any signals. I despised you."

"On some levels maybe. I wasn't too crazy about how you treated me, or the rest of your detail. But you were getting to me. And that was in direct conflict with my job."

"And now?"

"Now you still intrigue the hell out of me, Veronica Rourke. I've followed your progress. I couldn't seem to help myself. Maybe I hoped you would prove to me that you were as shallow and self-centered as I wanted you to be."

"You seem to have found a certain level of disdain with little effort."

"It's easy to do when the subject is several thousand miles away."

Her heart was pounding so hard she could hardly hear herself think. Was he saying what she thought he was saying? And why did it sound so good? "I'm not several thousand miles away any longer."

"And I'm finding my reasoning flawed. My interest in who you were then is a small thing in comparison to my interest in finding who you are now. What were you thinking when you looked at me back then?"

"I was thinking that you had the most amazing eyes, and I was always wondering what was going on behind them." She raised a shaky hand to his face. "Maybe it's just as well I didn't know. Back then."

"And what about now?"

"Now I'm wishing you would kiss me again."

"I still work for your father, Nicki."

"But you don't work for me."

6

She'd expected a gentle exploration, a kiss that went a bit further than the first one.

But at the first touch of her lips to his, he cupped the back of her head, and took her. She would have thought she'd have hated something like that. She hated men who tried to dominate her, tried to prove their manhood with punishing kisses.

So why was she grabbing at his shoulders? Digging her nails into his sweatshirt? Why was she kissing him back with every bit as much heat as he was creating?

Because he wasn't punishing her. It was more like . . . a claiming. And she liked it.

He slid his tongue into her mouth and she groaned. Maybe she didn't have as much control as she wanted to. And maybe, for one glorious moment, she didn't want to.

She trusted him.

It was a stark revelation to make when her body was melting, her blood singing, and her muscles clenching.

She trusted him. The man she'd spent her adolescence escaping from was now the man she knew she could turn to. The man she knew would never hurt her. It made no sense.

Yet it made perfect sense.

His hands slid down her back and over her hips, pulling her tight against him. "It's insanity, Nicki. What you do to me," he said against her neck. He suckled her earlobe, then nipped it, making her gasp and hold on even tighter.

She was breathless. The things he was doing to her neck with his tongue . . .

"I . . . I like it when you call me Nicki. I mean, I hated it . . . but now—" She dropped her head back. "Now I have no idea what I'm saying. Dear God, how do you do that?"

"Do what?"

She heard the sly teasing in his tone and was surprised yet again. Now that she knew this side of him, now that she'd seen, felt, tasted . . . she wanted more.

His mouth sent sparks along her skin. "That. Oh, and that." Her control was slipping rapidly, and that was enough to have her putting her hands on his chest.

He held her hips close. "What is it?"

"It's . . . I don't know what it is. Am I the only one who can't believe we're doing this?"

"We haven't done much of anything yet."

"That's just it. I'm not sure I want to stop. That can't be right." She looked at him, barely making out the stunning blue of his eyes.

"I'll admit that this is the last reason I came here. And I didn't plan on speaking with you, much less . . ." He let the sentence drift off, but she didn't need him to fill in the blank. "I won't lie and say I wasn't intrigued by the possibility of getting to watch you again." He traced a finger over her cheek. "And I won't lie and say I didn't find myself glued to that monitor yesterday as you rode that Appaloosa up the trail. You ride a horse real well, Nicki."

"You sound surprised."

"Maybe I am. Maybe I've spent so much time forcing you into that nice, neat socialite box I'd built that I refused to see anything else."

"And socialites don't ride horses?"

"On nicely groomed farms, or out in the gentrified hunt country. Not climbing rugged inclines."

"I've been coming out here since I was a kid. Maybe not as often during the White House years. This was my grandfather's spread before he willed it to my father. I love it out here."

"Do you, Nicki? What do you love?"

His drawl slid over her skin as smoothly as his fingers continued to trace her face. She felt safe in the dark, where anything could be asked, and anything could be answered.

"I love the mountains. I love looking out on them every morning. It . . . I don't know. Sometimes it all gets to be pretty heady. The whirl, the wheeling and dealing. You can get caught up in your own importance. But when you look at something so grand, so old, so enduring and lasting . . . it's like they put me in my place."

He said nothing, but she felt his body go rigid under her touch.

"What did I say?"

"Nothing. Everything." He pressed a light kiss on her mouth and gently moved her out of his arms.

It was like being thrust out in the snow.

"What did I say?"

"Why is it you never married, Nic?"

The question caught her more than a little off guard. "I came close. Why do you want to know?"

"Just tell me."

She frowned, then shrugged. "I don't know. Probably the same reason you never have."

"I doubt that."

Now she was curious and confused. "What makes you say that?"

"I asked you first."

She realized that, while he'd been slowly uncovering details of her life, he'd revealed little of his own. Excepting the bombshell that he'd been attracted to her. Maybe she shouldn't probe beyond that. But she found she still wanted some answers.

She shrugged. "I meet eligible men all the time. I love to be wined and dined as anyone would, and Washington men know how to wine and dine a woman."

"But?"

"But—" She lifted one shoulder.

"You said you came close."

"I did. There was a guy I dated in college for a while."

"Jeremy Rutherford, of the Hampton Rutherfords."

Her eyes widened. "You keep surprising me."

Dylan thought she was the one doing all the surprising here. "What happened?"

"Too young, I guess."

"You were never young."

She smiled. "My life-style did make innocence a rather difficult thing to cling to. Maybe that's why I clung all the harder. To some ideals anyway."

"Such as?"

"Love. The storybook kind where you want and need the other person more than your next breath and he wants you just the same."

Dylan stilled, then worked to shake off the reaction he'd had to those words. "Sounds obsessive."

"Maybe in a cynic's eyes."

"And you're not a cynic?"

"I think there's a part of me that still believes in that. And wishes for it."

His palms began to sweat. He rubbed them against his thighs. "And that's why you never married? No white knight?"

"Actually, when I was little, I dreamed of marrying a cowboy." She laughed. "Of course, I also wanted to *be* a cowboy."

"So, no cowboys in Washington?" He didn't quite pull off the easy tone he'd been going for.

"Not the kind I dreamed of. The men I meet all have political agendas, or they want the celebrity that comes with dating the President's daughter. I never felt that any of them were truly interested in getting to know me. The real me."

"Not even Jeremy?"

"Maybe he knew me better than most. But we had different paths we wanted to follow. And I don't know that I really loved him. Whatever the case, he married a woman he met while doing his postgraduate work. I'm happy for him. Truly."

"You kept in touch?"

She smiled. "What, your spies didn't intercept our letters or tap our phone conversations? Yes, we did. More a Christmas card kind of thing than a serious attempt to maintain a friendship. But I was glad we did."

He couldn't help it, he had to touch her. He tugged on her sleeve, and she came easily back into his arms. He kissed her softly. "I'm glad he's happily married, too."

She smiled up at him and his heart bumped hard against the inside of his chest. He should stop this now before it went any further. Before she started to think he was serious in pursuing something real— This was circumstantial. Like being trapped in an elevator with a girl you had a crush on in high school, ten years later. They were reacting to the moment, telling each other things that otherwise they would have never known. When it was over, and both had gone back to their own lives, this would be just an interesting episode. No harm done.

Which was total bullshit, and he knew it. He knew what he felt, and it was hope. Insidious and damning and inescapable.

"Your turn. What family emergency sent you home?"

His arms tightened again.

"I don't want to remind you of times you'd rather forget."

"No. You answered my questions. It's only fair."

"Not if it's painful."

He kissed her suddenly; it was hard and fast and over almost before it really began.

"What was that for?"

Because I had to, he thought. Because I need to. He already needed to again. "You keep surprising me."

"Because I don't want to hurt you? I'm not an ogre."

"Maybe it would be easier if you were." He started to push her out of his arms, only this time she held on.

"No, no walking away now." She turned his face toward her. "I wish there was more light in here."

"Why?"

"Those eyes of yours. I want to see if I can read them any better now than I could back then."

"What do you think you'll see?"

She didn't say anything for a few seconds, and he began to wish he hadn't asked.

"Just don't walk away from me, okay? I promise I won't ask difficult questions."

He pressed his lips to her forehead to hide his sudden smile.

She must have felt it. "Okay, I'll try not to," she said wryly. She stroked his face, then his lips, then pressed her own lips to where her fingertips had just trailed.

His pulse spiked at the gentle touch, the soft kiss. He could have used her touch about a million times these last couple of years. And insane as that was, it was even more impossible to imagine he could have them now.

"My mom and dad owned a large spread in Idaho," he said quietly. "Some cattle, mostly horses. Show horses, barrel racers. It's been in our family for four generations."

"That's quite a legacy."

"That and more." He stroked his fingers through her hair and felt her arms slide around his waist, as if she sensed how hard this was for him. He couldn't shake the feeling that he'd come home.

"My father had a heart attack. He didn't survive it. I had to go home and help my mom run the ranch until we could hire someone else to manage it with her."

"Oh, Dylan, I'm so sorry. Wasn't there any other way?"

"I have no brothers or sisters. My mom wanted a big family, but—well, it never happened."

"Did your parents encourage your career, or did they expect you to take over the family business?"

He kissed the top of her head, amazed that even now, with the memories still raw, she could make him smile.

She winced. "I'm sorry, I promised no difficult questions."

"It's okay. I wouldn't feel right if you didn't."

She reached down and pinched his butt, which made him

jump. She laughed, and he found himself smiling and pulling her closer.

"So? Did they understand?"

"Yes and no. My mom was really disappointed, but she understood I didn't want to stay on the ranch. I wanted to see the world. Or at least more of it than southern Idaho."

"And your dad?"

"He wasn't as understanding. I graduated high school early and started college just after my sixteenth birthday. My dad was happy because this meant I could get my degree and be back on the ranch before I turned twenty. But I wanted more. Or, I thought I did. Maybe I just wanted the freedom to decide on my own."

"Did you make up over it?"

He shook his head, and she hugged him tightly then, kissing the spot on his chest over his heart. There was a sudden sting behind his eyes, not entirely from the painful recollection.

"I can't imagine how much that hurt, to lose him when you both had unresolved issues. But you went back, to help your mom."

"She wasn't all that happy about it, either. I'd left to find my way, I was doing well, and she didn't want me back just because I felt obligated."

"It must have been a tough time."

"More than you can know." He traced her hair, then tipped her chin and kissed her. It was a slow, sweet kiss, different from the other ones. He didn't keep part of himself back. He wanted to, knew it was the smart thing, but he couldn't quite manage it. He'd shared. She'd understood. There was need here. In both of them.

A seed of hope began to bloom in his chest despite all the reasons he knew it shouldn't.

He knew then he was in serious trouble.

7

Dylan struggled to stay focused on the story. "We argued a lot and I would have left once we hired the manager, but then my mom was diagnosed with a brain tumor. It proved to be cancer."

"Oh, my God. It's like a nightmare."

"It was worse than that. So I stayed. She was operated on, underwent chemo, the whole nine yards. I stayed to run the place and take care of her. She got better, but the cancer came back."

"It must have meant a lot to her to have you there."

"It was pretty rocky for a long time. But, in the end, yes, it meant a lot to both of us."

She laid her hand over his heart. "Good."

"The funny thing was, after she was gone, I realized I didn't want to let the ranch go. I really wanted to be there. I'd been so caught up in all the problems we were having that I just jumped in headfirst without thinking about it. If I'd taken time to question it, I'd have been surprised that I even cared enough. I enjoyed the work. Maybe I always did, and just refused to believe it because I was so bent on thwarting my dad."

"So . . . why are you here in this truck?"

"That's the final irony. Just when I realized that keeping the McTaggert land was something I wanted more than anything, I had to admit that we were going to have to sell it, anyway. We'd had a rough time of it even before my father died, and the medical bills were staggering. It all just got too big to overcome."

"So . . . you sold it?"

The heartbreak in her voice echoed his own. She really did understand.

"I couldn't imagine not being able to come to Timber Springs." She cupped his face. "That's terrible."

"It's not sold yet. The bank owns it at the moment. The auction is later next month."

"Is that why you took this job? To raise money to buy it back?"

"No. I couldn't make that much money that fast. Your dad's offer came at a time when I didn't know what direction to take. So I'm going back into security work. Private, this time."

"It's not what you want."

"It was once. It can be again."

She shivered.

"You're cold."

She shook her head. "I'm fine. I'm worried about my dad, though."

He tilted her chin up. "If he comes looking for you, your tracks will lead him right to me." He put his mouth on hers . . . and kept it there.

She let him in, and kept him there.

He pushed her jacket off her shoulders just as her hands found the edge of his sweatshirt. He let her pull it over his head; she let him push the coat from her shoulders.

This was insane. Even as his hands went to her sweater, his mind was commanding him to stop. He couldn't do this, not here, not now. "Nic, wait—"

"We're unattached adults. I'm consenting. Are you?" She sounded so sure of herself, but he saw the flicker of uncertainty in her eyes. She tried on a smile. "You know me, impulsive is my middle name."

"I don't want to be just an impulse." He hadn't known how true that was until he'd spoken the words. "I want you, Nic. Maybe I always have. But I don't need more regrets in my life."

"I'm saying yes. Whatever happens, I want this."

"And later?"

"Now who's pushing? Just what are you asking for?"

Damn good question. "Nothing. Nothing."

"It's not nothing. And who knows, it could be the beginning of . . . something."

"Could it be? The socialite and the security guard? The President's daughter and her bodyguard?"

"I don't think in labels."

"But the rest of the world does."

"And since when have I ever let the rest of the world dictate what I do?"

"So, am I another rebellion?"

"No. You're a man who has gotten my attention. Maybe you always had it." She pulled his head down. "So why don't you just concentrate on keeping it, and let the rest take care of itself."

Yes, why didn't he? God knows he wanted to.

"You know, you're not like any man I've ever met. You might have tried to shove me behind a label, but you still know me better than anyone."

He smiled at that. "Even Jeremy?"

"Even Jeremy."

It had been six years of hell, and she was offering him heaven. He deserved the shot at happiness. He took her hand, then swung her up into his arms.

She let out a little yelp of surprise. "What are you doing?"

"Sweeping you off your feet." He moved to the back of the RV and pushed aside the folding door that separated the main cabin from the rest of the vehicle. "It's not a castle, but then, I'm no white knight."

Veronica smiled into his neck, nuzzling his skin. He was

more of a knight than he thought. "No," she said softly. "You're my cowboy."

He stumbled a bit then, but she held on tight. She'd always trusted her instincts. What was happening here was something she'd never have planned on, but she wasn't walking away from it. Life doled out opportunities at the oddest times. She'd learned long ago never to dismiss them out of hand.

She smiled to herself. Dylan was her cowboy. Her heart knew it. Her head could catch up on all the details later.

He laid her on the bed and moved on top of her. His weight felt wonderful, perfect, and she shifted until he fit between her legs.

"We have way too many clothes on here," she said.

"For once, I'm not going to argue with you." He rolled off her, much to her dismay, but she heard the rustle of fabric, then felt his warm thigh next to her hand. She reached for the button of her jeans, but his hand found hers. "Can I?"

She smiled. "I don't know. Can you?"

He laughed. And she knew it was going to be perfect. "Watch me."

God, I wish I could. "Next time I at least want moonlight."

His hand stilled, but only for a second. He slid her jeans and panties over her hips.

"I want to watch you take me, Dylan."

Her bra came off like a slingshot under his suddenly unsteady hands. "That mouth of yours is going to get you in trouble."

"God, I hope so."

He growled then and scooped her into his arms. Before she knew what was happening, he was flat on his back and she was astride him.

She ran her hands over him. Smooth, hard, perfect. He gripped her hips, then slipped his hands up over her breasts. He brushed at her nipples and her back arched of its own will, pressing them more fully into his hands.

"Come here, Nicki." He pulled her head down and lifted his hips until she slid forward. He took her mouth hard and fast until she was squirming on him, desperate to feel him inside her.

"I want you, Dylan."

Her hands gripped his biceps, her nails digging in as he began to enter her.

"Dear God," she breathed. "I'm not sure I can take much more teasing."

"You still want to be a cowboy, Nicki?"

The laugh came out of her in a burst. "You've got a mouth on you, too, McTaggert." He slid inside her then, and any hope of speech was lost.

"Ride me, Nicki."

And she did. God help her, she did.

Dylan's watch glowed two in the morning when he finally drifted off to sleep, his head on her stomach, hands still tangled in her hair.

It was almost too amazing to believe. And Veronica didn't regret a moment of it. Nor did she intend to let him ride off into the sunset when they finally got out of the RV.

She wondered what her father would make of this relationship. He liked Dylan, even more than she'd realized. She'd make it okay with him. Right after she apologized. Her father and Henry hadn't come to the RV, and there had been no unusual alarms. She prayed that meant everything was okay. Perhaps her father had seen her tracks and knew she was here with Dylan. She wasn't sure what she thought of that scenario, but it was better than thinking the worst.

She played with the hair at the nape of Dylan's neck. Her life had taken an amazing turn in the span of one night. She let her hand trail down Dylan's back. Could they have a chance?

Veronica and Dylan were jolted awake by a loud rapping on the door. "McTaggert? It's Lawrence. Is Veronica still in there with you?"

Even in the dark, Veronica knew Dylan turned his head toward her. "I don't want this to be a problem for you, Nic."

"Cowboy code?" she whispered lightly. "Yes," she called out loudly. "I'm here. Are you okay, Daddy?"

"Fine, fine."

Then she recalled his exact words. "What did you mean, 'still here'? How long have you known I was in here?"

There was a pause, then a clearing of a throat, then, "I followed your tracks last night. Saw where you went and figured you were in good hands."

Both Dylan and Veronica began scrambling for their clothes.

"What in the blazes happened? Why is the armor up?"

"It's my fault, sir," Dylan started.

Veronica started to giggle, but Dylan shut her up with a short but effective kiss. "Let me handle this, Nic."

"I can handle my own father." She was first to the main cabin. "I thought it was a tabloid truck," she explained. "I broke in and sabotaged his computers."

"I left the security system down while I fixed that monitor," Dylan said, coming up behind her, putting his hands on her hips and turning her around. "I'll take the heat," he whispered.

"Oh, I think we share heat pretty well. Why stop now?" She was ridiculously pleased. Both that her father was fine and that Dylan still couldn't keep his hands to himself. That he cared enough to try to protect her. It was a good start.

"I overrode his security system and triggered the Y2K bug," she called out. "It locked us up like Fort Knox."

"Hang tight. Jamie's here with the blow torch. We'll have you out shortly."

"Blow torch! There must be another way." Dear God, replacing his computer equipment was one thing. This was going to cost a fortune.

"Afraid not."

A couple hours, a chain saw, and a sledgehammer later, Dylan and Veronica were freed.

"I'll make restitution," was the first thing she said to her father.

He looked at her, then at Dylan.

"Sir, I—"

"We'll discuss it in my den." He turned his back on them and walked up the hill to the waiting Jeeps. "Ronald is waiting." He had two four-wheel-drive vehicles waiting. He and Jamie took one, leaving the other to her and Dylan.

She frowned. "He must really be mad."

"We'll explain everything. He'll be okay." Dylan didn't sound too sure of that.

She'd have agreed with him, except her father was acting very strangely. "At least it looks like nothing happened last night. Thank God for that. I'll make sure he knows this was all my fault."

Dylan turned and grinned at her then. "Now who has the cowboy code?"

She thought of all the palpitations her heart had experienced last night. None of them came close to how it felt right now.

His smile faded. "I will make it okay, Nic. I promise."

"No. It's not that. I can take responsibility for my actions. It's just—"

He stepped closer then, and touched her cheek. "What? Regrets?"

"None." Her hand brushed over his cheek. She noticed her fingers trembled. "You're beautiful."

He actually colored. "Isn't that supposed to be my line?"

"I mean it." She grabbed his hand when he would have turned away. "Dylan, wait."

He turned back and she tried to see past the sudden wariness in those beautiful eyes of his. "What?"

"No matter what happens with my father, don't just walk away."

The wariness faded. What she saw stole her breath, and what was left of her heart. He stepped closer, not caring who was watching, and kissed her. It was a claiming kiss. And she reveled in it.

"I'm not walking anywhere but right by your side, Nic."

8

Lawrence and Ronald were waiting for them after they freshened up.

Dylan stepped forward. "Sir, I'd like to explain—"

"I only want to know one thing. Do you love her?"

Dylan's gaze shot to Veronica. She looked just as shocked as he felt.

"I, uh, I beg your pardon, sir?"

"It was a simple enough question—"

"Daddy, I'm an adult. What I do is my own business. How dare you—"

He shifted his dark gaze to her. "I'll get to you in a minute." He looked back to Dylan. "I went to a lot of trouble to throw you two back together again. Did it work, or not?"

"We've made a wager." That came from Ronald.

"Hush, now, Henry. That was merely to keep you happy."

Veronica finally managed to snap her mouth shut and step up to her father's desk. "Are you saying you purposely put us together?"

"You've been hounding me day and night to settle down, when it was clear to anyone with eyes in his head that you were the one who needed to nest." He gentled somewhat then. "I love you, baby. But I'm too old to nest. It'd be like sitting around, waiting for the caretaker to carry away my bones."

Her eyes stung. "I never meant to make you feel that way. I want to spend more time with you, but I don't want you to do anything that would take away your vitality. I'm sorry I was so selfish. Can you forgive me?"

"There's nothing to forgive. I know you're just trying to do what's best for me. But you have to trust that I'm doing it."

She let out a sigh of relief. "I will. I promise." Then she folded her arms. "But the rest of this . . . Daddy, I don't think I deserved such a blatant manipulation—"

"It wasn't blatant. It was damn subtle if you ask me. I mean, I could have just invited him to dinner, but I knew you better than that."

She looked at Ronald, still unable to believe what she was hearing. "And you were in on this, too?"

Ronald smiled, obviously quite satisfied with himself.

She turned back to her father. "I deserve an explanation, at the very least."

"Yes, you do. But you must promise to listen with your heart. It's much softer than your head."

That brought smiles from both Dylan and Ronald, which she withered with a glare.

"I wasn't going to shove anyone down your throat," her father said gently. "But I know you better than anyone on this great earth, Veronica. And I know young Dylan here quite well, also. We've been keeping in touch."

"So he told me."

Lawrence's eyebrows raised. "Splendid, so much the better. So, I brought Dylan here on the pretense of work."

"Pretense?" This from Dylan. There was no twinkle in his eye now.

"I'm sorry. It wasn't meant as a slight to your pride, but I was only willing to do so much. I had a pretty good hunch, but the rest had to be up to you."

"There is no missile program?"

"Oh, no, the program exists. The plans were sent by private courier to Washington two days ago, just after Ronald arrived and signed the final papers."

"So there was no threat?" Veronica asked.

"None to speak of."

"And the intelligence reports?" Dylan asked, jaw tight.

"Ronald here took care of those. Quite a nice job if I must say."

Veronica grunted in exasperation. "You set this whole thing up because you wanted us to meet—what, by accident?"

"I sent you on that trail, figuring you'd see the truck. It didn't take too much guessing to know how you'd react."

"I could have come directly to you." He just looked at her. Her cheeks grew warm. "Okay. But you still had no way of knowing I'd break in."

He lifted a disapproving brow, but said, "Oh, I knew you'd do something. Of course, we figured you'd confront him right away."

"You gave us a bit of a scare when you came back straight-away and didn't say anything," Ronald added.

She looked from one to the other, then to Dylan. "Am I the only one here who thinks you two have lost your minds?"

"Are you so sorry about it?" Dylan asked.

That set her back. "Are you saying you don't care that we were manipulated into this?"

"We were manipulated into seeing each other again. Your father and Mr. Henry here had nothing to do with what happened after that."

He didn't seem in the least embarrassed that both her father and the former Prime Minister were watching them closely.

"Nothing could be more true than that," her father said. "Your little espionage trip last night outdid even our wildest expectations."

"I can't believe this!"

Dylan turned her chin toward him. She could get lost in his blue eyes and never come back.

"Maybe it wasn't straightforward of him," Dylan said softly. "But I'm having a hard time holding a grudge."

She wanted to be mad. But he made too much sense.

"Do you wish he hadn't done it?" Dylan asked.

"No. No, I can't say that."

"I want the chance with you that he's given us. A chance we'd never have taken otherwise."

"The cowboy and the socialite?"

His smile faded. "I'm not a cowboy any longer."

Her father interrupted by clearing his throat. "So, can you answer my question, McTaggert?"

"I don't know that I can offer her the kind of future you'd like her to have."

"Hogwash. She can have whatever future she wants. If she'd wanted to settle down in Washington with one of those slick-haired sharks, she would have done so by now."

"Father, I'm only twenty-six. Not exactly an old maid."

"You were going on twenty-six when you were sixteen. You needed someone who would give you what you really wanted, Veronica. A life out of the spotlight, a person you could be yourself with. A man to build a family with. Did I guess wrong?"

She whispered, "No. No, I don't think you did." She looked at Dylan, who squeezed her hand, then back at her father. "How is it you know me so well and I'm still figuring you out?"

"Parental privilege. Something I hope you come to understand while I'm still around to bounce a baby or two on my knee. I'm not getting any younger here."

She should have objected to the more than obvious nudge. But, somehow, she couldn't seem to find the righteous indignation. "Don't push your luck too far, here," she warned, but there was no heat in it. "One night does not a lifetime make."

"Life is a series of one nights, and one days," her father said. "I wish I hadn't wasted so many of the ones I could have had with your mother wondering if I should tell her how I felt."

"You weren't sure about Mom? You always told me it was love at first sight."

He chuckled. "Lust, maybe. Love took me at least a couple of hours. But it took me months to find the courage to tell her." He shook his head. "And she never let me forget who told who first. She got tired of waiting and delivered an ultimatum. I never regretted taking the challenge." His eyes softened. "You're a lot like her, Veronica." He rubbed his nose and cleared his throat. "And don't think I'm shoving you two down the aisle."

Veronica smiled. "Oh, no, we'd never think that."

"If you're suited, you'll do something about it. And I trust you won't dillydally around like I did. You've too much of your mother in you." He looked at Dylan. "I respect what you've done for your family. I'm sorry about your ranch. I know what land like that means to a man." He looked briefly at Veronica. "And a woman. Timber Springs has been in my family for a long time, too. It doesn't take a genius to see that your heart is in your ranch. But if you'd like, I can make a call, get you back in the Service."

"Sir, I'm grateful for the offer. But this one job was enough to tell me this isn't what I want to do." He turned to Nicki. "But I'll find my way. Both with my life, and with your daughter."

Lawrence shook Dylan's hand, then turned to his daughter. "Forgive a meddling old man?"

Nicki skirted the desk and went into his arms. "Of course." She laughed and cried as she kissed him, then smacked him on the arm. "But you can keep your strategizing to world affairs from now on, okay?"

He sighed and hugged her. "Gladly."

"If you don't mind, sir, I'd like to talk to Veronica outside."

"Fine, fine. And Dylan, please call me Lawrence."

His heart was pounding when Nic slid her fingers between his. His whole future was right there, where their hands joined.

Nicki stopped long enough to buss Ronald on the cheek. "Thank you, Uncle Ronnie," she whispered.

His eyes twinkled merrily. "Of course, my dear. Think nothing of it."

"Look out for my father, okay?" Then she rolled her eyes.

"What am I saying? It's like asking the wolf to guard the sheep."

He patted her on the shoulder. "Go on now with your young man. We're perfectly harmless. Going to do some fishing later, in fact."

"I'm glad. And I don't buy the innocent act for a second."

"Always said you were a sharp girl."

She was still smiling as Dylan shut the door behind them and kissed her deeply.

She wove her hands around his neck. "I could get used to this. A lot of this."

"This has all happened very fast, Nic."

She frowned. "What are you saying?"

"I don't want you to do anything you don't want to do."

"Has that ever been a problem with me?"

He grinned. "No. But—" He rubbed his finger over her bottom lip. "Why are you smiling at me like that?"

"I'm just picturing how stunning you'd look climbing over me with the sunlight at your back."

He swallowed. Twice. "You're making this—"

"Hard?" She grinned. "Good."

He fought his own smile. "I meant what I said in there. I will find my own way. I'm thirty-four years old, and basically out of work. Not the catch of the century, here."

"I've been giving that some thought." She leaned back. "Uh-oh, that wary look is back in your eyes."

"You might as well get used to it. I have a feeling you'll be seeing it a lot."

"You're probably right. But hear me out. If you could do whatever you wanted, what would that be?"

He answered her from his heart, and made a promise right then that he always would. She didn't pull punches; neither would he. "Work the McTaggert ranch."

"The bank auction is next month, right?"

His eyes narrowed. "If you're going to say what I think you're going to say—"

"Does the bank have a buyer?"

He shook his head. "No."

"No chance that whoever buys it would hire you on as manager? I mean, no one would know the place better than you."

"I'm not hanging my hopes on that."

"I want to help you." She held on to him when he would have pushed away.

"I'm no charity case, Nic."

"I should hope to hell not. I give enough to charity. In fact, I think it's high time I started to think about myself for a change."

His jaw stayed tight. "Don't do this to me, Nicki."

She huffed. "Honestly. Men and their pride. Listen to me, Dylan. I can do this. I can make a dream come true. Do you know how hard I work for people, knowing that they'll probably die before anything I've done can help them? Let me do this. It's not like you're going to walk back in and it will be golden. It will be sweat and tears and probably some blood. Maybe some of mine, if you'll let me help."

He said nothing. But he didn't walk away. He couldn't.

"Take me to Idaho, Dylan. Let me see if I fall in love with McTaggert land as fast as I'm falling in love with you."

When he remained silent she said, "If the situation were reversed, could you sit back and do nothing while my dream vanished? When you knew you could rescue it?"

"I don't suppose so."

She grinned. "You don't suppose."

He still frowned. "No. What about your charity work, Nic? You can't just walk away."

"No, but maybe it's time I came at it from a new angle. You have lots of space, right? Well, maybe some of those kids who benefit from the charities I raise money for could also benefit from some time in the fresh mountain air. We could get support for a program for kids out there, and for the charities, too."

He leaned in and kissed her. It was slow, deep and he felt his heart shift fully into its rightful place. "I should never have doubted your heart," he said softly. "We'll help your kids, Nic. I'll see to it."

"Maybe you can help me with my other dream, too."

"Your other dream?"

"To become a cowboy. And who knows? Maybe I'll go for broke and try to marry a cowboy, too."

She reached up and kissed him.

His defenses were gone. Truthfully, she'd decimated them when she'd said she was falling in love with him. He kissed her until she was breathless with the same need he had for her. "Veronica Rourke, cowboy." He smiled down into her eyes. "It'll be different."

"Different is good. In fact, it's essential."

"What you said earlier . . . about McTaggert land . . . and McTaggert men . . ."

"Yes?"

He grinned. "Let's just say your father is right. You take after your mother."

"Is that a proposal?"

He scooped her up in his arms. "Let's go home to Idaho, Nic."

"I thought you'd never ask."

Lawrence and Ronald both turned from the monitor that surveyed the hallway outside the office.

Ronald clapped his hand on Lawrence's back. "Looks like I owe you a few pounds."

"That you do, mate. That you do."

"I'll wager they make you a grandfather before your seventy-fifth birthday."

"They'd best not wait that long!"

They both laughed and sat in the pair of leather chairs fronting the fireplace. The flames crackled as they each lit a congratulatory cigar.

"So," Lawrence said, pausing to puff the cigar to life. "That went quite well if I do say so."

"A shame about the RV."

"Small price to pay."

Lawrence clenched the cigar between his teeth and

rubbed his hands. "So, have you come up with a plan for your lovely daughter, Claire?"

Ronald grinned. "Valentine's Day is coming."

Lawrence grinned right back. "Why, yes, yes, it is indeed."

They bent their heads and got to work.

About the Author

Donna Kauffman has been in one or two tight spots in her life, which is probably why she delights in tormenting her characters with similar restrictions. Now if she could just figure out a way for her sticky situations to end as smoothly as those of her characters. . . .

Donna was born and raised in Maryland, and now lives on the other side of the Potomac in Virginia with her husband, two sons and two Australian terriers. She loves to hear from readers and can be contacted via her website at www.donnakauffman.com

Trouble at Midnight

Jill Shalvis

1

The train sped through the night, racing away from 1999 and into the new millennium. It was New Year's Eve.

Only a handful of people were on board the luxurious passenger line, all of them associated with the new rail system designed to bring the rich and famous of San Francisco up to the casinos of the Nevada shoreline at Lake Tahoe. Everyone was dressed to the nines. Food and drink flowed, as did laughter and high-wheeling deals. But Dora Wickers felt none of that excitement for this inaugural trip, nothing but a rising panic she couldn't control.

Dora stared out a window into the landscape flying by. The moon was high, casting silver shadows on the tall, twisting silhouettes that were the Sierras. Though the shimmering, nighttime scenery couldn't be beat, she was only here because she had to be. As the interior designer for the passenger cars, she had to make a showing for her clients, and hopefully gain new ones in the process. But more important, she was here for Adam Morgan, who, as the bank's representative, had gotten the entire deal financed.

He was also the man who wanted her to marry him.

Dora's claustrophobia doubled. The walls she'd so

lovingly designed seemed to close in on her. The windows shrank before her very eyes, swallowing her view to the outside.

God, she wanted off this train.

She could see him out of the corner of her eye. It wasn't difficult; Adam was as tall as she was . . . well, not. His dark hair gleamed and his features eased into a pleasant smile as he spoke to the engineer's wife. He wore a well-fitted charcoal gray suit without a single wrinkle. In his breast pocket was the slight bulge of his reading glasses, and, if she knew him well, he also carried a neatly folded handkerchief, a complicated pocket calculator, and his favorite writing pen. In his hand was a glass of champagne that someone had pressed on him. Dora knew he would take no more than a discreet sip, and though a special warmth for him burst within her, it did nothing for her growing restlessness. He'd been her closest friend for over a year now. That friendship had deepened when Adam's bank had funded her struggling designing business, and maybe the affection between them had even turned to love. The logical evolution of the relationship was marriage.

Staring sightlessly into the bright night sky, Dora slipped her hand into her purse and felt for the bulk of the tiny, beautifully wrapped box.

A New Year's Eve gift from Adam.

It could be no more than mere ounces, but the weight on her heart seemed to be a hundred pounds. A thousand. More.

Anything could be inside the box, anything at all. And yet she feared she knew exactly what lay there: a diamond ring that would make their casual discussions of marriage official. If she opened it, she'd have to pick a date.

She would become Mrs. Adam Morgan.

It would be a good thing, a glorious thing. Certainly the nicest to happen to her in a long time. But God, oh God, she wasn't sure she was ready.

In the reflection of the window, she saw Adam pause in conversation and glance over. Dora turned her head and met his gaze.

Slowly, warmly, he smiled, and it was so genuine, so sweet and just for her, she smiled helplessly in return. That special bond, the affection, the friendship, the warmth, only grew with time.

So what was her problem?

The train jostled slightly as it shifted up a steeper elevation. Outside the windows, and far into the night, the Sierras rose beautiful and wild and free in a way Dora had never been.

Complacency had become her middle name, but right then Dora vowed to change that. She promised herself she'd do the one thing she'd never had the guts to do before. She would live her life to the fullest, the way *she* wanted to.

Starting now.

Only she didn't know, could Adam be a part of that life?

Midnight came. Hugs and kisses abounded. So did the joking about the infamous Y2K bug, but the train ran right on target.

Two minutes later the laughter faded abruptly when the train came grinding to a halt. Everyone simply froze, then the lights blinked once and went out, pitching them into blackness.

Before fear could hit Dora, Adam was there, squeezing her hand. "Don't worry."

That was Adam: assuaging, protecting. He'd been there for her when she'd had no one else after her parents' deaths. They'd been a huge part of her life, always loving, always sheltering and protective. Then they were gone and Adam was there, just as loving, just as sheltering and protective. Always supportive, easygoing. More than anything, Dora appreciated his tenderness, his nonexistent temper, his sweetness.

Around them, a general panic began. When the party started, most were gathered in the car Dora had designed as a conversation room. There were comfortable sofas and chairs—not that she could see them now. The train was so dark she couldn't see her own hand in front of her face.

A sob sounded clearly, then a rising thin voice. "We'll suffocate!"

Dora held her breath. She knew it couldn't happen, but it sounded terrifying. She became thankful for Adam's hand in hers.

So why did she feel as though she was hiding from life? *Her* life.

She no longer wanted to be coddled. She wanted . . . adventure. Excitement.

She had always told herself that she wanted a man just like Adam, one who would cherish her, take care of her. But now . . . It no longer was enough to be merely compatible. She wanted passion. A wildness she'd never experienced but yearned to. *Sizzling heat*. She wasn't going to get that with Adam, which of course was her own fault. She had held back. No matter how much she secretly yearned and burned, experience had taught her that she wasn't good at physical relationships.

Adam let go of her hand after one last gentle squeeze. "Sit," he told her quietly before he left her. "And breathe!"

"I am!" she lied. Her palms were damp, and sweat trickled between her breasts, but she gulped in air.

"Of course you are." In the dark she heard the smile in his voice. "Did I tell you tonight how proud I am of you? Of what you've accomplished?"

What was the matter with her? He was wonderful. He was everything she needed.

Except for adventure, a horrible ungrateful voice whispered in her head. Where's the heart-pounding, thrilling excitement? You aren't going to get it with Adam Morgan, a man who could have been the model for the mild-mannered Clark Kent.

The thought of hurting him made it all the more difficult to breathe. Yet she couldn't argue the truth, that with every beat of her heart, she wanted, *needed*, more.

"I'll be right back," Adam said in her ear. "You'll be fine, Dora. You're strong."

Well, she was glad *he* thought so. Knees annoyingly weak, she leaned against the wall and hitched up her long black velvet dress so she could sink to the floor. At least she'd dressed right, she thought inanely. Velvet didn't wrinkle, and the dark material managed to highlight her few strengths, while hiding a multitude of flaws—namely, too many curves.

Yet no matter how she tried to occupy her thoughts, her wild restlessness grew.

She needed off this train.

This crazy desire for adventure shouldn't have been a big surprise. Her parents had been college professors, quiet and reserved. She had no siblings. Her entire life had been planned out for her, and it was time for a change.

Adam couldn't possibly understand this secret side of her, not when he was every bit as quiet as her parents had been. He was happy with his life, and hers.

Why couldn't she be?

Next to her, a man groaned. "Should have given that damn Y2K bug more credit. It'll take days to fix everything. Assuming, of course, that we're ever found."

"It'll be like camping," came a woman's excited voice. "We'll just keep partying. We have plenty of food."

"And beds." A man laughed deeply. "We have places to sleep. Or to do . . . whatever we want."

Men, Dora thought, rolling her eyes in disgust. Granted, she didn't have much to judge them by; there'd only been one in her life before Adam. Derek's idea of foreplay had been shucking off his pants in less than two seconds, leaving nothing but black nylon socks sagging around his ankles. He'd kissed like an eager Saint Bernard, too much slobber and tongue. Though he'd been an esteemed professor, and therefore, according to everyone she knew, perfect for her, they'd stayed together just long enough to convince Dora she didn't need physical contact in a relationship.

She knew Adam planned to convince her otherwise, and in the few times they'd embraced, she had to admit, she did feel different. Weak. Tingly. Even excited. But in spite of her yearning for passion, she hadn't been able to persuade herself those feelings would remain for the rest of the sexual activities.

Around her, some of the panic died as people began to

understand that they were not in any immediate danger. Most seemed content to extend the party.

Not Dora. Her throat was closing, her pulse leaping. The gift inside her purse pressed relentlessly against her hip. Outside the stars twinkled in a familiar pattern. "The Big Dipper," she whispered, twisting to plaster her face to the window. Long ago, her family had vacationed semiannually in Lake Tahoe. Squinting through the dark, she frantically searched the landscape that she'd known like the back of her hand. There was the bridge they'd climbed under on their hikes! And the cliff they used to photograph—she could see that, too! It was a miracle, but she knew exactly where they were.

She surged to her feet. They were only miles from one of her favorite small towns. And since the winter season had been record-breaking mild this year, none of the snow had stuck.

She could get off the train and walk. It would be fun, exciting. An adventure. By morning she could be in a cab bound for home, happily buried in work by midday—

The lights came back on, startling her from thought.

Everyone cheered and passed more drinks around.

Dora made her way to the next car, which was blessedly empty. With singular purpose, she touched the side door—her way to the outside.

What about Adam? She had to tell him she was leaving, but she knew he wouldn't let her go. What to do? Whirling to check the door, she plowed right into a hard, warm chest. Arms reached out and steadied her.

"Going somewhere?" came a low voice of velvety steel.

"Adam!" She lifted her head and managed a smile. "I know where we are, so I thought I would just go—"

"No."

He said it so kindly that at first she hadn't realized he was firmly holding her back from the door she was itching to open. "But you don't understand—"

"Claustrophobia, right?"

"Yes!" Relieved, she relaxed. "I can't stand being confined."

"By the train."

"Yes."

Disappointment flickered across his features. "Dora." His gaze met hers evenly, those melting brown eyes daring her to name what she was *really* running from. "You know I can't let you go. It's dangerous."

"I *have* to," she said desperately.

A scream ripped through the air, halting whatever Adam might have said. Gripping her arm, he ran with her to the main car, where everyone was crowded around a woman sprawled on the carpet.

"My ankle," she cried.

"She slipped," a man explained to Adam when he hunkered down and carefully examined it.

"I don't think it's broken," he said after a moment, but he looked concerned.

"I'll go for help," Dora said quickly. "I know how to get to a nearby town."

The engineer and brakeman entered the car. "We're here for awhile, folks," the engineer said regretfully. "The computer shut us down at the track switch." He held up a hand when several people started to speak at once. "No need for panic. We have plenty of food and water."

The brakeman nodded his agreement. "It's inconvenient, but the wait won't kill us."

"But I'm hurt!" the woman wailed, carrying on until someone brought her a glass of champagne.

"I can get help," Dora said again.

"We couldn't let you off the train alone, ma'am," the breakman said, dismissing her offer. "That's firm. I'm sorry."

Dora jaw hardened with determination. She was getting off this train.

Adam's gaze met hers. A silent clash of wills ensued and finally he sighed. "All right. I'll go to town with Dora, on foot." He spoke with such authority that, amazingly, the alarm settled and everyone listened. "We'll go get help."

Adam came toward her, his expression shuttered. He took her hand, and once again she found herself being tugged through the cars. They stopped in the kitchen compartment where he grabbed an apple, two granola bars, a candy bar, and a package of string cheese, and opened her purse to shove them in. The present lay there, staring at them. Dora reached for it and slipped it into her coat pocket. "Adam—"

Refusing to talk, he grabbed her hand again.

As they moved through the cars, she stared at his back, which was straight, flexed, and shockingly full of power. "Will that woman be okay?" she asked him breathlessly, since she was forced to run to keep up with his stride.

"Sure. If she lays off the booze and stops trying to dance on the tabletops, she'll be fine."

Sarcasm? From sweet, kind, patient Adam? She just managed to catch her coat as he tossed it at her. Pulling it away from her face, she stared at him. "Why do you have a grease spot on your cheek?"

"I helped the brakeman start the generator." He swiped absently at his face.

Dora would have sworn Adam couldn't have changed his own oil.

He opened the traveling door with an ease that might have startled her if she wasn't so busy being relieved to see the great outdoors. There was no snow base, and the air was clear and gorgeous.

Freedom, Dora thought, until Adam leaped down, took out his favorite pen, and—turned it on? "It's a flashlight," she said, stunned. "What do you do with that?"

He lifted a hand to her. "Follow stubborn women into the wilderness." Wrapping an arm around her waist, he helped her down. Their bodies met at the contact, and so did their gazes. His embraces had always comforted her, assured her she wasn't alone, that she had her closest friend, Adam.

But this didn't seem like such a friendly embrace at all. Now she was suspended off the ground, completely against him, and she experienced a shiver of anticipation that confused her. Her long dress rode above her knees as he slowly slid her down his body. Her breath caught, and she heard his do the same. One strong, warm arm held her tight to him, his hand splayed wide on the base of her spine.

If she thought she hadn't been able to breathe before, she was *really* challenged now.

He set her next to him on the tracks. When his hands left her, she felt oddly chilled. *What was that about?*

A light wind blew his hair. His eyes shimmered in the moonlight, and for once they weren't mirrors to his emotions but completely inscrutable. The rest of his features were cast in shadow. He looked nothing like her easygoing Adam. And for a moment Dora could only stare at him.

He stared at her, too, then slowly lifted a finger and touched her face. More tingles raced through her, which was silly. He'd touched her before, plenty of times.

But never with that strange, faraway expression on his face. "Adam?" His name was a whisper on her lips. "What's happening?"

His expression changed, tightened. "You got your wish. You're off the train." He straightened away from her, his hand falling to his side. "Let's go."

2

Adam let Dora lead as they made their way off the tracks and down a slight incline. He figured the walking would be easier there, but he was still unhappy to say the least. "This is the dumbest thing I've ever done," he muttered.

Dora slapped away a branch, letting out a sound of annoyance when a different one smacked her in the face. "It's an adventure," she corrected cheerfully.

Adam didn't say a word as he reached forward and grabbed yet another branch before it got her as well.

Above them the night sky was brilliantly clear, lit by a bright moon. The air blew around them, whistling through the trees. Their feet crunched noisily on the ground, through the heavy bed of fallen pine needles and the occasional patch of snow.

"At least the walk is easy enough." Dora pulled her coat closer around her long, clingy black dress, hiding her toned, curvy body from view, which in Adam's opinion was probably a good thing since he'd done little but wonder what the heck she was wearing beneath it. She'd changed her heels for the tennis shoes she'd had stashed in her bag, but thanks to the slit in the skirt, Adam got a nice view of her legs with every step she took.

"I could do this by myself, you know," she said. Her wild red hair blew in her face and she shoved at it, exposing a hauntingly beautiful face and vivid green eyes, which were filled with tenacity and annoyance.

"Yes," he agreed. "You could." He had no doubt. She was the most independent woman he'd ever known, not to mention the most stubborn. She was also intelligent, funny as hell, compassionate, and all he'd ever wanted. It'd been that way since the day he'd first met her, when she'd come to his bank with her last dollar in her purse, desperate for a loan for her business. There'd been so much in her expression that day—fear, loneliness, strength—and Adam had felt like her kindred spirit from that first moment.

He'd made sure she got her loan, then begged for a date, *begged* being the operative word because she'd been so incredibly shy. They'd been together ever since. She wasn't an easy woman to get to know, but Adam had no trouble seeing past her veneer to the passionate, enchanting woman beneath, even if he had yet to figure out how to *get* to that woman. He'd hoped commitment would help, but so far Dora had done little more than panic at their talk of marriage.

"It's only two miles at the most," Dora said breathlessly. "We'll be—" The sentence ended on a little scream as she tripped over a log. Material ripped, Dora let out a scream of pure frustration, and pushed to her feet just as Adam reached her. She spread her skirt wide and groaned. She'd ripped the slit up to her hip, revealing one thigh-high stocking lined with black lace, and a little scrap of silk masquerading as panties. "Oh, great!" she cried. "Look at this!"

Adam could do little else, and right there, in the midst of this disaster, heat surged through his body. Before he could say a word, she'd whirled off, rushing through the woods. Her hair whipped behind her, as did the now torn skirt of her dress.

"Slow down," he called after her. Naturally she didn't. "Damnit, Dora, would you be careful!"

She stopped abruptly, then turned slowly around to gape at him. "Are you . . . yelling at me?"

"You're going to kill yourself!"

"You *are* yelling at me," she breathed, looking both shocked and intrigued.

With some difficulty, he lowered his voice. "I am not."

"Hmm." She started walking again, much slower, which was little relief since a smooth, long leg and a peekaboo hint of lace flashed with each step.

"I can find help for the train and still be back in the city by afternoon," she told him. "Assuming that everything is running by then, of course."

Adam looked at her and then wished immediately that he hadn't. Her deep red hair glowed in the moonlight, falling in rich waves past her shoulders. The twigs and bristles that were stuck in the rioting curls only endeared her to him. So did the smudges of dirt on her cheek.

Unfortunately, her expressive eyes were filled with secrets, reminding him that he was losing her with every breath he took. "You've made your point, Dora," he said quietly, slipping his hands into his pockets rather than haul her back to the safety of the train, which was what he really wanted to do. "You'd rather be alone."

"Adam . . . It's nothing personal—"

The temper he rarely ever felt surfaced sharply. "Oh, it's personal. But if you think I'm going to allow you to walk by yourself in the dark in the middle of the damn mountains, forget it."

"*Allow* me?" She sent him an almost comically incredulous look. "*Allow me?* Please. I'm a big girl now, and—"

"Then act like it." He was getting cold. So was Dora, if her blue lips were any indication.

"And what does *that* mean?"

"You didn't have to go on this inaugural ride. Yes, I know you had clients there," he said when her mouth opened. "But you could have gotten out of it. You *chose* to go, Dora, and you have no one to blame but yourself now, so stop taking it out on me."

She blinked. "You're . . . yelling at me again."

So he was, damnit. Good job. Way to keep her. "Sorry. But it's the truth."

"I'm not taking anything out on you!"

"Aren't you?"

She looked guilty for a moment before she turned around and started walking again. After a moment, she pulled out her cell phone for the fifth time and tried to get a signal. Adam knew she wouldn't, not in this mountain range. Muttering something about the whole world being attacked by the bug, she kept going.

Keeping the train tracks in sight, they went on in silent single file, Dora watching her feet and Adam watching the gentle swing of her hips.

"I wanted to support you tonight," she said after awhile.

"I don't want you obligated to me."

"It wasn't that."

"Really? Then open your present."

The crunching of a small patch of snow beneath their feet was the only sound. Adam smiled at Dora's back, but it was a painful smile. "Can't do it, can you?"

"Adam, I—"

He reached out and gently turned her around to face him. He cupped her soft, cold face in his hands. Her smaller hands came up to touch his and her eyes softened. It wasn't often she touched him of her own accord. "Open the present, Dora," he said quietly. "You'll be surprised, I promise."

She stared at him, mute and miserable, and he swore to himself. "Fine, then. Let's go." He spoke gruffly, bitterly disappointed in her lack of trust. Did she think he didn't know her? That he would accept less than one hundred percent of her love and affection? He had needs, too, damnit.

"You're shivering," he said angrily as she stalked along. "We should go back."

"No. We're halfway there already. See that clearing?" She pointed off to the right, where a small natural valley dipped, highlighted by the moon's glow. "The town is on the other side. We'll save time cutting through."

"We're not leaving the tracks."

She shot him a frustrated look.

He sighed. "Look, we're talking survival here, Dora. It's nearly two in the morning and getting colder."

"I'm going."

He stared at her, then realized that to her, this was an adventure, one she desperately needed. One he'd been hoping she'd have. How could he thwart her? "It's your party," he said, knowing even as he spoke the risk he took. She would get them good and lost. And he would let her. How else to encourage her to run her own life!

Ten minutes later, she hesitated and bit her lip, looking around her warily.

"I think it's that way," she said eventually, and started trudging up a heavily wooded hill.

"You sure?"

She was quiet for a long moment. "Yeah."

He smiled grimly at her back and followed her.

The temperature dropped as they shared the candy bar and their breath became clouds of fog in front of their faces. The train track had all but disappeared behind them.

No town came into sight.

When an owl hooted, sounding sinister and haunting, Dora stilled, and Adam thought maybe she'd turn to him then, but she continued moving along, more slowly now. It wasn't until something howled into the night, the call echoing eerily around them, that Dora stopped again and carefully, purposely backed into him. "Yikes."

It wasn't often he saw her let down her guard enough to show vulnerability. Her hands came down and back, gripping his thighs close to her bottom. She squeezed, and he would have sworn he could feel her heart ricocheting against her back and his chest. It brought forth the most surging sense of protectiveness. He touched the delicate gold robins dangling from her ears. "You love animals, remember?"

"Beyond reason, but that doesn't mean I want to meet a big, hungry one in the middle of the night."

He slipped an arm around her waist and held her against him. The feel of her was so good that he secretly hoped something else would make a spooky sound. Maybe she'd even turn around and crawl up his body. Yeah. *Come on, howl again*. "Ready to give up?" he asked huskily, knowing he could have them in town in an hour.

"Nope. We're close," she insisted, again going the wrong damn way.

Sighing at her slim, stubborn back, Adam let her go, not saying a word when she grinned victoriously at the sight of a narrow trail and insisted they follow it.

With frightening speed, the stars and moon disappeared beneath a huge black mass of cloud. Thirty minutes later, lightning split the sky. When thunder boomed, shaking the ground beneath them, Dora whipped around and plastered herself to Adam. "Don't be afraid," she whispered shakily.

Adam couldn't help it; he laughed and pulled her close. "How can I be afraid with you to save me?" His amusement faded when he felt her shiver. "Come here." Turning, he pressed her gently to a tree, then wrapped himself around her, holding her when she would have squirmed away. "Let me warm you."

It wasn't often he got to hold her, even though there was a strong attraction between them. At least for Adam it was strong; he could hardly touch her without feeling a jolt.

But when he heard her sharp intake of breath at the close contact, he took heart.

She wasn't as immune as she'd like to be.

The rain came, soaking them in seconds. Once they were wet, the cold seemed to spread, invading their bodies with startling speed.

"We'd better keep moving." Dora grabbed his hand, but suddenly the rain was coming down so hard they could hardly see a foot in front of them.

It was time to call an end to the adventure. "Dora, stop." He pulled her back to him. "I can find—"

"No, I know we're almost there. Hurry."

One hundred yards later Adam's skin felt like ice and his clothes clung to every inch of him. He'd had enough. If Dora wanted to close her eyes to the truth about what she was running from, fine, but he wanted to be dry while she was doing it. She was rushing ahead, moving straight toward a thicket of trees. "Dora, stop."

"We're almost there!" she cried.

"We're not. We're not even close—" A bolt of lightning lit up the forest. The boom of thunder shook the ground beneath their feet. Safety became Adam's immediate concern. "This way. Dora!"

She glanced back at him, saw him gaining on her, and rushed forward, turning her head back just in time to crash directly into a low, heavy branch.

It knocked her to the ground and by the time Adam got there, she had an egg-sized bump on her forehead, and blood oozing from the middle of it. "Christ, you're bleeding everywhere."

"That's okay." She gave him a wobbly grin. "You have a handkerchief. You always do." Then she lay down in the growing mud and closed her eyes, oblivious to the rain falling on her face.

Heart in his throat, he scooped her out of the dirt into his arms.

"No, don't," she whispered weakly, pushing him away. She managed to stand, though she let him hold her steady. Carefully, she set her forehead to his chest, promptly bleeding all over it.

Worried and furious, he did his best to staunch the flow with his handkerchief. "You're shaking."

"No, I'm not. You are. I'm fine," she claimed. "Let's just—"

"No. Whatever it is, *no*."

She blinked at him. "Excuse me?"

"You're done. It's *my* turn to be in charge." At his forcefulness she looked shocked, but he didn't care, not when another crack of lightning burst, and the ensuing thunder resounded so close on its tail that goose bumps rose on his skin. "Let's go." With an arm around her waist to steady her, he backtracked on the trail to find the small wooden structure he'd seen. It wasn't nearly what he'd hoped, but it would have to do.

Dora stared at the small shack, her hair plastered to her head, water and blood running down her face. She was trembling badly, and while it fueled his concern, it also stoked his temper. What a ridiculous, unnecessary mess! She needed a doctor, and he couldn't get her one tonight without leaving her.

"Wh-what's this?"

"Looks like a gatehouse." Which meant that there had to be something that the gate house led to, but in the freezing rain it would have to wait. "For tonight, it's the Hilton." He yanked open the door and pushed the wildly trembling Dora inside. Her color was bad, pale and pasty, but at least the cut had stopped bleeding.

"Sp-spiders," she gasped. "And it's d-d-dark."

"Better than freezing to death in that downpour," he remarked much more calmly than he felt as he inspected her head. He checked out their small fortress with his flashlight. "No spiders; you're in luck. And look, all the amenities of home." Their six-foot-by-six-foot haven had one wood chair, a desk that had seen better days, and a metal trash can. Rubbing his hands together to warm them, he eyed the top of the desk. While he'd like to imagine what he and Dora could do on top of it, he knew she'd be horrified at his undignified if not wildly erotic thoughts. She was hurting, and they were both drenched through.

It took him only a minute to break down the chair into pieces, pile it carefully into the trash can, and start a fire.

Dora gaped at him. "You started that fire with your pencil?"

He shrugged. "The pen's a flashlight, the pencil is a lighter."

She looked as if she might have said more, if she could talk through her chattering teeth.

"Take off your clothes," he said.

Her eyes went wide. "Wh-wh-what?"

Her body had gone stiff, but not just from the shock of his words. From the way she winced with every movement, he knew her head hurt. She was cold, dangerously so, and in his fear for her he forgot his innate politeness. "You heard me." Shrugging out of his jacket, he kicked off his shoes and waited for her to follow his orders. They'd use all they had to keep warm: body heat. "Hurry."

"Why?"

Her mistrust stirred his frustration. "So I can jump you."

"You're crazy. I don't want to . . . *you know*. Not now."

That wrung a reluctant laugh out of him. "It was a joke, Dora. A bad one, apparently." They'd dated for most of a year and they'd never "*you know*." It had been a dilemma for him, a big one. Dora claimed she didn't want to sleep with him until they were married, but since she didn't really want to marry him, he had to assume she didn't want to do it, period. He knew she was unaware of the sexuality and passion that simmered just beneath her surface. He was aching to show it to her, but hadn't been able to find the heart to rush her, even though his self-imposed celibacy was killing him. "Take it all off or I will."

"You—I—" Dora sputtered a moment, then gave him her best scowl.

Then his hands went to the buttons on his shirt. The crackling fire highlighted his every movement.

Dora gasped when he shrugged out of his shirt.

Oh, my God, was all she could think. He was huge, magnificent, and she'd had no idea, none at all. How could she have known what an incredible body he hid beneath those suits? His shoulders, broad and tough, gleamed in the faint light of the fire, and between them was a wide bronzed chest. Why was a banker so tan? And that stomach—good Lord, it was perfect. She couldn't take her eyes off him, and since she was already dizzy, she staggered back a bit.

"Dora, sit down." His concerned face appeared before hers. "How many fingers am I holding up?" he demanded. "Come on baby, pay attention."

She was, oh, she was. "Three fingers," she whispered, enthralled. Until he dropped his pants and came toward her with an intent, fierce expression that made her squeak. Undeterred, he grabbed her, slid off her coat, and had her dress unzipped before she could even draw a breath. Cold air danced up her spine, bringing her back to her senses. "Hey!"

she cried, hugging the bodice of her dress to her chest before it could fall.

"Strip," he ordered in a rough whisper.

What had happened to her quiet, gentle Adam? The man standing before her, dripping wet in his marvelously sexy underwear, was a stranger, which in no way explained the strange jolt of excitement that shot through her. "We . . . you . . . I—"

Worry flickered, but his anger remained. "You're frozen. And you probably have a concussion."

That was it. It was the concussion distorting her view of him. She liked it. Or so she thought, until he spoke again.

"Now get your stubborn hide naked, Dora, so I can keep it warm."

3

Shaking violently, head aching, Dora stared at Adam. She couldn't have imagined him furious, but he most definitely was. She couldn't have pictured him turning that fury into passion, but he had most definitely done that, too. She could feel the startling heat of it shimmering between them, singeing her nerves, leaving her strangely breathless and . . . hot.

It thrilled and terrified her at the same time.

"The floor, close to the fire," Adam decided, opening his coat on the ground, apparently unconcerned with the fact that his entire body was visible to her. His briefs hid nothing, not a single sinewy muscle or one inch of rugged, tanned skin.

Divided between fascination and genuine, driving pain, Dora couldn't tear her gaze off him. "The f-f-floor?"

Tugging at her dress until it fell, he waited until she stepped out of it, then carefully spread the velvet over the desk. "We'll have more room." He kneeled before her. Jaw tight, eyes hot, body taut, he started on her stockings, rolling each one down her leg.

"Room for what?" He didn't answer, just ruthlessly pointed to the ground, then belied that toughness by helping her stretch out. She closed her eyes tight when she felt his bare flesh brush hers. Leaning over her, he frowned as he probed at the cut on her head.

"I'm fine."

"You're not."

"Yes—"

"Dora, be quiet." He put on his glasses and peered deeply into her eyes, checking each one carefully.

There was something about the way he looked: sleek, powerful, and half-naked, like a Greek god, with those prim wire-rimmed glasses perched on his nose like a computer geek. Such contradictions for some reason made her giggle, and once she started, it was impossible to stop.

He frowned at her as if trying to decide how badly off she was.

"You're so tan," she said inanely, because he looked so worried. He was awfully cute when stressed, she decided. How was it she'd never noticed that before? "Why is a banker tan?"

"The seminar I attended last week was in Hawaii."

He'd invited her; she'd declined. "You never said it was in Hawaii."

"Would it have mattered?"

She couldn't see his expression clearly, but she didn't have to. "God, what a mess," she whispered. Every part of her hurt, especially her pride. She had no one but herself to blame.

Adam came up on his side, facing her. His stare pierced her in the faint light, and she wished . . . oh, she just wished. A delicious body heat was pouring from him, and she scooted a bit, just a little bit, until she brushed against him. "Oh, Adam. I've been so . . ."

"Stupid?" he inquired mildly.

"I prefer stubborn."

He let out a low laugh, but it held little mirth.

Swallowing hard, she said, "I'm sorry."

"Save it, Dora, until you mean it."

He'd never spoken to her like that, with such censure and reproach. She couldn't say she appreciated it, and yet, it was enlightening and somehow endearing to hear his true thoughts.

When she shivered uncontrollably, his arms circled her body, sliding against her bare arms, her sides, causing her to nearly jerk out of her skin. "Shh," he said, his voice silky and rough as he pulled her into his warmth. "Just me."

Just him. Only it *wasn't* him; he was a perfect stranger. A perfect, nearly *naked* stranger who could alter her pulse. "I know."

"Do you really?"

"Of course."

"Because I'm not certain you know me at all."

He scooped her closer, tucking her against him so that every inch of her was plastered to every inch of him. His skin burned hers everywhere they touched. Though she still wore her bra and panties, the skimpy black silk was no protection. Her hips moved reflexively against his, and she went perfectly still at what she found between his tense thighs.

He was hard as a rock. And huge.

"Relax," he muttered against her hair, gently brushing it away from her cut. His fingers didn't seem too steady. "I can't help my reaction to you, but I can help what I do with it. Which will be nothing."

The pang of disappointment startled her. Adam's heat was seeping into her body, chasing away her tremors and replacing it with a hunger she didn't understand. Before she could stop herself, she pressed her face into his neck, and it smelled so heavenly, so overwhelmingly, so uniquely Adam that she scooted closer.

It was his turn to go rigid. "Don't," he whispered hoarsely and with such longing her bones melted away.

She couldn't stop herself. One second she was lying there cold and confused and hurting; the next she'd captured his mouth with hers, kissing him with all her pent-up fear and frustration. She had a moment to think that his kisses were like paradise, and to wonder why she'd avoided them for so long, before she found herself beneath him, her breasts brushing against his hard chest, her legs entangled with his.

Outside a storm raged, and inside was no different. A strange sense of need built. He returned the kiss, a deep, wet, erotic one that had them straining against each other. The feel of his hard, hot body against hers, and the sounds he made as he pressed close, sent excitement spinning through her. Heady with it, Dora shifted, trying to angle even closer, when something poked into her hip. "Ouch," she said, reaching into the coat beneath her. "There's something . . ."

"I've got it," he murmured, brushing her hand aside. Their hands reached for it at the same time . . . and closed around the small, wrapped gift.

It might as well have been a huge, gaping chasm.

"You could just open it," he suggested quietly.

She could, but . . . *but what?* What was it, exactly, that held her back? Slowly, she let out her breath. Adam shifted off her without a word. On his side now, he wrapped an arm around her waist, and turned her away from him. Then he pulled her snug against his chest so that her bottom fitted to his lap. "Rest," he demanded tautly. "I'm going to wake you every half hour."

Her injury wasn't what worried her. There was still something poking her, and it was hard and hot and throbbing against her bottom. A tense silence fell. Her head was pillowed on his arm, and his other hand was splayed on her belly in a protective, almost possessive grip.

"Adam?"

His fingers flexed but otherwise he didn't move. His voice was quiet but steely. "Unless you want to face what's between us, don't. Don't talk. Don't think. And whatever you do, don't move."

But what if she wanted to do exactly that? What if she wanted to turn over and explore this surging heat between them? What if she wanted to press her mouth to his and let him take her?

After all, he had needs, too. It shamed her to realize she'd never given them much thought. She could think of little else now.

It was a long time before she fell asleep, and given the rigidity of Adam's body behind her, it was even longer for him.

He was awake long before dawn's first light, listening to the driving rain and Dora's soft breathing, smelling the intoxicating scent of her shampoo and skin. He lifted up on an elbow and stared helplessly down at the beauty sprawled in his arms. She had a hell of a shiner, and a lump to go with it. The cut itself seemed to have closed, but her eyebrows were puckered as if even in sleep she couldn't find peace.

She stirred, and blinked up at him.

"Hey." He smiled into her confused face. "How many?" He waggled a couple of fingers in front of her eyes.

She shifted her thigh, which was snuggly pressed to his groin. "One," she whispered, sliding against him.

He closed his eyes and groaned. "I think maybe you should get concussed more often." But she looked truly miserable. She was pale, and clearly weak. The lingering pain in her eyes had him rising and checking their clothes.

Stretching, wincing, he pulled on his still-damp pants, then brought Dora her dress. "It's a mess, but it's nearly dry."

He helped her glorious body into it. She didn't want to, but he made her eat the apple in her purse. Afterward some of her color came back. So did her determination.

"I thought we could—"

"Nope. I told you last night: I'm in charge. Get your shoes on." He checked the trash can, making sure the ashes were completely out. Then he pulled out his wallet, leaving both some cash and a note of apology for the owner.

The rain still came down in droves when he opened the door. He glanced at the bedraggled Dora, and at the look of misery on her face, he let out one concise, incredibly rude oath.

Her mouth fell open. "I . . . I can't believe you said that. I've never heard you use that word before."

He had always tempered himself with her, not wanting to seem too coarse or rough. It had seemed the right thing to do, but now he thought he'd probably made a serious error in judgment. He wanted to be himself, and wanted her to love him for it. Since that wasn't about to happen, he had nothing to lose by showing her how he really felt. "I use swear words, Dora. I also make mistakes."

"You get angry, too."

"Yeah. Are you afraid of me?"

"Of course not."

"Good. There's too much hiding between us. I'm not going to do it anymore. I wish you wouldn't either, but I can't control you, and don't want to."

Clearly she had no idea what to make of him, and he decided he liked her silent for a change. "This way," he told her, pulling on her hand when she would have backtracked on the dirt path.

"But I was wrong," she protested. "The town isn't that way. The best thing to do is to get back to the tracks."

"No, this trail has to lead to something. I'm hoping it's a house. With a phone."

"Adam, let's go back."

He had a feeling they were closer to help than to the train. "Where's your sense of adventure?" he asked, pushing the one button he knew would get her going.

She stared at him, water running in rivulets down her face. "My sense of adventure." A little laugh escaped her. "That's funny, because I always thought I had one and you . . ."

"Yes?" he pressed. "And I—?"

"Nothing." She searched through her bag, pulled out the two granola bars, and slapped one against his chest.

"Tell me," he insisted, opening his breakfast.

Dora tightened her lips.

"Oh. I see." He studied her quietly. "You thought I was boring."

"Not boring."

"Don't lie, Dora. I can see right through you."

"You're different here."

"Am I?" he asked softly. "I don't think so. Less gentle, maybe, but the circumstances demand it."

"But . . . that's not it." She looked uncertain, and the tug on his heart irritated him.

"Maybe your eyes are just open now." He wrapped an arm around her and steered her on.

About half a mile up the road, they came upon a boarded-up cabin.

"It's empty," Dora said, sagging against him in defeat. "God, I'm so tired."

And hurting, he'd bet, though she hadn't complained. The cabin was huge. It looked as though it'd been converted into some sort of camp, but was most definitely closed up now. They walked around the perimeter of the place. On the back door was a rusty lock. Adam studied it, stood back, and gave it one good roundhouse kick. The lock fell to the ground.

Dora stared at him. "What was *that*?"

"Let's check for a phone."

When he turned away, she grabbed his sleeve. "You kicked that door! Like you knew what you were doing!"

"It's a trick I learned in kickboxing."

Her mouth fell open. "When do you do kickboxing?"

He shrugged and stepped inside. "After work sometimes." They usually only saw each other on weekends, which Adam knew had been Dora's way of controlling her feelings for him. "It's a good way to keep in shape."

"You . . . kickbox."

"Yeah." Adam felt her studying him, felt her confusion. She hadn't followed him inside, but was standing in the doorway, the rain pounding the earth behind her. Her eyes were huge, and exhausted.

"Come on," he said, as an even mix of compassion and annoyance filled him. She looked so small and vulnerable. So why was *he* hurting? Impatient with the both of them, he turned away from her. "Shut the door. It's cold."

"You went to Hawaii. You can start a generator. You can build a fire with a chair and you *kickbox*! My God . . . How have I missed all this?"

He pulled a chair away from the table and made her sit before she fell on her face.

She just stared at him. Out of her pocket came the present, which she glanced at briefly before meeting his gaze again. "Who are you really, and what have you done with Adam?"

4

Adam might have laughed, but the genuinely baffled expression on Dora's face disturbed him. "I'm exactly who I've always been. There's just a lot about me you haven't seen."

She lifted a hand and touched his chest. "You're different," she insisted.

"Why?" He grabbed her hand. "Because I took charge?"

"Partly. I'm not used to that, certainly not from you. You've always been dependable and responsible, but—"

"But what? Tedious? Stodgy? A *banker*?" Frustrated, he let go of her and stepped back, wishing she'd see him for what he was—a man who loved her, and always would. "You saw what you wanted to, and didn't try to get to know the rest. I don't know how we ever got as far as we did."

"You're angry again."

"Frustrated as hell, not angry." With no choice but to turn away, he eyed the kitchen. It was perfectly clean and perfectly empty. "Damn, I'm starving." Not surprisingly, there was no phone.

When Dora slipped her arms around his waist and laid her face against his back, he went still.

"Oh, Adam, I'm sorry. I like everything about you, I do." She hugged him gently. "I like how you let me . . . just be. You always understand me, even when I don't understand myself. And you give me the space I need."

There was a window above the steel sink. He stared out into the driving rain, trying unsuccessfully to harden his heart against her. "Yeah, well, that was a mistake. A big one."

"No, it wasn't. Without it, we'd never have been together so long." She sighed. "All my life I was told what to do. Nicely, of course. But I never chose for myself."

"I know." That's what made this so difficult.

"*You* never did that to me; you let me make my own path. It's what I like most about you."

He turned to face her. "So why are we in this mess now? In two separate places, one of us ready for the next step in our relationship, the other ready to take off?"

Dora rubbed her head, and, mad at himself for pushing her, Adam backed off. "Never mind. I'm as much to blame as you. I let you keep me at arm's length because I didn't want to scare you away. I wanted—" Shaking his head, he stepped away. "This isn't the time or the place, not when you're in pain."

She gave him a small smile. "You're so assertive. Sure of yourself. You saved my life, you know."

"And you think that's unlike me?" He scowled. "I don't think I'm flattered."

"No, I meant . . . I meant that I used to think being with a strong person meant *I* had to be weak."

"You're the most *un*weak woman I've ever met."

"Oh, Adam" she whispered. "That's the biggest compliment anyone has ever given me."

Then she fainted.

When Dora opened her eyes, she was in a bed. Adam sat on the edge of it. At the sight of her, he closed his eyes briefly, then smiled at her. "You're going to give me gray hair, Dora."

"I feel better."

"You stay right there. I'm going to go check and see if there are any other houses near here." He touched her face softly, and was gone.

She stared at the closed door and waited impatiently. And waited.

He didn't come back.

She got up, ignoring her throbbing head. The place wasn't as large as she'd thought. On the second floor, where apparently Adam had carried her, was a series of bedrooms, with a bathroom at each end of the hall. Sparsely furnished, but nice. She explored a bit, then went back down to the kitchen.

What could be taking him so long? One peek out the window assured her it was still pouring. In fact, the temperature had dropped enough that there were spots of ice everywhere. What if he'd fallen? Bumped his head? What if he'd run into a bear? What if he was seriously injured and—God, it was all her fault.

All he'd ever done was care about her. He was still her quiet, caring, sensitive Adam. But he was also the stuff her dreams were made of, adventurous, tough, strong-willed . . . passionate. *Hers*.

"Just let him be safe," she whispered, staring out the window as if she could will him back.

She wasn't proud of it, but it had taken this misguided trip to realize how she felt for him. The very things she'd taken for granted—his dependability, his quiet strength, his compassion—were the things she loved most about him. She wished she would have done things differently. She wanted to open her gift. She wanted to wear her ring. She never wanted to take it off.

She wanted him back, damnit, *safe*.

The back door opened and Adam stepped wearily inside. "C-c-cold."

At least that's what she thought he said, but he was shaking so badly he couldn't talk, and he was soaked to the bone. "Oh, Adam." That strange surging warmth invaded her again, the one that made her yearn to hold him close.

"No houses," he managed, laying his cheek on top of her head, his arms banding around her.

"You scared me to death," she admonished, hugging him. They staggered back up to the bedroom, leaning on each other. "I thought something awful had happened to you out there."

"W-w-wouldn't leave you."

"I know. I know." She got him to the bedroom and went to work on his coat. Nervous now, she watched him beneath lowered lashes as she struggled to get him out of the wet, clinging material. He seemed content to let her, remaining silent. Next she attacked his shirt. When she finally got it open, she slid her hands inside, sighing at the feel of his smooth, sleek skin.

His harsh intake of air was the only sound in the room, except for the swoosh of his shirt as it pooled at his feet. "Dora—" He sounded hard-pressed for air. "Don't."

"Don't what?" Her voice was every bit as low and hoarse as his, as she slowly unzipped his pants. "Don't talk? I have to. I have to tell you I was wrong about never wanting to kiss you, because that kiss we shared last night was . . . well, incredible. I was wrong about a lot of things. Adam?" She tipped up her head. "Kiss me again."

"No." He reached for her hands when she awkwardly tried to reach inside his pants. "You're hurt."

"No more than last night."

"Dora!" With a yelp, he managed to get ahold of her curious, eager, *cold* hands. "You're vulnerable right now. It's some sort of a danger thing."

"No." Tugging on him, she kissed whatever she could reach, which at the moment was his neck.

She loved his deep, heartfelt moan.

"I don't want to take advantage of you—" He sucked in another breath when she opened her mouth on him, spreading hot, wet kisses to his shoulder.

"Stop," he said weakly.

"Strip," she ordered. "Now." Then she grinned, appreciating the irony. "I need to warm you up."

"You wanted to save this for marriage, remember?" he asked desperately, his voice breaking when she reached behind her and unzipped her dress. "All these months you've been saying that."

"I changed my mind." Oh, he was so beautiful. His eyes told her every little thing he felt; so did the hitch in his breath whenever she touched him. That she could do that to him, render him weak and trembly, was a huge, powerful rush. She wanted more.

She traced the line of hair down his chest to where it disappeared past his zipper. He closed his eyes and made a strangled sort of sound that made her smile. "I want you to kiss me again," she murmured. "Please?" She looped her arms around his neck. "Show me everything I've denied us before." She backed them to the bed.

"Dora—"

"We could have died last night, Adam. You realize that? We still could." Gently she pushed him onto the mattress, then followed him down, thrilling to the groan he let out when she slid her body to his. "It would be my fault. I couldn't stand it if something happened to you."

He flipped her gently, so that he towered above her. "I don't want you to be afraid."

"But I could have lost you—"

"Shh." He gave her a hard, possessive kiss. "We're safe."

"And together."

He went still, then slowly opened his eyes. "So we are." He stared down into her face, which he touched with reverent fingertips.

She kissed his fingers. "I don't want to spend the rest of my life hiding, not from you."

He touched her, trailing soft, mind-blowing strokes over her throat, her collarbone, then further, cupping a breast.

She moved convulsively, pressing into his hand while her hips surged to meet his. "I want you, Adam."

"Do you?" His fingers continued their magic on her body. Their remaining clothes flew across the room. "Tell me why, Dora. The real reason."

She could hardly think at the sight of his gloriously naked body, but when she didn't answer, he lifted his head and waited until she looked at him. "Tell me."

"Well . . . you're sweet." He rolled his eyes, making her laugh. "I mean it!" she said. "You're kind and good. And sensitive."

"Sounds like you've got me confused with Santa Claus."

She laughed again, and ran her hand over his broad shoulders, down his taut back. "You're strong-willed," she said. "And confident enough to let me be whatever I want to be—"

His fingers dipped between her thighs and she gasped, opening for him. "God. Adam . . ."

"You were telling me something important." His fingers continued to torment her. "Don't stop now," he said thickly.

She might have said the same thing. It was a struggle to concentrate when she was already on the edge. "I would never have known this without you," she managed. "Adam . . . you're so important to me."

She could feel his body trembling with need, and with a low murmur of pleasure and desire, she kissed him. Her heart hammered, her pulse raced, and that it was Adam that made it so was all the sweeter. Only he could chase away her fears and loneliness, push them to a place where neither could hurt her, but this wanting of him went far past the mere physical, for she could have had that from him long ago. In his arms, she felt special.

It never occurred to Dora that it was not the time or the place for this. She wanted to give herself to this wonderful, caring, passionate man, and she could think of no better place to do it. This is what she'd been searching for, yearning for, only it'd been right in front of her all along.

He touched her, first with his hands and then his mouth, bringing her to a point of soaring release far before she could have believed possible.

"You were so ready," he whispered with awe when she'd stopped shuddering.

Then, before she could catch her breath or reason, he started over. She could never have imagined him this way, with such fluid moves and bold thrusts. The way he brought her out of herself and lifted her to another plane would have frightened her if he hadn't been just as wild, just as out of control as she. There was a spot inside her starving for this, for *him*, she discovered, and she accepted it. There would be no turning back.

They rested, maybe for a minute, maybe an hour, Dora had no idea. But when Adam turned to her again, she was more than willing. She was shaking uncontrollably, for him. He soothed her, his voice full of erotic, sexy promise, his hands and mouth on her breasts, her belly, between her thighs.

At the end, when they were connected body and soul, when he drove her higher and higher with each thrust, when she was mindless, wild with it, he followed her over the edge, her name a ragged sigh on his lips.

5

"I don't have the foggiest idea where we are," Dora said, disgusted with herself.

Adam's lips curved in a reluctant smile. "Nice to hear you admit it."

They stood in the small clearing in front of the cabin. The late afternoon was chilly, but at least the rain had stopped.

After the most passionate, soul-shaking experience of her life, they'd shared the string cheese and were trying to decide what to do. Or *she* was trying to decide; Adam hadn't said much. She had a feeling he knew exactly what to do, but suddenly her forceful adventurer had gone silent.

"Do you think the train is running yet?" She hoped he'd say something to give away his thoughts.

"Hard to say."

"It's a holiday, and all the computers are down. They're probably still waiting."

"Probably."

"Wonder if the entire world is at a standstill." It felt strange to be so isolated. Stranger still to feel so isolated from Adam. She ate her last bite of cheese. "That was it for the food."

"Hmm," was all he said.

Clearly he had something on his mind, and Dora was afraid she knew what. In both her heart and mind she was finally ready to open her present, but had no clue how to tell him. "Adam?"

He turned to her, then cupped her face in his large, warm hands, searching her gaze for a long moment. Full of pleasure at his touch, she smiled.

He ran his thumb over her lower lip, then spoke her name. She loved the way he said it, all throaty and husky. He kissed her softly on the mouth. "How are you feeling?"

Ready for more, came her shocking thought, which was amazing to her. She'd never considered herself a sensual woman but what she'd just done with Adam had certainly proved her wrong. She hadn't recognized the uninhibited wild woman she'd become in his arms. "I'm fine."

As if he could read her thoughts, his smile flashed, slow and sexy. His eyes gleamed with satisfaction, and she imagined herself being the recipient of that smile for years to come. The idea thrilled her. *Now*, she thought. *It'll never be more perfect than now.*

"I'll be right back," Adam said before she could open her mouth. He squeezed her hand gently. "Let me have your phone."

"But—What are you doing?"

"I want to try to get reception. I'm going to go up that hill over there. You'll stay here?"

A question? After all the bossing he'd done in the past twenty-four hours? "But—"

He gave her another kiss, which numbed her mind a bit. "I'll be back before you know it."

"Sure," she said to the air, since he was already gone. "I'll just . . . hang out. Enjoy Mother Nature. I'll just . . ." The present in her pocket was burning a hole there now. She thought of how afraid she'd been of it. Seemed so silly now.

Adam was indeed everything she'd feared. Thoughtful and intelligent. Happy with his life. He also had incredible inner strength, an amazing will, and a sense of self she greatly admired. He cared for her deeply, enough to want her to be a part of his life, and yet he wanted her to be her own woman.

Thank God he hadn't given up on her, she thought, pulling out the gift. She knew she should wait for him, she had no business opening it alone, but for the life of her, she couldn't. Couldn't wait to see her beautiful ring, to slip it on, couldn't wait to pick a date for her wedding.

The ribbon fell away. "Whoops," she murmured. "Can't leave it half opened, can I?" Before she could stop herself, she unwrapped the paper. She lifted the top of the box . . . and slowly let out her pent-up breath.

There was no sparkling diamond. In fact, no ring at all. On a bed of velvet lay a delicate gold pin: an eagle, its wings spread, head high, as it sailed through air on some uncoursed path. The detail was breathtaking. Picking it up with shaking fingers, Dora read the inscription on the back.

" 'If you love something, set it free and watch it soar,' " she whispered, as hot tears stung her eyes. Not an engagement ring at all. Not a push for her to make a decision she hadn't been ready to make, but a gift far more heart-wrenchingly perfect.

She'd thought she wanted her freedom, and Adam had handed it to her, no questions, no strings attached. He loved her that much. Oh, God, he loved her enough to let her go. That she no longer wanted to go was her own private anguish. Nearly blinded, she looked up.

Adam stood there, on the edge of the clearing, watching her. Waiting.

Never had she felt such overwhelming, abiding love. "Oh, Adam . . . it's lovely."

His inscrutable gaze holding hers, he came close and took it from her fingers. "May I?" he asked quietly, taking the pin, gesturing to her dress.

Heart in her throat, she nodded. To protect her skin, he slipped his fingers inside the bodice. His knuckles brushed the curve of her breast. A disturbingly needy sound escaped her, and they both lifted their heads to stare at each other.

"It's not nearly as lovely as you," he whispered. His gaze

caressed her every feature. "You don't look quite as happy as I imagined. I expected this to give you great relief."

"Relief?"

"You've made it very clear that you aren't ready for marriage, Dora."

"But *you're* ready." She looked from the beautiful pin into his face. "You knew right away, and for the life of me, I don't know how."

"I love you," he said so sincerely, with such conviction. "I always will, Dora, but watching you fight it is torture. I thought maybe if you were uncaged . . ." He shrugged. "You were very sheltered growing up, it clipped your wings. You wanted more—No, don't deny it," he said when she opened her mouth to do just that. "Then your parents were gone and I was there. *Sheltering*." His smile broke her heart. "You need to have your adventures, at least for now. It's the right thing." He touched her cheek then, one soft, sweet touch. "Be free, Dora. I want you to be happy."

Stepping back, he slipped his hands into his pockets.

"But—"

"I couldn't get reception," he said quickly. "We'll have to walk. I think it's time I lead, don't you?"

Dora stared at him, her throat burning with the need to cry. How had this happened? "You know the way? But yesterday—"

"Yesterday you wanted an adventure. You wanted to find your own way. I hope you do, Dora. I want that for you."

"Adam."

"If we hurry—"

"Adam, *please*." Dora ran her hands up his arms, waiting until he looked at her. "The pin is beautiful, I'll treasure it always, but—"

"But we're in a dangerous, exhausting, even volatile situation." All of a sudden, he looked incredibly weary. "You feel differently because of it. It'll pass."

He was all the adventure she ever wanted. How had she not known that until now? "I—"

"If we hurry we can get there before dark. I don't know about you, but I'd prefer dry clothes tonight." He walked away.

Left without a choice, Dora touched her pin—her freedom, the one thing she no longer wanted—and followed him.

By the time Adam led her to the tracks they'd left the day before, Dora was beyond exhaustion.

She staggered to a halt and sank to a large rock. "Great. Nearly full circle."

"Are you feeling sick?" It was the first time he'd spoken since they'd started walking.

Already he'd mentally pulled away from her, and the realization brought a strange sense of fear to Dora. She had to reach him somehow, had to—

He hunkered down beside her. "Can you make it into town?"

She looked at him watching her so closely, his eyes filled with regret and worry. "I can make it."

He held her hand, guiding her when the tracks wound upward. Adam didn't seem to be bothered by the walk, by the chill of the late afternoon air, by the fact that he'd crushed her hopes and dreams, just as she'd allowed them to bloom. He just continued to move in that easy, graceful stride of his, away from her and out of her life.

"Finally."

So deep in her musings and worries, Dora blinked and realized they'd come to a stop at the top of the hill.

"We're here," Adam said. "You should be able to get home soon, Dora. Just as you wanted."

Yeah, just what she wanted.

How had she messed everything up so badly?

Sighing, she followed him down the embankment and headed for the main road.

Behind them, they heard the unmistakable sounds of an engine. Two seconds later, the train—*their* train—passed them.

6

Okay, you've got two choices," Adam told Dora. "*After* you see the local doctor."

They stood at the main intersection in town, looking at the train station. Or *he* was looking at the train station. Dora was looking at her feet, silent and thoughtful.

"You can wait for the next train. Or you can let me get a rental car to drive you back."

She shot him an indecipherable look. "No doctor."

"Dora—"

"I go for door number three."

Great. It wasn't enough to break his heart, she had to torture him, too. "Which is?"

"A motel."

"I thought you couldn't wait to get home."

"I've lost the rush."

She'd been unusually quiet on the last leg of their walk, but then again, he hadn't exactly given her much room to do anything but huff and puff as he'd rushed them into town. Now that he'd given her the pin, things would be different between them, and he didn't quite know how to deal with it. "You need to be checked out."

"I'm fine. Just a bump, that's all." She bit her lip, looking at him with huge eyes the color of the tall pines behind them. "I'd really like to wait until tomorrow morning to go home. I'm tired. Not hurt or sick, just tired." She paused. "Are you—Will you stay too?"

Was she asking him? He wanted to be noble enough to let her go. Taking a good, hard look at her now, he knew he couldn't do it. For him, the past day and a half had been just a mild inconvenience, if that. Not for Dora. Her dress, the one that had stolen his breath on New Year's Eve, had seen its last day. Her coat had dirt streaked down the front and a tear on the spine. Her fiery hair had gone wild long ago, littered with pine needles and even a stick or two. She had dark rings beneath her eyes and dried blood on her arm and cheek.

She'd never looked more grubby, or more beautiful.

And now she stood there in all her miserable glory, waiting for an answer he couldn't easily give. How could he spend one more night looking at her, yearning for what would never be?

Yet could he leave her? Not a chance. "Let's go," he said gruffly.

They found a small bed-and-breakfast, a white Victorian with a wraparound porch and at least three fireplaces. It even had a porch swing. *Madder's House*, the sign said, and since there wasn't another place in immediate sight, Adam had no choice. But damnit, did it have to be so romantic?

He used the house phone to call the police. He told them about the train and their lengthy walk, and was glad he did, because the engineer had radioed the authorities as they'd passed through. Search and Rescue would have been looking for them for naught.

Dora smiled at him, a sweet, beguiling smile that twisted his heart strings. "Two rooms," he said to the receptionist.

"One," Dora corrected.

"*Two*."

The woman laughed. "Which will it be?"

"*Two*," Adam insisted.

Dora pressed close, the scent of her, the feel of her driving home the need for two rooms. "It's not necessary—" she whispered, a whole host of promises in her eyes.

His body tightened, his heart ached. He ignored the avid interest of the receptionist. Ignored also the way Dora gripped his hand, apparently unconcerned at how the mere contact pulled on his already spinning emotions. "*Two*," he said firmly, pretending not to hear Dora's soft sound of protest.

He saw Dora to her room first, then went to his, which, as luck would have it, was right next to hers. Short of causing a further scene at the front desk, he had no choice.

He attempted to lose himself in a long, hot shower.

He bowed his head beneath the spray and let it pound his shoulders and back for long moments. The tension in him remained.

He'd given her the pin, and she'd accepted.

It was over.

Too late to regret it.

He got out and wrapped a towel around his hips. Steam engulfed him, but not so much that he couldn't see the small present sitting on the bathroom counter.

It hadn't been there before, he was certain of it. Picking it up, he stared at it, wondering why his heart was suddenly slamming against his ribs.

"Open it."

Whipping around, he found Dora sitting on the opposite counter, wearing no more than he was, a small white towel that barely covered the essentials and enhanced far more than it hid.

"No, I didn't parade down the hall dressed like this," she said, a nervous smile playing on her lips. "I convinced our hostess that you really didn't want to be separated from me. She gave me the key to the door between our rooms."

"Dora . . ."

"Open it, Adam." A hint of laughter sparkled in her eyes. "Unless you need to stare at it for a few days first. I have to admit, it'll be torture, but I understand the need."

She scooted closer, her freshly washed hair brushing his

arm. She barely came up to his chin; his petite, brave, lovely Dora. And when she tipped up her head, capturing him with her wide, expressive gaze, he was lost. "Dora—"

Reaching close, she pulled on the bow of the present. "I loved your gift, Adam." Her cheek lay against his chest now. "It's been a long time since someone cared about me as much as you do. Maybe since forever. I wasn't used to it, not a good excuse for how I panicked, I know, but the truth is . . . Adam, do you think you could open it now?"

God, it was hard, so terribly hard to pretend he wasn't dying at the thought of his future without her.

She waited until he lifted the tissue paper and stared down at the eagle pin he'd given her, his every nerve painfully alive and kicking. "What is this?"

"I don't want my freedom. I want you."

Talking was difficult, he discovered, with a lump of emotion stuck in his throat. "This is because of what we went through. You think because I rolled up my sleeves and figured out which way was north I'm some sort of Indiana Jones. Don't deny it," he said quickly, when she opened her mouth to do just that. "I saw how you reacted to me when I took charge. But I'm still that other man, the sometimes quiet, sometimes unassuming one you couldn't bring yourself to say yes to."

"I want both of you, Clark *and* Superman. And to tell you the truth, Adam, I like Clark the best."

He had to close his eyes because she pressed that body up to his. It wasn't the body he wanted so much as the heart and soul behind it, and it hurt far more than he could have ever imagined. "Dora, please. Go back to your room. Get dressed. I'll get a car and drive you home."

"You don't understand."

"I think I do." Walking away from her now, before she touched him again, seemed the only thing to do.

But she touched his arm, twisted in front of him, making him look into her eyes. Her drenched eyes. *Shit*. "Dora—"

"I love you, Adam."

His hearing had failed him. That had to be it, because in

all the time he'd known her, she'd never said those words. "You . . . what?"

She took a deep, clearly calming breath, looking more confident than he'd ever seen her. "I love you. I love you with everything I am. I want you to take the pin back. I don't want my freedom. I want *you*. Forever. Will you marry me, Adam? Today?"

"Today?"

"Do you already have plans?"

His blood was pumping, his pulse racing. He was grinning like a fool and he couldn't help himself. "No, no, I don't."

Her smile widened. "Good." She lifted a shoulder. Tossed her wet hair behind it. "And I think getting married on the first day of the new millennium is fitting, don't you?"

He realized, even managed to swallow and take a full breath. "Oh, yeah, it's fitting." Scooping her close, he kissed her softly, then not so softly. "I love you, Dora. So much."

"Does that mean yes?" she asked breathlessly when he dropped first his towel, then hers.

"Yes." He nudged her close. "Forever, yes."

About the Author

Jill Shalvis is the award-winning, bestselling author of over a dozen romances. She lives at Lake Tahoe with her husband, three young children and far too many raccoons.

Now that you've met Serena and Richard Merlin in "Arts Magica," experience the magic of their own story.

The Wizard of Seattle

By Kay Hooper

Available now from Bantam Books

From the moment Serena Smyth appeared on his Seattle doorstep, Richard Patrick Merlin recognized the spark behind her green eyes, the wild talent barely held in check. And he knew he would help her learn to control her gift, despite a taboo so ancient that the reasons for its existence had been forgotten. But neither suspected that in their rebellion they would risk everything, even a love none of their kind had ever known. Serena and Merlin will take a desperate gamble and travel to a long-lost world to change the history that threatens to separate them. But they risk being torn apart forever, destroyed by a cursed land . . . and their own fierce passions.

Here's a sneak peek at this enthralling novel.

Seattle—1984

It was his home. She knew that, although where her certainty came from was a mystery to her. Like the inner tug that had drawn her across the country to find him, the knowledge seemed instinctive, beyond words or reason. She didn't even know his name. But she knew what he was. He was what she wanted to be, needed to be, what all her instincts insisted she had to be, and only he could teach her what she needed to learn.

Until this moment she had never doubted that he would accept her as his pupil. At sixteen she was passing through that stage of development experienced by humans twice in their lifetimes, a stage marked by total self-absorption and the unshakable certainty that the entire universe revolves around oneself. It occurred in infancy and in adolescence, but rarely ever again, unless one was utterly unconscious of reality. Those traits had given her the confidence she had needed to cross the country alone with no more than a ragged backpack and a few dollars.

But they deserted her now, as she stood at the wrought-iron gates and stared up at the secluded old Victorian house. The rain beat down on her, and lightning flashed in the stormy sky, illuminating the turrets and gables of the house; there were few lighted windows, and those were dim rather than welcoming.

It *looked* like the home of a wizard.

She almost ran, abruptly conscious of her aloneness. But then she squared her thin shoulders, shoved open the gate, and walked steadily to the front door. Ignoring the bell, she used the brass knocker to rap sharply. The knocker was fashioned in the shape of an owl, the creature that symbolized wisdom, a familiar of wizards throughout fiction.

She didn't know about fact.

Her hand was shaking, and she gave it a fierce frown as she rapped the knocker once more against the solid door. She barely had time to release the knocker before the door was pulled open.

Tall and physically powerful, he had slightly shaggy raven hair and black eyes that burned with an inner fire. For long moments he surveyed the dripping, ragged girl on his doorstep with lofty disdain, while all of her determination melted away to nothing. Then he caught her collar with one elegant hand, much as he might have grasped a stray cat, and yanked her into the well-lit entrance hall. He studied her with daunting sternness.

What he saw was an almost painfully thin girl who looked much younger than her sixteen years. Her threadbare clothing was soaked; her short, tangled hair was so wet that only a hint of its normal vibrant red color was apparent; and her small face, all angles and seemingly filled with huge eyes, was white and pinched. She was no more attractive than a stray mongrel pup.

"Well?"

The vast poise of sixteen years deserted the girl as he barked the one word in her ear. She gulped. "I . . . I want to be a wizard," she managed finally, defiantly.

"Why?"

She was soaked to the skin, tired and hungry, and she possessed a temper that had more than once gotten her into trouble. Her green eyes snapping, she glared up into his handsome, expressionless face, and her voice lost all its timidity.

"I *will* be a wizard! If you won't teach me, I'll find someone who will. I can summon fire already—a little—and I can *feel* the power inside me. All I need is a teacher, and I'll be great one day—"

He lifted her clear off the floor and shook her briefly effortlessly, inducing silence with no magic at all. "The first lesson an Apprentice must learn," he told her calmly, "is to never—ever— shout at a Master."

He casually released her, conjured a bundle of clothing out of thin air, and handed it to her. Then he waved a hand negligently and sent her floating up the dark stairs toward a bathroom.

And so it began.

The angel Noelle from "Gabriel's Angel"
casts her spell over the little town of Bethlehem
in two heartwarming novels.

Some Enchanted Season

Father To Be

By Marilyn Pappano

Available now from Bantam Books

Here are sneak peeks at both.

Some Enchanted Season

When Maggie left Ross that fateful Christmas Eve, their marriage was over. But a near fatal accident on an ice-slick road changed everything. Now another Christmas approaches. While Maggie hasn't regained all her memory, she's already testing her strength at home—with Ross as her only companion . . . and her husband-in-name for a few months more.

Maggie wanted friends. She thrived with friendship—grew more serene, more content, more absolutely beautiful. With these people she was like an exotic flower unfolding under the sun's life-giving light. Having friends made her a different person—No, that wasn't true. Having friends enhanced the woman she'd always been.

Ross wondered if they could improve the man he'd become.

As soon as they finished their hellos, J. D. Grayson approached them with a tray of delicate Christmas china cups. "How about a cup of the sisters' special egg nog?"

Ross accepted a cup and sipped from it, expecting something to rival Maggie's flavored egg nogs. What he got was . . . "This is just egg nog."

"The sisters don't believe in the use of spirits," Grayson said, "except for the rare medicinal dosing. How are you, Maggie?"

"I'm fine."

"Are you ready to be dazzled by the fifty-first annual Tour of Lights?"

"I've been looking forward to it all day."

All the lights in the world couldn't be as dazzling as the smile she gave the doctor, Ross thought stiffly. Grayson reacted to it the same way *he* had earlier, staring, murmuring a response with absolutely no idea what he was saying.

Feeling perverse, Ross took Maggie's arm and pulled. "Come on. We need to find Miss Corinna and Miss Agatha and say hello."

As they made their way through the living and dining rooms on the way to the kitchen, he examined the emotion that had led him to put as much distance as possible between them and Grayson—between *her* and Grayson. Surely it wasn't jealousy. He'd never experienced it before—she'd never given him reason—and there was no reason for it now. For a very long time he and Maggie had been married in name only. There was little emotion and certainly nothing physical between them. In a few more months there would be no legal bond either. For all practical purposes she was a free woman now—free to start living her own life. Free to start looking for a man to take his place in it. She wanted it. *He* wanted it.

He had no logical reason to be jealous because she'd smiled at some other guy the way she'd just smiled at *him*. No reason at all, just because that guy looked at her in the same stunned, turned-on way that *he* looked at her.

No reason. He wanted out of her life, remember?

Didn't he?

He should be pushing the two of them together, not pulling them apart. Grayson was everything Maggie wanted—solid, dependable, a family sort of guy. He preferred small-town life over the city, wasn't interested in being rich or powerful, kept regular hours in his medical practice so he could have a personal life, and loved all these people in the same way she soon would. On top of all that, she thought he was handsome and admired his obvious affection for kids. Grayson was perfect for her.

Perfectly *wrong*.

"What are you scowling at?" Maggie asked as they squeezed between guests and a table loaded with mouth-watering food.

"I'm not—" He *was*. Consciously he forced his face to relax. "I'm not scowling."

"You don't like him much, do you?"

"Why should I?"

"I don't know. You're both intelligent, successful, respected. You're both mature adults. With that in common, I'd think you would get along fine."

And in a few more months would they also have her in common?

Just last weekend, when she'd asked what he wanted for Christmas, he'd given her a simple answer: *I want you to be happy*. He'd given that answer knowing that for her being happy meant being in love, married, and having babies—being in love with and married to another man, having babies with another man. He knew that. He'd accepted it.

But not Grayson. He was her shrink, for God's sake—though, granted, so far they'd had only one short session and would probably end the doctor-patient relationship after their next visit. He was— was— Hell, Ross didn't know *what* he was, besides unsuitable for Maggie.

He was saved from continuing the conversation by Miss Corinna's appearance. "Oh, you're here," she said, hugging Maggie, squeezing Ross's hand. "You're in for a treat tonight. We're very proud of our town, and the snow will make it perfect."

"That's what the kids said. Can I help with anything?" Maggie asked.

"No, no, we're all set. We'll eat just as soon as I make an announcement. Come along." She drew them both back the way they'd just come, then left them near the table while she took up a position on the broad arched doorway. "Can I have your attention please?"

A chorus of hushes spread through the rooms, followed by silence.

"Agatha and I are pleased to have you all join us for our fifty-first Tour of Lights opening night party," Miss Corinna said. "Some of you may have noticed that the Walkers aren't here. There's a good reason for their absence this evening. I just got off the phone with Mitch, and he told me that Shelley has given birth to a healthy, beautiful, eight-pound-eight-ounce baby girl whom they have named Rebecca Louise. Mother and daughter are doing fine." She waited a moment for the whispers and exclamations to die down, then said, "Time to celebrate. Let's eat, friends."

Ross moved closer to Maggie, who'd gone still at the announcement as the guests crowded around the table. "Are you okay?"

"Of course," she replied, and she managed a pretty good impression of being just fine. But he recognized the wistfulness in her eyes and the envy that underlaid it. "Why wouldn't I be okay? I'm not the one who just went through the rigors of childbirth."

"Precisely."

In the crush she reached for his hand, squeezed his fingers tightly. "My turn will come. Maybe by this time next year . . ."

At that moment Grayson came into sight across the room. Brendan Dalton was sitting on his shoulders, and Josie and another young girl were plastered to his sides.

Ross deliberately moved to block him from Maggie's view.

Father To Be

J.D. Grayson agrees that the Brown kids, abandoned by their parents, deserve a loving home. He's not just sure one man is parent enough for four young children . . . or if he could pass muster with Caleb, fierce guardian of his young brothers and sister, and Kelsey Malone, Bethlehem's newly arrived social worker.

The *hello* came on the third ring, the voice strong and vital.

"Dad, it's me, J.D."

His father chuckled. I may be old, but I'm not forgetful, not even in the middle of the night. I remember my only child's name. How are you, son?"

Parents asked their children that simple question all the time, and it was nothing more than that. A simple question with a simple answer. *How are you? I'm fine*. Or *Not too bad*. Or *I've been better*.

But when Bud Grayson asked, it wasn't so simple. Neither was the answer.

"I'm . . ." Relatively healthy. Slowly healing. Sometimes finding life worth living. All those answers were true. So was the one he gave. "I'm having some problems."

"What sort of problems?"

"I've got temporary custody of four kids whose parents abandoned them."

After a long silence, Bud's question came hesitantly. "Do you think that's wise?"

"No."

"Then, why . . . ?"

"I don't know. I felt . . . I don't know." It was the only explanation he offered. Pitiful as it was, it was enough for his dad. "They're good kids, Dad. They're smart and innocent and scared as hell. They'd break your heart."

"But have you forgotten, J.D.? Your heart's already been broken."

And that was the problem. The repairs he'd managed in the last two years and four months were still fragile. It wouldn't take much at all to undo all his hard work, to put him right back where he was when he'd come here. It wouldn't take any more than Caleb, keeping him or giving him up. Helping him or letting him down.

"Tell me about these kids, son."

He settled in the darkened living room by the window. "Gracie's the youngest. She's five. She's a pretty little girl, brown hair, brown eyes. Noah's six. He thinks leaving and being left are the most natural things in the world. He doesn't expect anyone to stick around."

And what would he think when Kelsey came to take them to a new home? Would he believe that just like their mother and their father, J.D. had abandoned them too?

The hell of it was, he'd be right.

"Jacob is eight. He's a big baseball fan. He's never played, though, because the kids at school wouldn't let him. He watches it on TV every chance he gets, and with cable, he gets *lots* of chances."

J.D. fell silent again, but his time it stretched on. Finally Bud cleared his throat. "That's only three. What about the oldest one?"

Tension knotted the muscles in his jaw, his neck, his fingers. "His name is Caleb. He's twelve years old, and he hates me." *And sometimes I hate him too. I hate him for reminding me of Trey. For being wounded like Trey. For not* being *Trey.* And yet, for the same reasons, he felt obligated to him. He owed Caleb.

"Kids that age can be difficult," Bud said quietly.

Oh, yeah. And relating to them could be damn near impossible. And not trying could be even more impossible. And failing . . .

Neither he nor Caleb might ever recover.

"How long have you had these children?"

"Two weeks."

"And it took you this long to tell me. Were you afraid of what I might say?"

J.D. smiled in the dark. "I've made bigger mistakes and survived what you had to say. I'm not afraid this time."

"And that's what these kids are? A mistake?"

"No. They're the third hardest thing I've ever done." His father knew what the first and second hardest things were, so there was no need to explain.

"Nobody ever said being a parent was easy." Unexpectedly Bud chuckled. "The once-foremost psychiatic expert on kids should know that."

"I do know in theory. But in practice . . ."

"It's harder, isn't it? All that advice that seems so reasonable in your safe, secure doctor's office isn't reasonable at all when applied to living, breathing kids, especially kids who've been hurt." There was a creaking of bedsprings, then a barely hidden yawn. "I'll tell you what, son. Why don't I mosey on up to New York and give you a hand with these temporary grandchildren of mine?"

"You would do that?"

"I think the Tuesday-night bingo gang can get along just fine without me for a while."

"Quarters are a little cramped here," J.D. warned. "The only place left to sleep is the sofa."

"I've slept on sofas before." Another yawn. "I'll let you know when my plans are set. In the meantime, don't worry too much. Just treat those kids like the people they are. Like the gift they are."

Appreciating Caleb as a gift. That was even harder to imagine than giving him up. But he wanted to try—for his own sake, for Caleb's, for Trey's.

Look for Michelle Martin's
charming new romance

You Were Meant for Me

Coming in May 2000 from Bantam Books . . .

Here's a sneak peek

Zoe Jameson drove her cab steadily through the hot and humid August day, ferrying sweaty tourists, talking the usual surface chatter with her passengers, or saying nothing, depending upon what they wanted, keeping her eyes focused on the often treacherous Manhattan traffic, and making up stories in her head about where her fares were from and how they lived their lives.

It was the same old thing again. Each driving day blended into the last without a landmark or a sign post to show she'd even passed that way. Frustration mingled with resignation in her sigh.

She'd been following a two-tone Rolls-Royce Phantom Six up First Avenue for the last ten minutes and happy to do so, because she had a thing for the older Rolls-Royces. They were so much more elegant than today's interchangeable luxury automotive status symbols of the rich and vacuous.

She particularly loved the Phantoms, because they represented the aristocratic worlds she loved to watch in the classic movies that kept her glued to her TV when she should be writing, or sleeping. This one was a real beauty. She was a rich yellow on the sides and front, with a black hood and roof, and she had the sweeping sides ending in voluptuous fenders that Zoe loved.

Suddenly the Rolls began to weave wildly across the right

lane in front of her and halfway into the left lane before swerving back into the right lane.

Brake lights blared at her. She had a split second to realize that if she braked too, she'd be rear-ended in the tightly packed traffic. The only thing she could do was jerk the cab to the right, onto the sidewalk. Unfortunately, the Rolls did the same, almost in the same moment, and then she *did* have to hit her brakes.

She missed the Phantom's bumper by centimeters.

Her heart filled her entire chest and was pounding so hard it was bruising her ribs. Her clenched hands were trembling on the steering wheel. That was the closest she'd ever come to crashing.

She checked to make sure she'd pulled far enough over onto the sidewalk, then flung open her car door and got out.

A slender man in a gray chauffeur's uniform was lying stretched out on the front seat, groaning loudly. The Phantom's passenger was leaning over the driver's seat from the back.

"Easy, Thompkins," the passenger said in a soothing, evocative voice Zoe had heard somewhere before. "I've called for an ambulance. It should be here in just a few minutes."

"What the hell is going on?" she demanded. "You nearly got me killed."

The passenger looked at her then, his startled blue gaze nearly knocking her off her feet. He had thick dark blond hair cut short, an angular face with a strong square chin, broad shoulders, and beautiful hands with long tapered fingers.

She was looking at the embodiment of every hero she'd ever written on paper or in her head.

"My driver became suddenly ill," he said in a voice she now recognized as the one she'd been hearing in her head ever since she'd begun writing romance novels.

Within a few moments an ambulance had arrived on the scene.

Her romance hero stepped out of the Rolls with a cast on his left ankle and a walking stick in his hand. He pulled a cell phone from his jacket pocket and called ahead to the hospital to cut through bureaucratic red tape. He gave his chauffeur a reassuring smile as he pocketed the cell phone. Then he directed the transfer of Thompkins onto a stretcher and his careful placement into the back of the ambulance. The man was positively masterful. The paramedics closed the back doors of the ambulance and the sirens were screaming once more as it turned down East Thirty-Fourth Street.

Well. That was one of the more interesting experiences of Zoe's working life.

"Thank you for your help, Miss . . . Miss?"

"Jameson," Zoe said, turning back to her romance hero. Now that he was standing upright, she could see that he was about six feet tall and beautifully proportioned, the perfect English-looking gentleman with a very commanding air. *Wow*. "Zoe Jameson."

"Ah," he said. "Ms. Jameson, were you by any chance driving the cab parked behind us?"

"I was."

"You're a licensed hack?"

"I am.""

"Then it would be legal for you to drive my car."

"Um, sure," Zoe said, bright lights popping all through her brain, "but—"

"It is vital that I be at JFK in time to meet a Singapore Airlines flight from Hong Kong that arrives," he glanced at his watch, "in thirty-five minutes."

"Fine," Zoe said, fending off vertigo. "You've got a car. Can't you drive yourself?"

"No."

"No?" Zoe said in surprise.

"No," he said firmly as cars and trucks swooshed past them. "First, I am a wretched driver, Ms. Jameson. Second, I am fairly incapacitated with this cast, even though it *is* on my left foot and the Phantom is an automatic. Third, the gentleman I am meeting, Mr. Ng Pei Lau, president of the Mandarin Bank of Hong Kong, must be wooed, impressed, and signed on the dotted line during his brief visit to New York. As one of Hong Kong's pre-eminent bankers, he expects to be treated like royalty and royalty requires—"

"A chauffeur. Got it. But I am hardly chauffeur material."

"I don't have time to be choosy, Ms. Jameson. I need a driver to get me to the airport and then to ferry me for the rest of the day."

This was beginning to feel like an out of body experience. "The day? I can't drive your Rolls for the rest of the day. I've got a cab to drive, rent money to make, a tyrannical landlord to appease."

"Thompkins is incapacitated, I don't have a back-up driver, I need to get to the airport now, and I will need you until midnight or so. I will reimburse you the for use of your cab, and I will pay you an additional one thousand dollars for your services. In cash," he said, pulling a wallet from his inside breast coat pocket. He counted out ten bills—ten *one hundred dollar bills*—and held them up.

"Who the hell are you?" Zoe demanded with a suddenly dry throat.

"Matthew Rutherford Tobias Winslow the Fifth."

Zoe stared at her hero. "That is cruel and unusual punishment. You should sue your parents."

Not even a hint that the man knew what a smile was. "My name is a treasured family tradition and I, if you will recall Ms. Jameson, am both late and desperate. Are you or are you not driving me to the airport?"

From nationally bestselling author Donna Kauffman comes an enchanting new tale

The Legend of the Sorcerer

on sale in March 2000

Here's a sneak peek . . .

Did you pick up the pictures as I instructed? She was quite lovely. Such a pity you didn't respond to my last missive. Perhaps you need the challenge of a good deed, a soul rescued. Yes, I see now that I was wrong in underestimating you.

I have her here. She loves your work, but she's far from alone, isn't she? Ah, they fantasize about the man who writes of such a powerful and seductive sorcerer. But she sees only the fantasy you created. I understand the reality. You are *the sorcerer. I have always known this, I alone believed. I have been waiting for your sign and you have finally given it to me.*

Bring me the Dark Pearl, Malacai L'Baan. Surely you don't want her to suffer for her misguided, foolish, mortal emotions. Bring me the Dark Pearl and she will be set free. And we will be free to begin our future as ordained.

A bestselling author, Malacai L'Baan had received fan mail bordering on obsessive before. But none had ever seemed so personal. Until now. Had some deranged soul out there actually kidnapped one of his readers because she believed he was a true sorcerer? And what pictures was she talking about? He'd never received any pictures. He leaned back in his chair with a deep aggravated sigh.

He flipped through the top few pieces of the day's mail,

went to toss a piece of junk mail in the trash, then froze. He pulled it back and looked at it, remembering a postcard he'd tossed out over a week ago. A postcard alerting him that his pictures were ready. It had been from some one-hour shop, but he hadn't dropped off film to be developed. He'd tossed it and not given it another thought.

Cai hit pay dirt at the second shop. There was a stack of postcards on the counter of the ZippySnap that looked like the one he'd received.

"I'm here to pick up some film. Last name is L'Baan."

The woman behind the counter was very blonde and very tan. Her nametag said Sherrill. She looked him over, then tilted her head with a toothy smile. "Say, do I know you?"

"It's possible. I live around here." He nodded toward the file drawers. "I'm kind of in a hurry."

She gave him another lookover, ending with a direct look that made it clear if they hadn't met before, she was more than willing to remedy that situation. Cai shifted his gaze to some of the framed pictures on the wall. He heard her sigh, the sound of the envelopes being flipped through.

"Here you go," she said brightly, putting the thick envelope on the counter.

Cai spun back. "Really?" His gaze landed on the envelope with a mixture of relief and dread.

The clerk glanced at the envelope. "They were left here almost two weeks ago. We got them done that day."

"I . . . I know. You sent me a postcard, but I didn't get around to getting here until now. I'm uh just glad you still have them."

"We would have called you, but you didn't leave us a number, just your PO Box address."

Cai looked at the handwriting on the envelope. The neatly printed block letters weren't close to his own scrawl. He debated asking her a few questions, but decided he'd better look at them before doing anything.

He sat on his motorcycle and fingered the selfstick flap. Maybe she should just go directly to the police. He was probably being ridiculous and this was some sick prank. He tore open the flap and slid out a glossy stack of prints. He wasn't at all prepared for what greeted him.

She was quite lovely.

Yes, she was, that and more. A gamine face with short auburn hair that was lifted by the wind, blowing in soft spikes around her face. Her cheekbones were high and sharp, her mouth small and full. She had a graceful neck, or maybe it was the wispy tendrils that clung to it that made it appear so. She wore a skinny-strapped white tank top and no bra, although there wasn't much there to require one. She looked short, with well-toned arms and a flat, tanned belly, shown off by the baggy khaki shorts she wore slung low on her hips. The heavy leather sandals should have looked like clodhoppers on her feet, instead they made her seem all the more earthy and natural. Her crooked smile was somewhat shy, as if she knew a secret. But there was a twinkle in those eyes, as if it were a secret she was just dying to tell.

It took several seconds before he pulled his gaze from the woman's face and noticed the background. The glass door behind her had the words The Mangrove Hotel stenciled on it. It was a relatively new place, just opened the year before.

So, she was here. Or had been here.

He flipped through the rest of the photos. They were mostly shots of the shore; sunrises, sunsets, narrow focus shots of wildflowers, the occasional manatee or waterfowl. What was the point of all these other pictures? To burn up the roll of film? It didn't seem like that. They looked like someone's vacation photos. A chill raced over his skin. Had this nut snatched some innocent vacationer right off the beach?

The Mangrove was minutes away from the ZippySnap. How had the e-mailer set that up all the way from Wales? Then he realized the obvious. She didn't have to be in Wales, just have an account there. All she had to do was dial into the service provider in the UK and sign on to her account. Any e-mail she sent would originate from there. The kidnapper could have been here in the Keys all along. In fact, maybe there was no victim. Maybe the pictures were of Margaron herself and this whole thing was a sick, sick joke.

Oh, how he wanted to believe that. Yet, he thought of the smiling woman in the photo and couldn't imagine that either. She didn't looked mad or deranged. He had to go to the police. He'd deal with Eileen later.

The road to the Mangrove PD took him right past the Mangrove Hotel. He found himself turning in. The photos were left almost two weeks ago. The chances of the woman still being here were slim. But he had to find out.

He swung off his bike and locked his helmet on the back rack before pulling out the photo. He felt the pull of her gaze once again. "Who are you?" he asked under his breath.

Then he looked up . . . and saw her.